PICKLES

PICKLES

RAYMOND MENDOZA

PICKLES

Copyright © 2012 by Raymond Mendoza.

All rights reserved. No part of this book may be used or reproduced by any means, graphic, electronic, or mechanical, including photocopying, recording, taping or by any information storage retrieval system without the written permission of the author except in the case of brief quotations embodied in critical articles and reviews.

This is a work of fiction. All of the characters, names, incidents, organizations, and dialogue in this novel are either the products of the author's imagination or are used fictitiously.

iUniverse books may be ordered through booksellers or by contacting:

iUniverse
1663 Liberty Drive
Bloomington, IN 47403
www.iuniverse.com
1-800-Authors (1-800-288-4677)

Because of the dynamic nature of the Internet, any web addresses or links contained in this book may have changed since publication and may no longer be valid. The views expressed in this work are solely those of the author and do not necessarily reflect the views of the publisher, and the publisher hereby disclaims any responsibility for them.

Any people depicted in stock imagery provided by Thinkstock are models, and such images are being used for illustrative purposes only.
Certain stock imagery © Thinkstock.

ISBN: 978-1-4620-7685-7 (sc)
ISBN: 978-1-4620-7686-4 (hc)
ISBN: 978-1-4620-7715-1 (e)

Library of Congress Control Number: 2011963122

Print information available on the last page.

iUniverse rev. date: 09/22/2015

Is it you who cries, when the sky is gray?
Is it you who wonders, Why is it this way?"
Is it you who is in need of love?
Is it you who questions what's above?
Is it you who is desperate for a sign?
Is it you who seeks a stronger wine?
Is it you who cries every night?
Is it you who feels, he's lost his fight?
Is it you that asks, who is He?
It is you, my child, who holds the key…

~Raymond Mendoza

I dedicate this book first and foremost to
The Lord Jesus Christ, who is my strength and inspiration.

Second, I dedicate this to my beautiful wife,
who is an endless source of support and love.

CHAPTER 1

THE WEATHER AROUND THIS TIME is always bleak. Everything is so cold and gray as the chill of the northern wind crisps the air by the minute. The heaviness of the moisture in the air paired with the swiftness of the wind; they grounded and lifted me all at the same time. I'd seen beaches before, but none like this. Maybe it was the beach, or maybe it was just because she had been here before.

As I looked around, the view was simple. Big waves, sunset, endless amounts of sand on a beach that stretched as far as the east from the west. If you didn't know any better, you'd swear this was the end of something and the beginning of something else. There was so little to see, but so much to look at all at the same time. Scanning from side to side, I just couldn't' take the experience in fast enough. I kept stopping and lifting my head into the wind, thankful that it was offseason here, and no one was around. I could feel the agonizing sting of the cold, as winter was making a stand by to sticking around longer than it was welcomed. I liked it. The temperature reminded me of my hearts current state, cold and lifeless. Perhaps I could get used to this, having the weather as a common companion.

As I started to stroll, I noticed all the little seashells. I picked one up and tossed it back into the waves as if to put in back in its place, wishing at the same time, I could do the same to my life... If only to pick it up and find the right place again. That was why I drove. It is why I came here. In search of a new beginning by letting go. As I peered at the sunset, I couldn't help but wonder if I'd find one here.

The horizon was beautiful. The reds, oranges, pinks, blues, purples all merged into a beautiful painting. It reminded me what I loved about art. Colors in the right pattern could create a masterpiece. Having an art studio with my father, I had to learn about all types of art. Contemporary, abstract, Rembrandt to Michelangelo. I knew so much, but there was nothing like the right picture. It didn't matter the era or type; it was the emotion that was invoked. Those were the images that sold, and they are what I looked for to put in my gallery. I always believed beauty begins when you see with your heart; that is why not everyone can see it. Looking around, this picture was certainly one of those scenes. Pure beauty. It drew me in and made me want to stay.

Continuing to walk and toss seashells into the sea, I was lost in thought and memory. The last time I had walked on a beach was probably when I was 8 or 9, and my mom was still alive. Before cancer came, I remember one of her favorite things was to go to the beach. We would drive every month or so, and the sound of the waves brought back the memories. Looking at the seashells, I recalled when I was little someone telling me that you could hear the ocean inside of one. But I couldn't remember it that was true or not. Again, thankful no one was around; I lifted it up to my ear... And waited. Honestly, I heard the ocean, but probably because I was at the ocean. Dumb. I threw that seashell harder.

It's funny how one person's opinion of something can become a belief that never dies. I suppose that's kind of like a memory, an experience. It's yours and who ever you tell it to, it becomes their view the same. Strange. "Wait what?" I thought to myself. "What I am thinking?" Maybe all of this cold air is getting to me. I'm not much of a philosophical or spiritual type, nor have I been described as curious, but here I am listening to seashells and talking like Socrates. Is this is what grief does to you? Maybe after all this time, I'd become shallow in my thinking.

The sun was almost out of sight. It was time for me to head back to the hotel; I'd checked into a few hours earlier. It was a beautiful room, but just thinking of being cooped up in a tiny space with four white walls, made me want to keep searching just a little while longer. I have been here for a few hours now, and I hadn't seen what I have been looking for... until now. There it was in the distance, high on a cliff. For a second, I felt a glimmer of hope. As I got closer, I pulled out my wife's photo to see if it was a match. I couldn't believe, it was the same as it looked in the picture. Old and dead, but strong and stubborn. I smiled, personifying the image of the big dead tree my wife so famously talked about.

"How many things this old guy has witnessed? What all he had seen?" The branches were tall, and I'm sure with the beach winds, the roots were just the same, but in the opposite direction. It had beauty and stealth as it stood high on the cliff, before the land broke and gave way to the beach. There were parts of me that envied it. How many tragedies has this tree seen, yet it still stands? And here I am, falling apart over one. I knew I needed to move on, to let go, but it was so hard. Too many eyes, it would appear as that I have it all. I have a great, thriving business. I've been blessed with healthy finances. I have a good family, nice friends. As far as looks go, I've always been complimented. Standing tall, with dark hair, fair skin, and muscular build. Turning 31, I was not young and dumb, but not yet old and wise. Halfway there to everything. I've always been confident. I've never felt shy or insecure. I've always seemed to know who I am, and where I'm going. Until...

The bark broke the silence and busyness of my thoughts. I looked up, seeing an old, skinny dog. It was running as fast as it could towards me. A little nervous, I braced myself. I didn't know if the thing was ravenous, or just excited. As it came closer, I could see it's wiry hair, dabbled with tan, reddish dots on an ivory background of fur. Slowing down, he seemed to be growing tired and weary. The dog and the tree seemed to be the same. Old, lonely and nowhere to go... Maybe that was me too.

The dog came up and sat in front of me as if I commanded it to do so. I looked around for an owner, but no one was in sight. The old dog looked skinny and tired but acted like he was on a mission of some sort.

"You and me both, buddy." I bent down, to look at the collar. He had a nametag, so it was hopeful that he belonged to someone. I flipped it over. "Pickles."

He wagged his tail a couple of times. "Pickles." "Pickles?" The dog turned his head to the side, curious. "What a strange name for a dog," I thought. But isn't that just the theme of this whole evening. Take something full of life, and leave it in a cold, bitter, lonely environment, isn't that just what it becomes? Pickled. The tree, this dog, and me. We all had something in common; that was for sure. However, for some reason, I felt hope's presence. Something that I hadn't felt in a long time. I turned to face the lake, and a huge gust of wind blew, almost knocking me over. I faced it fighting, but embracing it at the same time, as if it would take me a flight and solve all my troubles. I resisted the urge to lift my hands in the hair and act as though I were sailing. My eyes closed. Cool and Warm. Strong and determined. Then, all of a sudden, it was gone.

I slowly opened my eyes. Pickles was just staring at me. I looked at the tree as if it were doing the same thing. "What was that?" I asked in a tone that expected an answer. I sighed. "Who knows?"

Whatever it was, I felt a refreshing feeling come over me. Just for a minute, I could breathe again. Over the past year or so, it seemed as though I wasn't. A person can breathe, but still not take in a breath. They can be alive, but yet still not be living. That was me. That has been me, for the past year since she's been gone. Alone in thought, I began to head back to the hotel. The dog followed me. I walked for some ways, but he never left me. He'd followed me about three miles, meeting my swift pace.

"Well, I guess I could use some company." Pickles barked as if he knew what I was saying. "But only if the hotel allows it. If not, you're on your own old guy because I'm not driving around tonight looking for a home." He barked again. I chuckled. Shocked by the sound. Man, when was the last time I had laughed?

"Well, come on Pickles, time to go." The hotel was about half a mile away. I could see the glow of the lights. Subtle, but there. It was like the feeling I had. Subtle, but something. There was a shift in me. Intrinsic, but tangible. Maybe I did need to come here. Maybe stumbling upon that old journal was a sign. Maybe this is what I needed. Maybe, the answer was here. Maybe, just maybe, this was the end of something and the beginning of something else. Like the beach. Maybe that's what this is for. Maybe that's why she led me here. I couldn't help but notice the hope blooming in my heart with the mere word... Maybe...

1 Year and 3 Months Previous

CHAPTER 2

"BEEP, BEEP, BEEP, BEEP, BEEP."

"Ugh," I sighed, trying to get over to the alarm clock to shut off the obnoxious noise. It was already time to get up again and start my morning regime. I hurried out of bed, to start my usual day. It was just after 8:00 a.m. and I needed to get down to the studio before ten.

I brushed my teeth and put on some running clothes. Having a rather large house, without anyone in it, I could allocate one bedroom as a gym. Every morning I did a few reps with free weights and ran two miles. The small workout always seemed to jumpstart my day. After, I drank a bottle of water and went to the shower.

Getting out, I combed my hair in my usual side part. Put on Polo and jeans, with my loafers. That was my typical dress, except for Sundays. I've always been a casual guy. Nothing too fancy works for me. Breakfast is always a hard-boiled egg, and a slice of toast with light butter. High cholesterol runs in the family, so I do what I can to avoid that battle. I suppose my morning ritual is evidence of that.

As I reached the garage, I checked my watch. 9:20. With the art studio only ten minutes away, it wouldn't take me long to get there. One thing that I loved about living in a town this size was the lack of congested streets. I never had to worry about being caught in the crossfires of road rage filled people off to their busy highway lives. Life here was simple and controlled. Nothing was ever too out of the ordinary.

I liked order. Control. That's just who I am, always have been. Lack of punctuality and scheduling made me feel unprepared. As I pulled up to the art studio, I was welcomed by our sign, 'Harvey Art Investments' every morning. For whatever reason, I always felt a joy when I saw it. It was like a trophy, as to what my Dad and I had accomplished and grown over the past few years.

After my mom had died of cancer in the summer of 1979, we both felt lost. Though I was only eight years old at the time, I remember things just feeling chaotic. My parents had just started an art studio business at an old building they rented in town. My mom ran the business while my Dad talked art with the artist. She also held our family together too. With her gone, Dad and I had to find a new balance. We had to find a new way of living. I remember he started taking me to work with him and showing me the ropes. He said, "It's you and me now kid. We gotta make this work." It was true. We did. And, we had. After years of learning the odds and ends, my Dad and I had one of the finest art studios in the state. With the bigger cities, not too far from town, we would get all kinds of artists who would want to showcase their newest creation. With the local vineyard close by, it was a perfect trip for those big city people. A little 30-40 minute drive... a glass of wine, then a stroll down to us. Our set up was perfect. Dad couldn't have planned it any better.

Over the years, our name had become known as a high-end destination for the next big artist. With many reviews, we had a packed house at every open event. We had scheduling's every day to consider new painters, photographers, and other art forms. Profits grew and grew. We were blessed and very comfortable. For me, things couldn't have been better. I loved my work. I loved being with my Dad. I was content.

Opening the door, the smell of the hardwood always welcomed me. There was newness with the refinish, but oldness, being that the floors were original to the building. I'll never forget when we bought it. I was sixteen years old and so excited for Dad and I. I knew that this was my life, and I was happy with it. Dad and I fixed it up good. White walls went up in a maze-like fashion that was still an open concept layout. Furniture was slim. Only a few sitting chairs here and there, with a few accents the same. In showcasing art, you have to do just that. You don't want someone ranting and raving out the interior decor of the art studio, as much as you want them paying attention to what's hanging on the walls. Everything was simple and classic, with a touch of traditional to keep everything flowing. Dad and I each had an office of our own. They were located in the back of the studio, where we seemed to spend most of our time.

Ironic, though, how different our offices where. Dad's was chaotic. Papers everywhere, sticky notes stuck to everything. I couldn't find something in there if it were the last thing I did. However, it worked for him. He had this weird way of knowing exactly where every little thing was. Me, on the other hand. Well, everything was organized, color-coded and in order. Dad always said I inherited the "uptight gene" from mom. Maybe it was true, but I just appreciated an organized, clean environment to do my work. It helped me keep track of everything. The strange thing was, though; Dad was able to do the same in his mess. The funny thing, office preference was just about the only thing Dad and I differed on.

We never fought or had disagreements. Dad and I were always on the same page. Over the years, we grew close. In every way, he was my Dad, but also my best friend. It was, just him and me like he always said after my mom died. I didn't know what I'd do without him.

Sitting, scheduling and planning, the time flew by as fast as those black birds swooping by in a grocery store parking lot. Before I knew it, it was 9:45. Dad came in. Always 15 minutes before opening. He was always in a rush.

"Hey, Michael, how's the mornin?" He asked as he went to the coffee pot. Normal. He'd drink two cups before noon.

"Pretty good, Dad. Same ole same," I said while watching him.

"Well, we can't complain about that now can we? Same is good."

"No sir, we sure can't. Hey, do you know what time Ms. Smith is coming in today? She wants us to review her new collection."

Chuckling, "No time for small talk, huh son? Always ready for business," He gave me a grim smile.

"Well..." I said, really not knowing what to say.

"It's alright son. I love that about ya. She is coming in at 11:00. We have plenty of time. Probably need to call Old Man Salvador though, to get him prepared."

"Okay, will do." I went back to my office. I had known Old Man Salvador my whole life. He was our carpenter, framer, and all around handy man. He helped Dad, and I fix up the studio and he was our frame builder. You couldn't get a better frame, than one that was custom made by Salvador. He was the best in the state. You couldn't find a kinder man either. He was an all-around good guy. A war veteran, he had been through hell but praised God in heaven all the same. I dialed his number.

"Hello, Michael, how are ya?" He answered, always in a chipper tone.

"Good morning, Mr. Salvador! I'm doing pretty good, how about yourself?" I asked.

"I'm doin well son. Just drinking coffee and praising The Good Lord."

That was always his response. "Well, good. I'm sure He appreciates it. But hey, do you think you'll be able to come by in a bit? Dad and I have some new measurements and styles for you."

"Yeah, no problem. Say, about 10:30? Does that work?"

"Sure does. I'll see ya then."

"Alrighty. See ya." He hung up. What a good man he was, but I have always been surprised that he wasn't a preacher of some sort, rather than a carpenter. He was always talking about God. Not that I minded it. I go to church every Sunday, pray a bedtime prayer, and write a tithe check every month, but Old Man Salvador. He was just different. I'd swear any day, that he heard God. Like, he talks to Him. The things he'd say, and the times he'd say them. There was holiness about him, but also humbleness. The kind of man that I think most of us only wish we could be.

* * *

Before I knew it, the hours had gone, and Ms. Smith finally came with a marvelous collection. We went ahead and scheduled a showing for next Thursday. We had a little over a week to get everything handled. Old Man Salvador had come as well, took measurements and gave compliments as he always did. Dad and I had three more appointments of new artists. Two were great... One, not so much....

I never like turning people away, but sometimes, business is business. Father and I do it in the kindest of ways, but it's still hard. The girl walked out of here crying like we stole her best friend. But, her pieces were so abstract that they were just strange and not in a good way.

"She doesn't know who she is yet," Dad had said. It was true. Young, and not even through college, she had a ways to go. The other two were great. We had a landscape photographer that moved here from Texas. His work was beyond words. He will be a keeper, no doubt about that.

The other was a portrait artist. She was a woman in her early fifties that had a real gift for art. Her paintings were so detailed; you'd think they were taken from a camera. She also had a few floral paintings as well, that I knew would sell for interior design purposes. Dad talked awhile with her. I sensed a little crush, so I let them talk.

Dad hadn't dated that much since mom died. It had been almost 20 years, and I could count on one hand how many dates he'd taken. He said, "Your mom stole my heart, and she left with it." What can you say to that? They had real love. The kind that most people dream about all their life. But, even so, I knew he was lonely.

For me, I dated on and off in college, but really; I just hadn't met the right person. I was too focused on work to have any time to search for true love. If I was lonely, I didn't notice it. I figured I'd meet the right girl someday, but no need to go looking for her. Sometimes I think looking is like a needle in a haystack kind of thing. One can get pretty preoccupied. It was just not something I was interested in doing. My work kept me busy. Life was good. I had good friends from high school that still came around. They'd tease me every now and again about being an old bachelor, but it was all in good fun. Being with someone, would be in good time.

The clock was ticking. When we didn't have openings, we closed at seven, but on the days we did, it always ended up being a late night. It was 30 minutes before closing, so I started packing things up and preparing for tomorrow. I was back in my office when I heard the doorbell ring, as someone walked in.

"Who could that be?" I thought. "It's awfully strange to have someone stroll in at this time...

CHAPTER 3

I STACKED THE REMAINING PAPERS on my hand and put them in tomorrow's folder. I was just finishing up. I grabbed my keys and put them in my pocket. I was ready to leave when the last customer left. The dry cleaners closed at six-thirty but was willing to wait only a few more minutes past seven, so I needed to get over there soon.

Shutting my office door, I strolled out to meet and greet. Turning to my right, I saw her. She was beautiful. I froze studying her. She had auburn hair and was tall, and slender. Fair skinned, wearing jeans, winter boots, and a light blue sweater that complimented her. Being that this is not the biggest town in the world, I am familiar with most of our customers. However, occasionally, we have city guests that come as they're driving through. Some were familiar; some weren't. However, I was quite certain I'd never seen her before. I would remember. I stared, watching when suddenly, she turned. I was almost at a loss for words.

"Hello," She said in a soft, sweet voice.

"H..." I cleared my throat. "Hi. Ugh, how may I help you?"

"Just browsing," She walked around the wall, to the other side. "You have beautiful artwork."

"Thank- "I had to clear my throat again. "Um, Thank you."

"Are you the owner?" She asked.

"Yes, my father and I own the business. He's James Harvey, and I'm Michael Harvey."

"Nice to meet you," she said with a smile, as she walked over and offered her hand for a shake.

"You too," I said as I grabbed her hand. I quickly pulled away. Touching her made me very uneasy. "Well, ugh, feel free to look around."

"Okay. Thank you."

Her eyes were something else as if you would have not problem getting lost in them. She drew all of my attention. Her touch. It was soft, but powerful somehow. "You're welcome."

I stood over by the front check out desk. I tried not to watch her, but I really couldn't help myself. I needed to get my attention off of her. I checked underneath the calendar and flipped through a magazine as if searching for something. The tension I had made the minutes drag on. I pulled out the cash register. Checking the time, I put it all back. I transitioned over the computer, alternating between looking at it, my watch, and her.

"Are you always on time?" She asked.

"Ugh, I..." I didn't know what to say. Was she watching me too?

"I mean, I don't know. Why?"

"Well, you keep looking at your watch. Do you have somewhere to be? I can come back if so." She said in a concerned, polite tone.

"No. Don't come back. Wait I mean... come back. No, I mean..."

She chuckled.

"Ha," I gathered myself. "I don't have anywhere to be. You can come back, but don't feel like to you have to leave now."

She smiled. "Okay. Well, I am new in town, so I'm glad you told me I could come back. I don't know what I'd do if I couldn't."

"Oh, new to town?" I asked instinctively.

"Yes."

"Wow, well, welcome to the city of churches or at least that's what they say about our town. What brought you here?"

"The wind."

Confused, I asked, "The wind?"

She laughed, "Well, the wind is to say that there was no reason."

"Oh, I see." I responded. "How strange," I thought.

"Yeah," she was changing the subject, "But regardless, I'm an interior designer, and I'm always on the lookout for great art. This place is fantastic."

"Oh, wow, that's awesome. And thank you."

"Thanks. How long have Y'all been in business?

"Most of my life," I said as if she was a local and knew who I was.

"Well, how long is that?" She said with a grin.

"Oh yes, haha, ummm, well over 20 years. My parents opened the gallery when I was a child."

"Wonderful. How sweet."

"Yes, ugh," I checked my watch.

"Are you sure you don't have somewhere to be?" She followed my eyes to my watch.

"What? I mean, no. No." Immediately, I had a new level of hate for my nervous tick. I always checked my watch when I felt anxious. She read me like a book.

"Are you sure? I don't want to be a bother."

"No, no, I'm sure." I tried not to sound rushed.

"What time do Y'all close?" Her slight southern accent warmed my heart.

"At seven, when we don't have a showing."

"Oh, then, look at me! I am keeping you!" She pulled up her purse over her shoulder to secure it.

"No, you're not. It's fine." I tried to convince her.

"Oh, but I don't want to keep you late. I would like to buy some of these, but I think I'll come back tomorrow. I need to clear space for them back at my apartment."

Oh gosh, she was leaving. Did I make her feel rushed? "Ugh, are you sure? I don't have anywhere to be."

"Of course. No problem. I just saw this place walking by, and I wanted to peek in. I will come back tomorrow or later on this week." She said as she moved closer to the door.

"Okay, well, anytime is great. We open at ten and close at seven unless there is art showing."

"Oh, on Thursdays I see." She looked and saw the advertisement on the front counter.

"Yes."

"Okay, well, I will see you then." She said, as she pushed against the door and started to walk out.

I scrambled. Why did I act hurried? I wanted her to stay. But wait, what? No. I mean... I was frantic.

"See you, Mr. Harvey." She said as she walked out.

"Call me...." The door had already shut before I could said anything... "Michael."

That couldn't have been worse.

"Michael you idiot!" I thought. "What a complete fool!" I was the clumsiest I had ever been. Ridiculous. Geeze. I felt so dumb that I was not brave enough. Wait, when was she coming back? Tomorrow or Thursday? I was so nervous I didn't catch it.

"Great job, Michael. Way to be smooth." I mocked myself. I closed the doors and shut off the lights, as I replayed the whole thing in my head.

As I got in my jeep, I noticed the time. Great. 7:23. I missed my dry cleaning. How did such a smooth day get so off? On the drive home, I played my music a little louder. "Frank Sinatra, get me out of my head!" I thought. I was still flustered just thinking about her and about what happened. However, I was more flustered with the fact that I was flustered with her...

I pulled into my garage, and went and fixed a sandwich. I didn't feel like cooking any. Usually, I was quite the chef. Dad said I inherited that from mom as well. I enjoyed cooking and being single; it was either cook or eat out every night. I preferred the comfort of my home. Especially today. I couldn't risk running into her again. How awkward.

I finished the turkey and cheese, and went and sat on the couch. A little TV would do. I flipped the channels, and nothing was on the television. Not even the sports center could keep me entertained. I just couldn't relax. I was so tense that I decided to take a hot shower, to whine down before bed.

Getting out and drying off, still, my mind was racing. "Michael, just let it go. Forget about it!" I coached myself. But, I just couldn't. There was something about her that just loomed in my mind. I laid down in bed, just tossing and turning. What was it about this girl that had me so wound up? She was beautiful, sure, but there were a lot of pretty girls. There was just something different about her that I couldn't name... Name! What was her name? I didn't know. I didn't ask. Ugh, dumb, dumb, dumb!

Could it even get any worse? When I saw her again, I'd feel so bad to ask. When would I see her again? Tomorrow, next week, next month, who knew... She might not even come back, with the way I handled myself.

* * *

The next morning, I awoke tired. The whole night I had tossed and turned. The last time I had slept like that was when Dad and I were waiting for the approval by the city to remodel our studio. It had been a long and grueling process. However, for whatever reason, this girl had me just as anxious. It made me annoyed and frustrated with myself. I got ready and headed to the studio.

I couldn't concentrate, and I needed to. It was Tuesday, and I needed to get all of the details worked out for the opening on Thursday. Charlotte Cruz was one of our biggest artists, and she loved perfection a little more than I did. There was a lot to handle. That part was easy. What I couldn't handle was my thoughts, drifting back to her.

Every time the doorbell rang, I felt a little wave of excitement and nervousness fill me. I was so quick to get the door, to see if it was she. It wasn't. All day, I was up and down, checking the door. Up and down, also, was my stomach at the mere thought of seeing her again? Dad even asked, "Son, everything okay? You seem to be on the edge a little?"

"Yeah, Dad, I'm good." I tried to play it off. I tried to convince myself, but I just couldn't let it go. Before I knew, the day was over, and a new one was soon to follow.

For the second night, I laid in bed for the wondering... would I see her again?

CHAPTER 4

Three days had passed by, and she had not yet returned to the gallery. At this point, I felt it was a lost cause. I don't know why I was so anxious to see her. I was starting to wonder if I was weirdly obsessive. However, I couldn't help it. There was something about her that intrigued me. Something, I just can't name but thinking about her just felt right. I am not surprised that she hadn't returned, considering the way I acted, I doubted she felt the same. I was strange and awkward with her, and I stammered all over the place. I am sure I made her feel uncomfortable. Why else would she not come back? It had been so long since I was taken aback by a woman. I don't know if I've ever been so.... "Cat got your tongue" so to speak. The whole thing was a business loss, but not as much as it was a personal one.

I had been thinking about the entire scene all week, but I have particularly been focusing on what little I knew about her from that one moment. I knew enough about her that I had barely enough hang on. Even the thought of thinking about her all day was tugging at my shirt, like a child who was trying to get the attention of a parent who was purposely ignoring that child. I was that parent and the thought of her was that child. I knew I needed to focus today. I coached myself getting ready this morning, "Just forget about it!". Tonight was the big showing, and I needed to get a grip! I couldn't afford to think about it anymore. I needed to focus. Though I gave it my best effort not to think about her, it was hard not to. I couldn't determine why my single equilibrium was so shifted by her. I had to acknowledge the struggle and the fact that I struggled to push a girl away. This was all too new for me, and that was saying something. Single women come into the gallery all of the time, and none ever truly intrigue me. Sure, some are attractive, smart, and I'm sure they are great, but... I don't know... She was different. The very fact that she caught my attention in that way is shocking, and I had let the ramifications of those feelings direct my thinking all week. Now, it just had to stop. There was too much to complete for tonight.

I went to work and made sure all the paperwork was done, along with last minute errands and phone calls. We had our catering done through the winery and the local grocery store owned by the Williams'. Mrs. Betty Williams was an amazing baker, and she always made little petite desserts for us. Mr. Williams was the butcher, manager, and everything else the store needed. They had a modest size shop at the corner of 8th and Central Avenue. I always ordered an array of deli meats, cheeses and fruits along with a set of petite desserts. They always came, as Mrs. Williams wanted everything showcased just right. Being that it was six o'clock, they should be here any minute. The showing was scheduled to start soon.

The doorbell rang. I got up, and sure enough, I could hear Mrs. Williams' taking her post and ordering things around. You just had to do what she said, and we all did, Dad included. Desserts here, plates here, cheese there. By six thirty, everything was all set. I went and put on the surround music. Classical. It always had to be classical, as it always set the right mood and tone. I double-checked the framing, to make sure everything was in place. Old Man Salvador had a gift. He knew just how to make it all come together, and it sure had, as it always did. Dad and I put in a lot of work, but Salvador and the Williams made that work look beautiful. It's not just the art you sell in a gallery; it's the experience for the customer. The atmosphere. One of the most integral parts of art is the emotion that goes into the painting, but also the emotion that comes from looking at it.

Thus, the mood and tone of the atmosphere can't be apathetic. It must have a certain welcoming quality to feeling and invite people to express what they see. Wine, excellent food, and good music set that stage while framing and layout decorated it. Every time, it came together the same way, but each was different with the art responsible for the fluctuation. That was the measure, in which I used to ensure that we were doing everything correctly. Like a variable I suppose... If you keep everything else consistent except the paintings, you will see what impact each artist has. For me, I enjoyed that the most in the business.

Before I knew it, the show was ready to begin. On the dot arrived Charlotte Cruz, dressed to the nines, as usually. The Columbian woman was about 40 years old, with the curves of a 20-year-old. And, she knew it. I often wondered if she came here to flaunt her artwork or herself... Probably both with emphasis on the latter. She was loud and vivacious and not my type though she was certainly persistent at asking me out. I don't know how many times I told this old cougar no, but she still asked. I wondered if it was the chase of a younger man she liked. A cat, mouse kind of thing.

"Darling," she oozed, "How are you? You're looking dashing, as always." She leaned in deep, with her low-neck topped red dress and matching lipstick. Her dark curly hair was all over the place, as she tossed it seductively.

She always made me feel so uncomfortable, but not in a good way. "I'm doing well, Ms. Cruz. How about you?"

"Oh Michael, how many times do I have to tell you to stop calling me Ms. Cruz. You say it like I'm an old lady. I'm Charlotte, darling.... You can call me Charlotte." She said so in a tone that was suggested I do more than that.

She was the only person I knew that could make even the simplest sentence sound like she was calling you to the bedroom. "Well, I know Ms. Cruz, but I always want to be polite, as my mother taught me."

She chuckled, "Of course."

"An excellent collection this time round. You have outdone yourself." I tried to change the subject.

"Thank you, dear. I try, you know I do. I wanted something different from my usual, so I went a little bold. Somewhat more fierce."

"How more fierce could she get?" I thought. "Well, it looks great." I responded.

"You know what else looks great," she put her finger, on my arm, tracing my muscle.

Ding! "Hey Michael, everything set?"

Thank God. Dad had come just in time. "Yes, Dad looks like we're all set. I'll start opening the wine." I slowly eased away from Charlotte. I always tried to keep a safe distance, and tonight would be no different.

Before I knew it, guests started to pile in, and the studio was alive with music, people, photographers, journalists, and critics. Everything was booming in beaming. For the first time this week, I felt normal in routine. My old pace was back, and I wasn't thinking about her. Good; hopefully, things would be back to normal for me. I couldn't imagine how one girl could be such a distraction.

I met and greeted everyone, all that I could. It was so important in this business to socialize. Artists come to see other artists and it was an excellent way to get our name out there. Dad was great at it. The man never met a stranger. I was getting better, but it wasn't my natural state. I preferred to sit back and observe. Sometimes, you learn more that way. Caught in the business of journalists and customers, I turned around to grab another glass of wine when I was stopped dead in my tracks. There she was.

Dressed in a beautiful navy dress, that came to the middle of her shins, with nude heels. Her hair was pulled up, showing off the back of her neck. She carried a cashmere light coat with her, a small purse dangling at her side. She had a gentle smile on her face, the kind that could be put in a painting. She was even more beautiful than I remembered. I couldn't look away. She was studying the art pieces as I studied her like the masterpiece she had so quickly become to me. I didn't know if she was critiquing it or if she was captivated by it. The way she shifted her weight from side to side made her look indecisive, but not incapable of making decisions. She was weighing the options, and she looked beautiful doing so.

"Michael, can you get more wine?" I heard but didn't respond. "Michael." I met my Dad's glaze. "W-i-n-e." He mouthed. Curious by my lack of attention to him.

I forced myself to look away, but I couldn't help the longing of my eyes to look back. Wine. I coached myself. Get wine. I walked over to the bar and grabbed a bottle of Spanish Merlot, one of the finest. Charlotte wouldn't have any less than that of course. I rushed over to Dad and gave it to him. I checked on a few guests, but I kept looking her way any change I got. I didn't want to lose her again. However, with all of the people and commotion, it was hard to keep track of where she was.

I fought back the urge to tell everyone in the room to leave, except her. I wanted to talk with her. I wanted to see her and to know her name. I wanted to know who this girl was who held my attention in the palm of her hands. I hustled around the room attending to guests but also keeping an eye. She went to every picture and studied it as if she were determining its fate. The evening wore on, and I tried so hard to be attentive to other guests, but it was proving more and more difficult. I was drawn to her. I was distracted by every mean... not in a lustful way, but in an interested way. I wanted to know everything she thought because I couldn't read her. For me, that was strange because I usually had the ability to see right past women, but not with her. Every observation pointed to the one fact I knew about her... She was different.

Finally, around nine or so, people started to leave. As the crowds grew smaller and smaller, I was so worried that she would go. I had to know her name. Now was the time. I couldn't miss out, or I'd never forgive myself.

"Come on Michael," I coached. "Get it together."

I sauntered towards her, with my heart pounding as loud as a kick drum. Every step I grew closer, the more beautiful she became. Okay, what to say. How do I start?

But, before I could say anything, she turned and smiled, "Mr. Harvey, so nice to see you."

I was stunned. Her beauty struck me. My memory failed me in recalling how stunning she actually was.

"Ugh, yes, yes," I shook it off. "Yes, it's good to see you. How are you?"

"I'm well, thank you." She smiled slightly.

I nodded. Like a fool. Come on Michael. Talk to her. "So..."

"It's a beautiful show this evening, and a great turnout." She jumped in, clearly seeing I was drowning in the conversation.

"Ugh, yes, yes, thank you."

"Ms. Cruz's work is exquisite." She complimented.

"Um, yes, yes, it is." I could barely swallow.

"Do you mind introducing me to her?" She asked earnestly.

"Ugh, yeah, yes. Um, yeah, let's ugh..." I searched the room for Cruz. Boy, I've never been in this situation. Most people know her, and if you don't know her, you can spot her. Ironically, I was never the one searching her out.

Over by the back, I found her. Surrounded by men, two of the critics. Cruz has a perceived "ability" to sway them in her favor.

"She's right over there," I pointed. "I'll take you."

"Great."

I was determined this time to keep her close to me. I didn't want to lose her again. As we walked, I couldn't help but notice her fluidity and grace and the subtle curves of her body. Me, and every other guy in the room. The jealousy caught me off guard; I didn't even know this woman, and I wanted her all to myself.

We were just a few steps away when Cruz shouted, "Michael, you've been a stranger all night darling," taking the liberty to have the other gentlemen move. Noticing her, she asked, "and whom do we have here?" She looked her up and down, with critical eyes.

"Ms. Cruz, this is...." Ugh, her name! I didn't know her name! "Ugh..."

"I'm sorry, I never told you did I?" She caught me right as I was about to fall. "My name is Rella Allan." She extended her hand. "It's an honor to meet you. I'm a huge fan of your work."

Cruz accepted her hand but didn't extend the courtesy. "Oh, yes. Aren't you so cute. Thank you. How do you know Michael." Cruz was quick to jump towards a threat.

Sensing hostility Rella quickly responded, "Oh, I met Mr. Harvey just the other day. I noticed your showing and wanted to stop by."

"Mr. Harvey..." Cruz gave me a sultry stare. "Well, that's nice dear. I hope you enjoy the evening. It was nice to meet your acquaintance."

Rella, "Yes, you as well." She turned to me seemingly uncomfortable. "Thank you Mr. Harvey."

"Ugh, yes, of course." Looking at her, I could sense Cruz studying us.

"Michael, darling. Won't you come, sit with me a while. I have so much to tell you."

Oh man, this couldn't be worse. Not now! "Well, Ms. Cruz, I was just about..."

"He was just going to show me to the lady's room. I'm sure he'll be right back," Rella said as she paused for me to turn with her and walk.

She saved me. Again. "Yes, I'll be back."

Cruz, not knowing what to say just nodded and smiled. We turned. "I can't thank you enough." I had uttered before I thought.

Rella chuckled, "It's not a problem. I'm not a fan of women like that, and I could sense that you're not either."

"No, and unfortunately, Ms. Cruz had yet to realize," I said under my breath.

She laughed. "Well, I can't blame her." She looked at me subtly.

Was that a compliment? I couldn't know for sure... I smiled. "Thank you... but I don't think it's anything to do with me, rather than I just happen to be male."

She laughed this time. "Yes, perhaps that's true."

We had made it halfway across the room, before I asked, "So, how do you like the showing?"

"It's wonderful... As much as I, perhaps wouldn't now want to admit, the art is truly exceptional."

I nodded understandingly. "Cruz is very talented. Most of her pieces will sell tonight."

"That's wonderful, for you?"

"Yes, business is always good." I agreed. "So how do you like the town?"

"It's great. I love it. There is so much to see and do here!"

I couldn't help but laugh. That wasn't the usual compliment I got, being that it wasn't the big city... "Really?"

"Yes. It's wonderful. There are so many small, quaint shops that I love. It's a great place to live. Plus, I can walk everywhere. It seems like everything is just a few blocks away. I love that. I've had my car parked; it seems, ever since I arrived."

"Yes... walking is nice, except in the heart of winter... You'll want to drive on the negative days..."

"Negative days?" She asked.

"When it's below zero," I instructed.

"Oh, right..." She laughed. "I will take your advice on that."

I smiled. "So, what all have you gone to see?"

"Well, today I went to the red lighthouse. It was so beautiful. I love how it stands so bold and has fought off age. The lighthouse concept too is lovely to me. It all depends on how the rainstorms find you but when some of those storms cause you to lose your way; go to the light as if you are chasing the sun. The Lighthouse will always help you find your way back home. I think all lighthouses are poetic."

Her insight struck me. "Oh, that's Big Red you're talking about. She is an old beauty and landmark of the town."

"I can see why, from today." Rella agreed.

"Yes... most people agree on that."

"I can imagine..." She hesitated. "I don't mean to cut this short, but..." She looked back over by where we walked from,

"Where is the lady's room? You'd better cover yourself. Ms. Cruz is staring us down."

"Oh, yes, right." I resisted the urge to look back and glare at her. "It's just through that back hallway, the door on the left."

She laughed, "Thank you."

Fortunately, I found other distractions while Rella was gone. I was taking orders, writing down purchases, and cleaning up. I had a way of finding things to do when Cruz was around. It was about 10 o'clock and the place all but cleared out. I noticed that Rella was back studying the art. She spent probably fifteen minutes at each piece. With our small conversation, that didn't surprise me. She seemed to be an intellect, looking and searching between the lines on the canvas.

While I wanted to talk to her again, there was a lot to do. I was comforted, though, just by knowing she was there. I couldn't help but wonder, though if maybe she was staying to talk to me again...

Cruz was lingering too. As she always did. I spotted my Dad and gave him a look; I knew he'd understand. He quickly went over to Charlotte and took his time talking and coaxing her towards the door. Cleaning, I kept watching for her. Rella. Her name was so unique; I assumed, just as she. There was such a grace about her. I loved that. The way she carried herself.

"Michael Darling!" My thoughts were interrupted. "I can't leave without a kiss." Cruz was too clever for Dad and was making her way across the room. Rella, Dad, Cruz and myself were the only ones left. One of us made it far too many.

"Looks like someone else is hanging around for you too," Cruz said it a biting tone looking towards Rella.

"She's interested in the paintings Ms. Cruz. That's all." I defended her.

"Of course... she is..." Cruz put her hand back on my arm. "You know, Michael... you have the perfect physic to be a model for a painting..."

I tried not to look shocked. Instantly, the Titanic came to mind. Oh no. I was no Leonardo... "Ugh..." I frantically searched for a quick scorch of her comment.

"So nervous..." Cruz said as she continued to touch my arm. "I would love to paint you..."

She coaxed me, but I knew her use of the word "paint" meant a lot more.

"Ms. Cruz, thank you, but that wouldn't be appropriate for our professional relationship." I tried to ease out of her touch.

She smiled, coming closer to me. "Oh, Michael... Don't be so uptight. Who knows if our professional relationship might just be the beginning of something more intimate."

I swallowed hard. How could I get out of this? How to get away from her. She was all but licking her lips, as I was her steak.

"Ms. Cruz." I heard Rella's voice. "What an impeccable display you have shown here." I couldn't help but detect the sternness and double meaning of her words.

Quickly, Charlotte turned. "Yes... Rella, was it?" Her tone drenched in annoyance.

"Ms. Allen." Rella corrected.

Challenge accepted. I could see it all over Cruz's face. There's no way this was going to end well.

"Well, Ms. Cruz." I tried to intervene.

Cruz cut me off. "So, tell me, sweet little girl," She said in a tone, "What brings you to town?"

"I just moved from Chicago. No, reason. I was just looking for a change." Rella responded with a cool tone.

"Oh, there must be some explanation..." Cruz suggested. "Boy problems? Are you on the run?" Her words were covered in ice.

"Ms. Cruz..." I said, but she interrupted.

"Oh Michael, I'm only teasing." She put her hand on my arm again as further provoke, as I tried to shake it away. "So, just moving for fun. Are you just out of college? You look so young..." She corrected and continued.

"I graduated three years ago from the University of Chicago," Rella stated.

"Interesting. So how old are you?"

Annoyed as I was, Cruz was getting more info than I did. I needed to get Rella out of this. "Now, I thought it wasn't allowed to talk about a women's age?" I said jokingly. "Charlotte, Wh---"

"Don't be silly Michael. I'm only inquiring about the girl." Cruz looked at Rella expectantly.

"I'm twenty-five. I graduated high school at sixteen. College at twenty."

"Oh," Cruz said quietly. "That's impressive... You must be smart."

I could tell the compliment hit a nerve with Rella. "My accomplishments aren't attributed to being smart, as much as they are God and hard work."

Cruz humbled and taken aback, "Of course. And what do you do?"

"I'm an interior designer," Rella said coolly. "I have my own business."

"Interesting," Cruz said. "How nice."

I could tell Cruz was getting ready to strike... A snake has a way of always lifting its head in pride before it lunges towards the threat.

"It's funny isn't it? Interior design..." Cruz said in a nonchalant tone.

"How so?" Rella questioned.

"How with marvelous art like this, someone would need help hanging it on the wall?" There was insult all over her words.

The blow was low. I was shocked that Cruz would have such audacity. I could feel the tenseness in the air. I gazed at Rella, ready to defend, but she beat me to it.

She smiled. "Well, yes, I do help them hang it on the wall. However, first, you have to pick the art out. That's where taste and tact come in. Two things that clearly, you wouldn't know anything about."

I had to tell myself not to drop my jaw in shock. Was this happening? I looked at Cruz. Enraged, she knew she'd lost the battle that she had started.

"Yes, well, that's just a matter of opinion. The critics don't lie."

"And neither does manners or lack thereof." Rella struck back.

Cruz was clearly defeated. I had to stop myself from clapping. This couldn't have been any more dramatic.

Cruz smiled, and slowly backed away. "Have a lovely evening Michael Darling. I'll be expecting a call." She leaned in and gave me a kiss on the check, knowingly leaving her red lipstick as trace and warning for the next round.

"Ms. Allen." Cruz smiled cruelly, as she headed out, trying to hide the tail that was between her legs. "Bye Mr. Harvey, have a great night."

Dad said bye, as he locked up. "That one's something, isn't she?" He asked rhetorically. He turned to Rella, "I'm sorry about that." Evidently he overheard. "She..."

"No need to apologize for someone else." Rella smiled sincerely as she corrected him.

Dad nodded. "Well, let me introduce myself. I'm James Harvey. It's nice to meet you." Dad reached to shake her hand.

"Rella Allan, and it's a pleasure."

"It's nice to meet you." Dad smiled with a little too much speculation as he turned to look at me. "Well son, I'm headed out. Do you mind locking up? We'll do the rest of the cleaning tomorrow. It's getting late."

I checked the watch. It was 10:30. "Yes, I can do that."

"And make sure you make sure this young lady gets home safely. Be a gentleman." He turned to Rella, "You tell me if he's not a gentleman, and I'll take care of it."

"Dad," I said with an embarrassed look.

She laughed. I loved the sound of her laugh. "Yes, Mr. Harvey, I will."

"Call me James. No one here around here is Mr. Harvey. That was my Dad. I'm James; he is Michael."

Rella laughed.

"Thanks, Dad. Goodnight, Dad." I said with a suggesting tone. I felt like I was in Junior High again, which was not a time I wanted to remember.

"Alright, son. See you tomorrow." He gave me a strange look.

"Night Dad, Love you." Smashing whatever he was suggesting.

"Love you too, my boy." Dad left through the back door.

"You're Dad is so sweet." She said.

"Yeah, he's a good guy. Drives me a little crazy, though."

"Well, the best parents do."

"True. That's true." I agreed.

"Well, I better get going myself. I'm sorry to keep you late again." She was lingering, all of a sudden embarrassed by it.

Oh no, not this time. I couldn't let the same scene happen again.

"You're not keeping me late." I fought the urge to look at my watch. "How did you enjoy the evening?"

"It was wonderful, overall." She said with a hint of sarcasm. "I had a lovely time."

"I'm sorry about Cruz," I remembered just what her evening held.

"Oh, don't worry about it. My Dad left my Mom for a woman like that. I've been exposed to that sort. I'm sorry for snapping like that. I'm usually not that rude."

I laughed cautiously, "It was quite the comeback. I've never seen anyone handle Charlotte Cruz the way you did."

"Well, sometimes you have to put people in their place, even if it isn't the most Christian thing. I feel a little bad, though..."

"Don't, it's alright. She was out of line. I am proud of you for having that kind of courage. Don't worry. I certainly don't think any less of you."

"Thank you for that. Women like that just always hit a nerve with me. It's hard to hold my tongue."

"Well, I just thank you for saving me. Three times, at that! I owe ya."

"What do you mean?" She asked confused.

"Well, first, I was rude and didn't get your name when we first met. So, in introducing you, I had no idea."

She laughed, "It's okay. That's not your fault."

"Then, with the bathroom, getting me away from Cruz. Lastly, well..." I hesitated not knowing how to put it, "the grand finally" I should say.

She laughed now. "Yes, that's all true. You're right. You do owe me. Let's say you walk me home and we call it even."

"I think I can manage that. Let me turn off the lights and get my keys."

"You don't walk?" She asked.

"Well, I sometimes do, but I like my Jeep, so I drive it as much as I can." The winter air was pretty cool this time of year as well, but I didn't want to tell her that and seem like a wimp.

"Oh, well, you don't have to then. No, it's not a problem at all. Let me just lock up."

"Are you sure? I don't want to be a bother." She insisted.

"Well, this is a safe town, but you never know. Cruz may be out on the prowl..."

She laughed out loud, "And with that, I'll take up your offer."

I closed the door behind her. "Lead the way."

"Are you sure you want to walk?" She looked to my Jeep. I did. I wanted more time to talk with her.

"Yes, it's a lovely night, and I could use a little exercise," I assured her.

She smiled. "Okay. Down this way..." She pointed. "I sure hope you're not crazy."

"What, why do you say that?" I asked concerning.

"Well, here I am letting a man, whom I don't know, walk me home in the dark to my apartment."

"You're right. This is how scary movies start."

She laughed again. "You're funny." Then grew serious. "So.... Are you saying you're not crazy?" She asked in a joking way.

"Well, I'm sure some would argue for and some against. You'll just have to trust your instinct."

"Ummm, well..." She studied me for a moment. "I'm going to guess no. You're too nervous to be crazy."

Shocked by her calling me out, I didn't know what to say. "I... Well..."

Chuckling, "I'm just teasing, Mr. Harvey."

"Oh, please, call me Michael. I'm sorry, I never told you."

"It's alright. Michael. I like that. Isn't Michael the huge angel in the bible who kicked Satan's butt?"

"Ugh, well, that's a different Michael," I said comically.

Again, she laughed. Harder this time. I loved her laugh. There was such a joy to it. I almost wanted to be funny just to hear it.

Catching her breath, she said, "Just this way. Two rights, then a left."

"Alright. So, are you getting around okay? Any questions about the town?" I knew that was a safe subject.

"No, none just yet. I'm just as curious as ever, so I nosey into most things and figure it out."

I laughed, "Well, good. Let me know if you need any help."

"Well, that's sweet of you to offer..."

"Yeah, I've lived here my whole life, so there isn't much I don't know about this town. It has its advantages and disadvantages, but it's home."

"Do you love it here?"

"I do. I couldn't see myself moving unless... I don't know. Unless I was forced to."

"Awe, that's nice. To be so attached to a place."

"You don't have that? A place you call home?" I wondered aloud.

"No, not really. When my Dad left my mom, and my grandmother passed, we moved around a lot. She was trying to fill the hole in her heart, so we went from place to place."

"What about school, friends?"

"Well, I was homeschooled, so that wasn't a problem. I've always been quick to make friends, so that's what I did. One friend in one town, another in the next."

handle it, and I sure wasn't going to go off the deep end looking dumb with a crazy plan.

I just needed to figure this out. I should have asked for her number. Dumb. I didn't. I was too awestruck. Isn't that just a love story? Guy meets a girl. The guy likes the girl. The guy doesn't know how to talk to the girl. The girl never knows the guy... The end. Ugh. I threw my pen down in frustration. I could only hope for another opportunity.

* * *

The hours ticked by as I alternated in thought all day between Rella and art... Rella and frames... Rella and pretending to think about not thinking about how I was going to ask her out.

"Ding." The doorbell went off. I couldn't tell if I was annoyed or relieved.

I headed out to the hallway, looking at my watch. The day was finally coming to an end. I tried not to sigh in despair.

"Hey, stranger. Am I on time?"

Her voice gave me chills and butterflies all at the same time. She was here. I couldn't believe it. I quickly looked up from my watch to look at her. There she was in a bright yellow blouse, appearing as the sun on my dark day. Her long hair was loosely curled, and makeup seemed simple if it was there at all. She was wearing jeans and boots that came to her knees. She was a woman with style and elegance. But most of all, one with natural beauty.

I smiled as I continued to walk to the front. Think, Michael. Think. Be smooth. Come on man, think. A line.

"Actually," I said, collecting myself, "You're early." It was perfect.

"Really? Early for what?" She asked quizzically. Her puzzled face was adorable.

"For dinner. With me. Tonight." How did I just say that? I thought. The words flew out of my mouth before I even thought them.

"Oh, wow." She seemed shocked and a little uncomfortable.

Crap. Crap. She doesn't like you. Bad move. I could see her body language shift in an unpleasant way. "No, I'm teasing." I forced a laugh to make her feel better. What was I thinking? That had to be the bluntest question I could have ever asked.

"Oh, you were?" Now she seemed hurt! What? I thought…

"No!" I said. "I mean, yes. I—I- ugh." What was going on?

She looked at me with eyes full of confusion.

"I've put my foot in my mouth," I said dryly. I knew what a lost battle looked like, and this was it. Time to fess up.

"I can see that," She laughed. "You look kind of cute when you're scared."

"How about when I'm embarrassed?" I asked in a way that begged for mercy.

"I'd love to go out with you, but I just can't tonight. I'm having a business dinner with a client."

"Oh, okay. Wow, that's great. I hope you two have a great time." I wondered whether the customer was male of female.

"Thank you. I'm sure we will.... A whole remodel. She just got divorced, so.... change of life, I suppose."

"Yeah..." I said, not knowing where to go... The awkward silence quickly filled the gap.

She laughed loudly. "Wow, you are awful at this, huh?"

"What?" I was concerned. Immediately, I started to wonder if she was letting me down easy. Girls did that. When they needed to get out of an awkward spot, they pin it on their moms or work or some other made up crisis. However, there was no way to know for sure.

"I don't understand?" I said, trying to maintain my composure.

"Well, aren't you going to ask me for another night?

"You want to go out with me?" I asked surprised.

"Yes, silly. I just can't tonight. But I can tomorrow."

"Oh. Okay. I thought you were just letting me down easy by saying you couldn't tonight."

"What? No, that's weird." She laughed.

"Oh." Man, how did this turn from smooth to slippery so fast. "So, you want to go out tomorrow?"

"Yes." She smiled.

"Okay. Well, I'm glad we've cleared all this up." I said comically, trying to cover my embarrassment.

"Michael you are so strange." She paused and looked at me with wonder. "I like you," she almost said in a whisper.

I couldn't help be embarrassed now. She was so beautiful. Her eyes. Her smile. I was completely smitten.

"I like you too, Rella." I noticed the sudden flush on her cheeks as I said the words. "I'm glad you came by. I was.... hoping to see you soon."

"Yes, well... same here. I enjoyed your company the other night. Plus, I still need someone to show me the ropes of the town."

"Hey, well, after dinner, I will. How's that?" I volunteered. That would take care of the whole, what to do after dinner phase.

"Great. So, tomorrow, at sevenish?"

"Yes!" I didn't want to sound too excited, but I was.

"Okay, well, I better get going. I just wanted to drop by say, 'hello.'"

"Well, I'm glad you did... I had no idea how to contact you again..." I admitted.

She smiled. "Well, you know where I live?" She questioned.

"Yes, but I felt that would come off stalker like."

She chuckled. "How so?"

"Well," I paused, "because I was trying to figure out a way to ask you out... and, I imagined what it would have been like if you said 'no'... Then to just leave... Seemed awkward." I shrugged my shoulders.

She laughed. "Yes, I can see that, but I can't imagine how you thought I would say 'no.'"

I didn't know what to say. I just looked down humbly, and we both chuckled in a flattered sort of way.

"I'll see you tomorrow, Michael." She said as she started walking towards the door.

"Yes, see you."

She'd hadn't made it far past through the door before she was heading back out of it. I couldn't help but watch her go. I heard my Dad roll into the hallway with his chair.

"That a boy, son!" He exclaimed. I heard the humor in his voice.

"Aw, Dad," I said in a tone.

Chuckling. He said, "I'm just saying. I gave the whole spill about love and your mom, and all. However, one thing is for certain; I was much smoother than you just were."

I couldn't help but laugh. I wadded up a flyer and threw it at him. "Shut up, Old Man."

"That was a train wreck, son. I thought you'd handle it better than that. I was about to come out and intervene."

"Well, it's not like I have a ton of experience. And she makes me nervous."

He smiled with a soft laugh, "I remember the feeling."

"Man, it was bad, though, huh?" I asked him again. I didn't want him back in grief.

He broke out in laughter. "I've never seen you so nervous. You handle business decisions so eloquently. With her, it's like the cats' got your tongue and wrapped it around your ankles."

We both laughed hard. "Yeah, I know." I paused for a moment and thought about it. "Hey, at least I pulled through, though."

"No, you didn't pull through. She did." He chuckled. "She's a good woman by that alone."

"Yeah, it seems so, huh."

"Sure does." He sighed. "Well, get out of here son. Get some sleep, too. You look awful."

"Gosh, thanks, Dad."

"You're welcome. I'll never lie to ya. Stop worrying and just go with it. I know that's not your thing, but maybe it needs to be for this."

"Yeah, maybe you're right. Well, I'm heading out. I'm exhausted."

"See ya tomorrow, son."

"See ya, Dad."

* * *

The next morning I awoke refreshed. Three days without sleep had taken a toll. I was so tired yesterday; I picked up something on the way, finished it before I arrived home and fell asleep before sundown. But the peace I gathered didn't last for long.

The moment my eyes opened, the scene from yesterday flashed back. I had a date. Tonight. With Rella Allan. Just the thought of her made me panicky. She was beautiful but in an elegant way. The few times I had seen her, she always dressed elegantly. She was beautiful in the way that a woman should be without revealing all that she has. Though my old high school and college buddies loved to see all a girl would offer by the measure of her clothes, I didn't like that. I wanted a woman that respected herself. Rella was just that.

I got ready for the morning with extra caution, somehow practicing for tonight. Man, I was just so nervous, already. I thought about the evening and what would make the perfect date. I remember reading somewhere that the first date, women make a lot of decisions or something. I didn't know if it was true of not, but I wanted to plan accordingly. First, I planned on taking her downtown to the local, DC's on B Street. It was the best in town. Tony was a top chef in New York but decided to retire here in Michigan, which proved to be beneficial to this city. He perfects every plate before it is served. The food was always unique and exceptional. I went there at least twice a week for lunch or dinner. I'd stop in this afternoon to make a reservation with him.

I didn't know how long dinner would last, but after, I just planned to walk around and show her the facts and interesting places of the town. Spring was on its way, but the prongs of winter still held on. I didn't figure we would talk to long because of that. However, I felt it a good idea. Talking about where I grew up was an easy subject and helped ensure me to have something to say. I could always chat about this place and its history, and that made me feel a little less nervous.

I got to work right on time, for the first time this week. I needed to get my pace back. It seemed like ever since I met Rella, I had been way off track. Not that it was a bad thing, it just wasn't what I was used to. I loved a plan. A schedule. A routine. It was soothing to me, somehow. This girl, she had me off my rocker. Deep down, I knew my heart was already lunging towards more serious feelings, and that scared me. At the same time, I also remember my Dad's advice to go after love. To take a chance with my heart. I never was a gambling type, but for her, I was willing to take a risk. There are people here in town that talk about love at first sight. Heck, my Dad and Mom had it, but I never really believed in it.... However, I just had this feeling that I was about to.

The door interrupted my thoughts.

"Dad-gum-it." Dad was here.

"Morning, Dad! Everything okay?" I asked as I peered down the hallway.

"Yeah, I'm alright. I'm just getting clumsy in my old age."

"I don't know if it's clumsy or just rushed," I said suggesting.

"Oh, Michael. Just because that watch on your wrist tells you what to do, doesn't mean that works for everybody."

He peered in my office with the look. The parent look that said, "I don't care how old you are, you sass me, and I'll take this belt off."

"Yes, sir... I'm sorry Dad."

"It's alright son. Just live a little.... Hey! How about that date tonight?"

Just when I thought, I was overcome being nervous about this date, I replied "Oh, yes." As I felt my heart flutter again.

"Well, where are you going to take her?"

"DC's," I said in a tone that begged for his opinion.

"Good. Tony won't let you down. Good food is the key. Truly it is. It's hard for anybody not to like you when they have an excellent filet mignon right in front, ya know?"

I smiled, "You know, that's pretty good Dad. You're right."

"You'll be fine son. I raised a good man, even if he is a smart little butt at times." He smiled.

I smiled back. "Thanks, Dad."

The doorbell interrupted our silent apology to each other.

"Hello?" Old Man Salvador's voice never got old, ironically. I'd heard it my whole life, and there was a comfort behind it.

"Hey, Salvador. We're back here."

I could hear his boots echoing closer and closer, on the hardwood floor. "Morning, boys." He nodded his head.

Old Man Salvador always made me smile. If there was ever a stereotypical Texan, he was it. He was always in boots, jeans, and a flannel shirt. No belt buckle, a cowboy hat or anything, but still a western man. His accent was thick. He was very tall and unyielding. One of those men that had worked his whole life. He had perfect carpentry skills. In twenty years, he never made a mistake. He was always too, a man of his word. When Mr. Salvador told you he was going to do something, you could count on it like you had a signed contract. He wore a small necklace with a silver cross on it. I believe it belonged to his wife. She passed away a few years back. I never forget seeing someone with that kind of grief, that kind of hurt, with that kind of love all while giving thanks to God. The loss of his wife had brought him and my Dad closer than ever before. Two widowed men. I admired them for the strength. I had lost one woman in my life, and I couldn't imagine ever losing another. I didn't know how my Dad and Old Man Salvador could go one, but they did. With all the grace, one could have, Mr. Salvador praised God. Thanked Him, even. It was beyond comprehension.

That was the other thing about Mr. Salvador. There was something about him, which just; well, reminded you of God. A kindness, but an authority too. He loved The Lord in a way that I don't think most people ever could. He talked to God, and I was sure, God talked back. You could trust him, like no other. And with anything. When I was younger, I remember thinking that if I wanted to hear God's opinion on something;

I'd just ask him. Honestly, it was juvenile back then. But, it was still true now. The blue twinkle in his eye held something that was.... I don't know... beyond religion and church. It was spiritual, somehow.

"Morning, Mr. Salvador. How are you?" I asked expectantly.

"I'm good. Just praisin' The Good Lord." He smiled, knowing that I knew that was always his response.

I smiled, knowingly.

"How ya been Salvador?" Dad asked.

"Au, pretty good. Just workin and livin. Livin and workin."

"Hey, well that's still a life, isn't it?" Dad asked.

"Sure is James. Sure is."

"Well, Michael's got a hot date tonight."

"Dad!"

He looked at me and continued. "With a real beautiful girl named Rella." He raised his eyebrows at me.

"Is that so, Michael? Well, how about that?" Salvador winked.

"Yes, sir." Man, if there were ever two men to make me feel like a little kid again, it was these two in the same room.

"Well, treat her good. You never know if she's the one." He suggested.

Just him saying that, made my stomach jump. "Yes, sir."

"I remember talking my sweet June on our first date." Salvador went on. "She was prettiest in all of Perryton, the town where we were both from. I wanted to marry her the moment I saw her. And I did, not too long after. God blessed me with a wonderful wife."

I could see the pain flicker across his eyes, as he changed the subject.

"Well, I got these frames for you, in the back of my truck. I also, here, got these new designs for Y'all to browse."

"Okay, Salvador. We'll do." My Dad said. "I got a check for you too, up front."

It was all back to business. As was the rest of the day. Everything went by so fast. And I knew because I was always checking my watch. I was counting down the hours. 10:00.

12:00. 12:30. 12:32. I don't know if I had ever checked my watch so much. I went to make a reservation with Tony. Everything was all set. I should have been relieved, but as the time passed, I just grew more and more nervous.

"Boy, you need to calm down," My Dad said around 5. "There is no need to be this nervous. It is just good food and good conversation. She likes you, or she wouldn't have agreed."

"I know, Dad. It's still just nerve racking. I haven't been on a date since... Well, I can't even remember."

"You'll be okay. Go ahead and go home. I'll take care of the rest here. Shower up and calm down."

I smiled. "Thanks, Dad."

I drove home and went straight for the shower. I needed the hot water to soothe me over. I got out and got dressed. I picked out a light blue shirt and khaki slacks, with brown loafers. My church ones. I put on my nice Rolex that my Dad got me when I graduated high school. I'll never forget opening up the gift and being in complete shock. The memory made me smile.

I went down stairs. It was 6:30. Great. It was getting close. I needed to... Wait! I never told her where to meet me or if I would pick her up.

"Michael, you idiot!" Oh my, what was I thinking? Dad was right. I was anything but smooth yesterday. Was I supposed to go to her apartment and pick her up? Was she going to wait for me at the gallery? I checked my watch. Thirty minutes till seven. I had better figure it out fast.

"Her apartment. Surely, I'm to pick her up." All of this was making me flustered. I didn't like not having a plan.

I drove way too fast down Main Street towards her building. I mean, I knew the building, but I didn't know what number she was in. I pulled up.

I went to the door. There was no way I'd know what apartment she was in... I would just have to hope for some guidance somehow.

I walked in and went up the immediate stairs. I came to the second floor looking for any sign. I checked my watch. "This is just what I need." I thought. "To be late on the first date." Great. I was late and lost. I saw the second flight, and right before I took the first step, I heard a door open.

She was looking at me in the most endearing way. Her expression struck me, but more so her beauty. She was wearing a red dress, which went just past the knees. It wasn't tight, but it was fitted. She wore a lovely tan coat just draped over her shoulders. Her shoes were low heels that just barely lifted her off the ground. As I gazed at her, I met her red lips that matched the color of her dress. I had never seen anyone look so stunning.

Her chuckle interrupted my gazing. "Are you lost?" She said in a flirty tone. "Confused maybe?"

"Uh," I fumbled around the stair railing. "No, uh, I was just looking for you."

She laughed. "Oh, I see... A little hide and go seek?"

"Ugh." I laughed. "I... I forgot to tell you where...."

"Yes, I realized that. But, you looked a little flustered. I was just going to meet you out at the front. I figured you would end up coming here first."

"Yes. Well, I ah.... I'm sorry." I stammered. I looked like a completely flustered fool.

"It's okay Michael." She said with an encouraging tone.

I met her gaze. Gosh, she was striking. I just wanted to grab her and kiss her. Calm down, my inner voice scolded me.

"Are you okay?" She asked, "You look a little pale."

Her comments snapped me out of whatever I was in. "Yes, Yes, I'm fine. Just hungry. What do you say we get going?"

"Sure thing." She smiled as she met me at the stairs.

* * *

Before I knew it, we were at the restaurant eating and enjoying fine wine. The conversation was so easy with her. There was no awkward silence. That "I don't know where to go from here..." It just flowed. I was so struck by her elegance and poise. She was unlike anyone I had ever met. But, there was a hint of my mom about her. The gracefulness, I think is what reminded me of her. Rella was talking about her family, her mom mainly, and how her Dad left when she was a young girl for a woman like Cruz.

"That's why I snapped, I think. I just... I don't know.... I've never had tolerance for that type ever since."

"It's okay Rella. She was taking stabs at you."

"Well, I think she's more interesting in taking a stab at you." She countered with a wink.

I laughed with a little disgust. "Charlotte Cruz is not my type. I associate with her only on business terms."

"I see, well if she's not your type, then who is?" She asked with such boldness.

I paused for a moment... "You." I said, with equal measure.

I couldn't help but notice the small blush reach her checks. The waitress came, and we ordered dessert. Rella said the food was the best she had ever tasted. I told her about Tony and how he owned the best restaurant in town.

We talked more and more about life. Goals and dreams. She had so many, and I loved that about her. It was so odd, that it already seemed to be serious between us. We both seemed to be drawn to one another. Like, it was though I had waited my whole life for the woman of my dreams, and all of a sudden she was here. I couldn't help but notice her interest in me. She kept looking at me in a way that I hadn't seen a woman look. Not in lust, but innocent curiosity.

Tony came out to meet her, and we gave our best compliments to him. The food was so exquisite. I couldn't miss his little winks my way that were saying, "Well done, my boy." I ignored them the best I could.

"Stay as long as you want," Tony said in his loud abounding Italian accent. "Michael over here is my best customer."

"Well, I can see why. The food is so wonderful." She complimented.

"Thank you, darling. It was a pleasure to meet you. Michael, as always," he extended his hand.

"Yes, sir." I shook. "Thanks for everything."

We stayed there talking, lost in conversation. The more I knew about her, the more I wanted to know. At ten, we decided for a walk. My initial plan was to talk about the history of the town, but now it was changed. I just wanted to hear more about her. What she liked and didn't like. Where she came from and everything.

"So, I graduated from the University of Chicago with a degree in interior design. I love art, but honestly, I have no talent there. Just, I just decorate with it." She laughed. "I'm sorry, I've been talking all night."

"No, no, don't apologize. It is great learning about you." I smiled.

"Well, what about you Michael Harvey. Tell me something I don't know."

"Ummm, well, I'm not as interesting as you," I warned. We were walking down 8th Street. I knew it was getting late, but I didn't want the night to end.

"Oh, sure you are." She urged.

"Well, I have a simple life. My Dad and I own the gallery, which you know. It's my job, and I truly love it. I love working alongside my father. My mom died when I was young, and we have been partners ever since. I think it helped us both survive the loss. Especially him. I went to Michigan State and got a Bachelors in Business. Dad insisted I go to college, even though I felt I didn't need to. I haven't had the time to go and explore other towns and other parts of the world. It's weird that everyone seemed to want to move away, but I never have. I love it here. It would take something dramatic, I guess, for me to leave."

"It's a beautiful town. That's why I stopped."

I smiled. "It is. That simple?"

"Yes..." She smiled.

"The best reason I've heard..." I looked ahead of us. "The simple things always turn out to be the most important."

"I couldn't agree with you more..." She said as we stopped and peered up at the moon.

I looked at her as if she had hung it there. “Not many women think so.” I bartered.

“I do.” She pointed up. “Look up at the moon, Michael.”

I followed her gaze.

“It’s the simplest thing. No complexity, no striking wonder, just there every night for us to look at. How many of us take that very simple thing for granted? How may of us forget that it is there? The moon was put there for many reasons but if you dig deep enough, you’ll find your reason. My reason is when I feel far from the Lord, I just go outside and look at the moon and remind myself that our Lord Jesus once looked at that very same moon. That always makes me feel closer to him again.”

“Wow.” I breathed. I had never thought of it that way.

“It’s a way... to bring you home...like a lighthouse,” She said quietly. “When you miss someone...”

“That’s beautiful, Rella,” I said.

She smiled. I couldn’t help but notice the distance between us shrinking. The coolness of the air sparked something. As my hand was on the small of her back, I guided her close. She didn’t resist. Slowly, our faces came together, portraying what in my head was my perfect picture. Her eyes closed softly, as did mine. We stayed there for a moment. Each was giving the other the opportunity to back down. However, neither of us did. We leaned in. One towards the other. Our lips met.

I was drawn, pulled, captivated. I pulled her closer to me to deepen the kiss. She pulled her arms up around my shoulders, pulling me even closer. It seemed to last forever in the way that you hope forever will forever be. I was lost in her. Perfectly and contently lost.

I felt a feeling that I had never felt before. As we kissed, electricity was surging through our lips as if it was some kind of stimulating shock. Her lips were soft but caressed mine strongly. I was trying my best to kiss slowly though I could feel my body hot.

“Beep, beep, beeeeep, beeeep, b-b-beep.”

"Whoohooo," We immediately pulled apart as we looked to the direction of the loud horn. A group of teenagers driving down the street spotted us. High school boys of course. "Whoohoo!" The were all whistling and yelling like a bunch of fools. Flashing their headlights.

We couldn't help but laugh, both a little embarrassed.

"Well, I think that's the best ending a date could ever have." She said comically.

"I agree with you." We laughed again. "Let me drive you back home."

DC's on B Street wasn't too far from where we were. We walked in silence, but not the awkward kind. The content type that makes you feel endless. When we reached the car, I opened the door and let her in.

"It is a bit cold, isn't it." She asked.

"Yes, it gets pretty cold here but fortunately, the brunt of the winter is behind us."

"Thank goodness. I'm more of a summer girl, myself."

"I can see that about you. Full of light." I smiled, as she blushed again.

The drive was only a few minutes away. I pulled up to her apartment. "Is it alright if I walk you to your door. I don't mean..."

"Yes, Michael. It's okay. I know you don't."

I was relieved when she picked up what I was saying before I had to say it. Not that I wanted to tell her, but I had never been... with a woman. In college, I dated because I felt I had too. I kissed and well... by all means, I wasn't the cleanest of virgins, but I had never gone that far. Never felt the need to. Never really, loved a woman enough, I guess. Regardless, that wasn't a discussion for tonight.

"Thank you, Michael, for such a wonderful time." She said as she took my hand as I helped her out of the tall Jeep.

"No, Rella, thank you."

"You're such a gentleman. I don't know very many men that will get out and get the door for a lady these days."

I smiled. "Oh, I'm just doing this because of my Dad's threat. He said he'd get me if I weren't a gentleman to you."

She laughed. "Yes, well, then, you better be on your best behavior." I couldn't help but notice the comical warning behind her phrase.

"Yes, ma'am." I smiled, knowingly.

We went up the stairs. "It's apartment 527. Now that I have verified you are not crazy, I will tell you the number."

I laughed. "Well, I'm happy to hear that."

We arrived at the door. As much as I wanted to kiss her again, I knew better. I'd never felt anything like I had just felt. And well, it wasn't anything I was used to, nor did I know how to control.

I smiled and leaned forward, kissing her on the check. It was safe, for the both of us. "Thank you, Rella, I had the most wonderful time. I can't wait to see you again."

She seemed so surprised by my action. I just knew I had to get out of there. She was beautiful, and this was all very tempting.

"Good night, Rella."

"Ah, goodnight." She said, with a confused tone.

I headed for the stairs, taking one last glance at her. She stood there with her hand on her cheek, where I had just kissed, with a blush following. I couldn't help but notice too, the faint smile on her lips, as I hurried away, wanting already, to hurry back.

CHAPTER 6

ANOTHER NIGHT OF NO SLEEP. I halfway expected that, but this time, it wasn't due to nerves. It was the excitement that kept me up, and it was the thought of her that made me excited. She was everything I could hope for in a woman. Everything I could ever want, she seemed to have. I tried to ground myself to the reality of just meeting her, with reason.

"How could you know she's who you want? You've barely known her?" My logic voice would ask.

"But her smile. Her personality. The kiss…." My heart would jump every time I thought of the kiss.

"Yes, the kiss…" The kiss was unlike anything I had ever experienced. It was as if an electrical current flowed through all of my nerves at once. A feeling that I had that surpassed all others that I could name. I don't know. Maybe it was just me or maybe it had been way too long since I kissed someone, but regardless, deep down I knew, she was different. Whatever was between us, was different.

Before I knew it, the morning had arrived. I didn't work out… In fact, I hadn't in a while. My body was so energized; it was like it didn't need the cardiovascular workout, as my heart was in overdrive. Heading to work, I could help but noticed that I had not stopped smiling. I couldn't.

Dad came in early. I knew there had to be a rhyme and reason as to why.

"So, how did it go?" He asked with the anxiousness of a teenage girl.

"Dad," I said in a tone that only pretended that I didn't want to talk about it.

"Come on, son. I'm your Dad. How did it go?" He egged.

"Dad.." I waited a long pause, and I grew solemn.

"What, what?" He couldn't read my expression.

"She... is perfect!"

Instantly, his body language changed to that of relief. He merely smiled as a way of telling me to go on.

"She... is gorgeous, smart, funny, driven.... But, she's unique in all of them the same. Like, she's beautiful in a way that most women aren't. She is smart, not by a measure of degree or IQ, but in her own right. There are no words to describe these hopelessly beautiful emotions she makes me feel. It would take a poet to describe her beauty, but not even the most skilled painter could capture it. I..."

I was cut off when I looked at my Dad. His eyes were filled with tears.

"Dad! What's wrong?" I begged, and I stepped towards him.

He cleared his throat and waited a moment before he spoke. "Michael... There are things in life that don't make sense. There will be things in this world that you can't define, can't understand and can't figure out. But... the word you're looking for... the thing you're saying you can't explain... It's love, my boy. It's love."

Part of me felt relief as he said it, but the other part of me felt this was all crazy. "But Dad, it's the first date! I mean, I know her, but there are so many things I don't know... and.... well, this just seems. Fast."

"Michael," he interrupted. "Michael. It's not about logic this time son. It's about feeling. Trust your feelings. There is a way that God leads you sometimes. He speaks to your heart, not by words, but by feeling."

I had never heard my Dad talk this way before. I was a bit freaked out by it... "God?" I asked.

"Yes son, God. The one you write that check to every month. He's real you know." He said so in a sarcastic tone.

My Dad had more of a relationship with the whole church thing than I did. It's not that I didn't have faith, but I guess I had a harder time believing that God was that involved. I would seldom pray and do what I was supposed to do. I just didn't see God as active as he did.

"So you're telling me that God is saying that I love Rella." I reasoned aloud.

He laughed. "Boy, some things fly right over your head. Only you can know what God is saying."

"Dad, this is getting weird," I said in a tone that mimicked a skeptic.

He laughed once more. "You'll see one day. Some things escape language, merely at the fact that it can't describe it." He paused. "So, when are you two seeing each other again?"

I looked at him a moment trying to decipher just what the heck had happened while also realizing that I had no clue. "Ugh..." I decided to move on... "Well, I don't know..." I smiled slightly. "I hope soon."

Dad laughed. "Well, until then, let's get some work done." We had a lot of appointments and meetings. We were booked for showings three nights a week for the next three weeks. Business was better than it had ever been. In between every meeting, though, my mind kept drifting back to her... Rella. I just needed to see her again and soon.

I skipped lunch hoping to get out early. Did I think maybe about going to see her or was that creepy? I just didn't know... There were dating "laws" that I had heard about, but honestly, I just wanted to be with her again. I wondered if she felt the same. I tried to keep myself busy, but our two 'o'clock appointment was late, making that more difficult than necessary. At 2:15 the doorbell ring, and I tried desperately to hide my frustration. I couldn't stand being late for anything. I got up, trying to hide my emotion. As I stepped into the showroom, I realized that wouldn't work. My emotion was all over my face when it came to Rella.

"Fancy seeing you here." She said when she spotted me.

The very sound of her voice took my breath away. She had already become my drug and by her presence alone I was relieved of my pain from missing her. "Yeah..." I said breathlessly.

"Are you okay? You look..." As I came closer, she examined my eyes further... "I don't know..."

"I'm all right." I smiled. "I'm ecstatic to see you."

Immediate blush hit her cheeks. I loved that. "Well, I was just in the neighborhood, doing some shopping for a client."

"I'm glad you were," I said as calmly as I could. The chemistry... The feeling in the air was so tangible. I just wanted to grab her and kiss her fervently. I wondered if she felt it too.

"Michael..." Her tone changed. "I need something from you."

Concerned, I answered, "Yes, of course. What is it?"

"Honesty." She turned away directed her attention to a portrait.

I didn't understand. She seemed mad. "Honesty?" I questioned.

"Yes. Honesty. The truth is important to me." She said, but it was as if she was saying something else.

"Rella," I went to touch her hand. Grabbing it, I asked, "Are you okay?"

She turned with tears in her eyes. "Yes. Yes, I'm fine. But I just need you to tell me the truth. Be honest."

There was some personal, internal conflict going on within her. She needed this answer from me. "Ask me anything, and I will tell you the truth, Rella."

"Always, you will?" She offered me a way out it seemed.

"Yes, of course," I assured her. "Rella, did I do something..."

"No, Michael. No... I... I... I just."

"It's okay, Rella. Tell me."

"I missed you."

Completely baffled by her statement, I asked, "You missed me?"

"Yes, yes, I missed you. After one stupid date, I missed you. I wasn't shopping. I wasn't in the neighborhood. I wanted to see you. I like you. I like you a lot. And you know, this is just how it started with my mom and Dad. They were like, in one date, all in love. You know?" She pulled away and was pacing as if she were ranting in her mind, and it was accidently coming out. "Like, overnight. They just 'fell in love'" she mimicked quotes with her fingers. "And you know it wasn't love... it was infatuation. Well, for my Dad, it was infatuation. And for my mom, it was love. And well, my mom, ended up hurt. And this... you. Well, I'm not my mother, Michael. I'm not" She looked at me sternly, "And I will not be fooled." She pointed her finger at me. "So, I need your honesty. Have you missed me? Do you have feelings... for... me?" She stuttered at the end.

I couldn't help the endearing smirk coming across my lips.

"What is that smile?" She asked in an accusatory tone. "Are you a player, Michael? Are you a chauvinistic pig like the rest?"

I couldn't help but chuckle. "Rella," This had just dramatically gone in a direction that I would never have guessed.

"You are, aren't you? It's too good to be true isn't it, love at first sight? It's stupid isn't it?" The fury in her voice was rising.

I immediately stopped at her word. Love. "What?"

"What?" She paused. "What?" She bartered me.

"You said, love. Rella."

"Just tell me if you've missed me! Tell me with complete honesty!" She was raising her voice.

I walked calmly back towards her. This was it. It was all the real deal. The feelings. The emotion. The way she felt. The way I felt. At that moment I knew she had felt what I had been feeling this whole time. It wasn't just me. "Cindy Rella Allan," I said her name in full, trying to catch my breath. "I have missed you, and I haven't stopped thinking about you. That is the truth. I will always be honest with you. I will not hurt you. I will not lie to you and... I love you, too."

I couldn't help the tears welling in my eyes. The emotion caught in my throat. The tears were rolling down her face, as I looked into her eyes.

"You mean it? You do?" She sounded like a scared young girl, who had been rejected her whole life.

"I do. I promise... I've been perplexed by this... It was only one date... But you... You're different. You're what I've been waiting for. I..."

She interrupted me with a hard kiss. I couldn't help but pull her in close and hold her in my arms. Her lips parted from mine. "Are we crazy?" She smiled.

"No... I think... sometimes..." I couldn't believe what I was saying... "I sometimes think God talks to us through feelings..." I looked deep into her eyes. "I think our feelings are saying that we have... found one another."

I leaned in and kissed her again. It was love. There was no way around it. There was no denying it. One date. One kiss. One love. She was all mine. It wasn't rational. It wasn't logical. It was right, and we both knew it. Our hearts knew it. Rella was mine. She had always been mine, but my heart had just found her after it had waited for so long. She had found me. Out of all the towns in this state, she chooses this one... And all the studios, she walks through this one... It was all part of a bigger picture... one not painted by our hands but maybe by the hands fate. Maybe that's God's nickname; Fate. This could be what my father was trying to tell me earlier. None other than less, out of all the paintings I've seen, there was never one as beautiful as this...

2 Months Later

CHAPTER 7

Rella and I, since that day, were inseparable. We were in love, from the moment we met. I know it sounds crazy, and maybe it was, but the evidence of our feelings didn't lie. I was old enough to understand the difference between love and lust... How I felt about Rella was solely rooted in love. However, we both still felt that dating and courting were necessary. We acknowledged that we didn't know each other well enough to get married, and we both wanted to further the friendship in the relationship as well.

Today marked the two-month anniversary since we made our first confession of love. I would never forget that day. Rella, full of emotion, came in demanding answers when she was just wondering if I felt the same as she. If it was all possible to meet someone and just know that you both were meant to be. I did feel the same, and as the months passed by, I still did.

Every day we had lunch and dinner together. She would often drop by, with clients of hers, to show them the artwork. But really, we both knew, it was just to see each other. I too started to relax a little on my tightly wound schedule. Rella and I would stay up late talking and planning. It was ironic that now Dad arrived to work earlier than I. Everything seemed to change, but the balance wasn't too far behind. Rella and I had developed a great friendship right along side our romantic love. It seemed like every time we saw each other we learned something new and fell a little more for one another.

Life, for me, was completely perfect. I didn't realize how lonely I was before Rella. It's funny how life can do that to you. You think you have it all, until the missing piece you didn't know was there, presents itself. I didn't know that I needed Rella until I found her. Now, there was no going back, even if we wanted to... Though, I couldn't image a situation where that would be the case.

This morning I was planning a surprise for Rella. It being our two months, I wanted to take her out to a neighboring big city. I figured a night in a 5-star restaurant would be perfect. I had already talked everything over with Dad and planned that we would need to leave around 5:00 to make our reservations for 6:00. The big city was around forty minutes away. Tonight was a big night, because... well, I knew it was time to tell Rella about my virginity.

Over the past few weeks, I could feel the intimacy building between us. It's not biased to say that usually the guy is the one that pushes for a little more and the fact that I wasn't doing so had to be a little suspect. I loved Rella. And honestly, as a man, I wanted more, but not until after we had the vows said and signed between us. I knew that we were not fallen victim to lust in our quick pace. And even if we did concede to more than kissing, it wouldn't have been due to infectious, physical appeal. However, I wanted to the first time to be more than that. Plus, I didn't know where Rella was at with... everything or where she stood on the issue.

She had to be wondering why I kept kissing and running. Literally, every time I felt a little too "heated" I would make an excuse to go. She had to be curious, but too ladylike to ask.

And, on top of all that, I felt guilty. Here I promised her honesty, and I was keeping a very important secret. Tonight was the night to get this all out in the open, so I wanted it to go very smoothly. Rella had already agreed to be ready by 5:00 for me to pick her up.

We didn't have any meetings or showings for the rest of the week, so Dad wouldn't have much to do when I left. I never liked leaving him with a lot of work. It made me feel guilty, and I didn't need that. I was already filled with enough emotion concerning this subject.

Around 4:00 I checked everything to make sure it was all set. I needed to go home, change and head to Rella's apartment.

"Dad, I'm going to head out, okay?"

"Yeah, sure thing. Where are you guys going tonight?" He asked.

"To The Sava in the city."

"Wow, the fancy 5-star stuff... You going to pop the question?"

I laughed nervously, "No, Dad. Not quite yet. I just wanted to have a special dinner. It's our two month anniversary." I played it off. No way was I having this discussion with my Dad. There was NO way.

"Oh, I see. Well, you kids have fun. Let me know if you need anything. I'll have my cell on me. Call me when you get back into the city. I worry about stuff like that..."

"Alright Dad, will do. I'll talk to you later then."

"Sounds good. Bye, son."

"See ya."

I grabbed my keys and headed out the door. It was important to get everything done on time. If there was anything that would make me unnecessarily rushed, it was being behind schedule. I went home and immediately hopped in the shower. The hot water helped calm my nerves. I needed that.

I grabbed my nice, newly tailored dark gray suit and white shirt. I put in on along with a light gray, silver tie. I grabbed my Italian leather shoes and combed my hair. As I looked in the mirror, I was pleased. I told Rella to dress up, and she seemed very excited. She told me that she was going to go buy a new dress.... Nothing better for a man than to give an excuse to a woman to go shopping. Surely, already, I had the upper hand with that alone. With a splash of cologne, I was off to her place.

As I got in my Jeep, it was the first time I felt perplexed about seeing Rella. I alternated between speeding there to see her and slowing down due to the anxiety of what would be discussed tonight. Arriving, I could feel my nerves rising. I didn't know when I was going to tell her, but I knew the right moment just had to present itself.

"Don't worry," I told myself. "It's not like tonight she's going to expect it. It's not like she's asking for more..."

My mind coaxed my stomach's butterflies. Relax. I took a deep breath and did so. What was there to be concerned about?

I strode up the stairs to her apartment door and knocked.

"Come in, babe." I could hear her yell at my knock.

I walked in. Her apartment was clean, but there was stuff everywhere. That's my girl. She was many things, but a neat freak was not one of them.

"Sorry," she said from the back room. "I'm a little behind."

That's my girl, too. She was always a little late, no matter what. It was just who she was.

"It's alright honey, take your time."

She laughed, "You don't mean that." She said jokingly.

"You're right," I said comically. "Hurry up."

She laughed again, knowing that she was in full control of the situation. I mosied around waiting for her, looking at various magazines and clippings of different furniture and style. That was one of her techniques for décor was keeping up with the latest home fashions. I picked up one labeled A Perfect Home out of curiosity, wondering what on earth a couch would have to do with that.

"Okay, I'm ready, but I need you to zip me up." She interrupted my thought.

Reading, I said, "Okay," unknowing just what I was about to see.

I turned and couldn't believe what was in front of me.

She was dressed in a floor-length, navy blue, silk gown. The dressed hugged her as if it was made for her. The soft curvature of her body was visible by the unseen. I felt the heat rush to me, as I have never experienced. He auburn hair, swept to one side, was intensified in color against the contrast of the blue. Her eyes sparkled. Her faint skin was highlighted somehow. She was the most beautiful thing I had ever seen.

I didn't notice that I dropped the magazine I was holding.

She chuckled, "Well, that's the nicest compliment ever." She winked at me. "But, I still need you to finish zipping me up."

She turned, and I saw the mid of her back. It was bare. No bra. My hands were quivering. This was going to be a lot harder than I imagined. I slowly grabbed the zipper and did everything in my power not to touch her skin. Here, alone in this apartment. I was more tempted than I had ever been before. I hesitated for a moment. Perhaps I wanted to move the zipper down, rather than up.

No. No. This was not how I wanted this to happen. I zipped up the dress quickly. We needed to go.

"Alright, you're zipped. Let's go." I said a little too sternly.

"Oh, okay..." She seemed concerned. "Let my grab my clutch."

I took her hand and kissed it as a silent apology. "Okay, baby," I whispered.

Before I knew it, we were in the car. For whatever reason, I thought this would be better, but it wasn't. I was so acutely aware of her. Her smell. Her looks. Her... everything. This was a bad idea.

"Tell her to dress up Michael." My mind teased. "Take her to a fancy dinner, Michael." It continued. "Get yourself into a tempting situation, Michael. Then, tell her you're a virgin, Michael."

Bad. This was all bad, and I was growing more nervous by the minute as we drove further out of town.

"Are you okay?" She asked. "You look a little... tense." She reached over a put her hand on my knee.

"Tense?" I choked. Boy, I was tense all right.

"Yes... Is everything okay?" She wondered aloud.

"Yes baby, I'm fine. Just hungry."

She laughed. "I should have known. You and your fancy food."

She always teased me about my gourmet food pallet. I just had gotten used to fine dining over the years.

"Well, I am excited about this restaurant. It's Italian, right?" She continued.

"Yes, it's Italian. They have the best fettuccini I have ever tasted." I went on. The food was a good subject to be on, considering the situation.

"Yum... Well, I am getting an appetite. How far are we?"

"We have about 30 minutes until we arrive."

"Wow, I thought you said it was about an hour drive?" She questioned.

"It is... I'm just driving fast." I turned and smiled.

She chuckled, "Man, you are hungry."

Gosh, if she only knew the real reason. I was driving fast because I was so nervous... And being this close to her with that dress.... I halfway wanted to turn around and go back. Stop Michael. I kept correcting myself.

"Well, what are we going to do after, Michael?" She interrupted my thoughtless thoughts.

"Ummm..." I stalled. "I don't know... What do you want to do?"

"Well, I was thinking we could just spend the rest of the night watching a good movie at my place?" She peered at me.

A movie? If this was bad, that was worse. Was this a... way to get me over there with her. Did she want more than a kiss... I just didn't know. I could only assume...

"A movie?" I asked, "We've never done that before..." I tried to sound casual.

"There are a lot of things we haven't done before, Michael." She said it in a way that made my heart almost jump out of my chest. How was I supposed to tell her? How was I going to... let her down easy. I wanted her... Would I even be able to let her down at all?

"Michael?" She questioned me. "Are you sure you're okay?"

"Yes, baby. I'm all right. We'll watch a movie when we get done eating." I would just have to tell her before we got back to her place. In the car. I would do it after dinner. That way, she would know... That way I could ... protect myself from all of this. I just needed to relax and get through dinner.

"So, what do you say to some Italian Classical, to get us in the mood?" I questioned.

"Yes, music would be great. I love Classical." She said in a chipper tone.

I quickly turned on my phone, to Bluetooth the music to the stereo. Nothing like Opera to calm one down.

Before I knew it, we had arrived. Rella and I didn't say much the rest of the way. The music was great filler.

As we walked into the restaurant, we were greeted by the hostess.

"May I help you, sir?" He asked.

"Yes. Reservations for Harvey." I replied.

"Yes sir, right this way."

The young man assured us to the table, and I couldn't help but notice that every man in the room turned his head to Rella. Jealousy filled me. She was mine. I pulled her in closer to me as we walked. Keeping my head up, as a form of signaling I wasn't threatened, even though I felt so. Rella was so beautiful, and I couldn't help but think she could move on... if she wanted to.

"Is this okay, Mr. Harvey?" The young man asked as he brought us to an exclusive table.

"Yes, sir. This will do." I responded.

He helped us to our seats. "Here is the wine menu. A server will be right with you."

"Thank you," I sounded as Rella smiled.

"Wow, this is very fancy." She smiled, grabbing the menu.

"Rella, you are stunning." I couldn't help but tell her.

She peered up at me over the menu. "Thank you, honey. You don't look so bad yourself." She winked.

The mere sight of her made my heart beat faster. I just wanted to eat. Then leave. Then tell her. I had to tell her. I was beginning to bust at the seams with anxiety!

I ordered the wine and an appetizer. I centered the conversation about everything except what we were going to do after. We talked about the art studio and the upcoming events. I talked about festivals that would come into town this summer that we could enjoy together. I questioned her about work and how everything was going. Honestly, I just kept talking... I couldn't take the silence. Not tonight. Not with her looking at me the way she was.

"Michael, you're talkative. You seem nervous." She said in a sultry tone.

"No, no... Nervous... Why would I be nervous?" I asked, taking a sip of my wine.

"Oh.... I don't know..." She said in a knowing way... Did she know?

Thankfully, our food was served. My stomach was filled with butterflies, but I forced myself to eat. Rella ate a few bites, but I noticed she was just really picking at her food rather than eating it. I kept noticing her look up at me in a certain way. It filled my blood with heat every time she did it. We talked just a bit... But, I was running out of things to say.

"Do you not like your food?" I asked her.

"Yes... Well... I'm not that hungry, on second thought." She said, setting down her fork.

"You're not? I thought you were excited about the restaurant?" I questioned her.

"I was... but.. I'm more excited about leaving."

My heart stopped. I couldn't breath. She wanted me. And Lord only knows I wanted her. I looked at her, almost painting like a nervous, hot dog.

"Michael?" She questioned.

I cleared my throat. "Yes?"

"Can we go? I'm ready for us to be alone." There was a hint of demand in her voice.

I gazed at her in shock. She couldn't have been any clearer.

"Is that okay?" She asked as I didn't answer.

"Yes, baby. We can go." Gosh, why did I say yes... I had to say yes. I couldn't say no to Rella... And that very fact was right now my biggest concern.

I grabbed the waiter and gave him my credit card. It was hardly 30 after seven, and we were walking out the door. The city lights were starting to come on, as the sun was dimming over the horizon. It would be dark before we left town.

"Do you want to do see anything in the city?" I asked, praying she would say yes, to buy me some time.

"No... I'm ready for that movie." She pulled me closer to her, as we headed back towards the Jeep.

"Alright, baby. We'll head back." It was all I could do but agree with her.

As we got in the car, I prayed for the moment to present itself on the drive back. I needed the perfect set up. The perfect intro into what would be one of the hardest, possibly most embarrassing things I had ever had to explain.

I was focused. As we crossed the city border, I knew I had about forty minutes to get it all out there. Rella was talking about movies and which ones she wanted to watch.

"What about you?" She asked.

"What about what?" I was so distracted by my own thoughts I was only halfway listening.

"Michael..." She scolded gently. "What kind of movie do you want to watch?"

"Umm," All I could think of is what I was going to tell her. "How about... No, you pick." I smiled at her reassuringly.

"Okay, how about a love story. Those are my favorite." She smiled.

"Of course..." I smiled. She has such innocence about her sometimes. "Your mom isn't the only romantic in the family, is she?" I smiled at her.

She teasingly hit me in the arm. "No... Maybe I like a little romance myself!" She said in a mockingly mad voice.

I laughed this time. I couldn't help but be so in love with her. She was perfect in every way... If.. I did lose my focus tonight; it wouldn't be the worst thing... I was going to marry this woman, no matter what. Regardless of vows, I was already 100% committed to her.

"Well, I'm going to pick the movie when we get back, okay? I have quite a few romance movies we can choose from, being that I'm a hopeless romantic." She said sarcastically.

"Rella, it's okay to be a romantic. I love that about you." I assured her.... I had about 30 minutes until we arrived back home.

"You do?" She asked.

"Of course..." This was it. "Love... it doesn't have boundaries, Rella. It is just full of complete acceptance, you know? And no matter what, nothing changes that. I have something to..."

The jerking of the jeep cut me off. I heard a sound as it was involuntarily slowing down.

"Oh gosh! Michael, is everything okay?" Rella asked, worried.

I felt the engine come to a stall, and then just stop. I remembered the same patterned when this had happened to me before in high school.

I couldn't help but laugh a little. "Rella... We're out of gas."

"What?" She exclaimed.

I must have been so nervous I didn't even check my tank. "Yes, I-I... I must have forgotten."

She smiled, "Well, well, well, Mr. Planner... Looks like you've missed the mark here?" She then busted into laughter. Man, I was never going to live this one down.

I couldn't help but laugh too. Gosh, how worked up was I not even to check the tank. "Okay, calm down." I teased her. "I'll call my Dad. He'll bring me some gas."

She was laughing hysterically. "Yeah baby, call your Dad." She laughed.

I shook my head. I had only planned on one embarrassing thing for the evening... Not two. I couldn't help but laugh though at how hard Rella was laughing. It was as if this was the funniest thing she had ever seen.

"Would you stop?" I teased her, poking her side.

"No!" She laughed, "I can't. This is great."

"Ugh," I sighed. "Well, time to make the call." Boy was this going to be something to explain. I dialed my Dad's number.

It had ringed twice before he answered. "Hello?"

"Hey Dad, it's Michael."

"Wow, well Y'all are back in town soon. How was dinner?"

"Dad, we're not back in town yet."

Rella was laughing in the background saying, "Go on, and tell him."

"Dad."

"Yes? What's going on son? Everything okay?"

"Yes, Dad. I'm just... We just... ran out of gas." Rella then lost it. I only thought she was laughing loudly before.

"Shhhhh!" I told her jokingly.

"You're out of gas?" My Dad questioned.

"Yes, Dad. I just forgot to fill up."

"You forgot?" he questioned. I could tell he was smiling.

"Yes, Dad. Can you please just come and bring us a can? We're about 30 minutes out of town."

He was chuckling now. "Okay, Michael. Give me about 45 minutes. I need to get a gas can and fill it up."

"Okay, Dad." Before I hung up, I could hear him laughing. At least Rella had slowed down to a chuckle.

"Is he coming?" She asked with a big smile.

"Yes. He'll be here in about an hour. He said 45 minutes, but for my Dad you always add and extra 15 minutes. He's usually late."

She laughed, "Okay. That's all right. Well, we'll just hang tight."

"Yeah... I'm sorry honey." I said embarrassed.

"It's okay Michael. This is good to see. You can't plan everything, you know?" She was looking at me so endearingly.

"I know... You're right. You can't." I agreed. Maybe now was the time. Might as well kill two birds with one stone.

"So, what were you about to say, before we stopped?" She asked.

"Ugh, oh... well." I stammered. Just say it, Michael! My mind was coaching while my heart was racing.

"Well..." Rella insisted.

"Well, I love you and no matter what... I..."

"What is it, Michael?" She seemed concerned.

"I... I... I..." There was a long pause. "I think we should look for satellites." Coward.

"What?" She seemed confused.

"Yes, satellites. We're out in the country, and it's a clear, spring night. Let me take the top off the Jeep." I hurried out before she could protest.

I got out and unlatched the top. I was too nervous. I needed to calm down.

I pulled it off. "Okay, now lean your seat back," I told her.

"Okay... This seems..."

"No, trust me!" I interrupted her. "You'll love it."

She smiled as if she knew that I was just distracting myself. I got back in the car.

"So, have you ever done this before?" I asked.

"I'm not sure what we are doing..." She reasoned.

"We are looking for satellites in the sky." I smiled at her.

"Satellites?" She questioned.

"Yes... Have you ever done this before?"

"Certainly not," she said comically.

"Okay, well, a satellite is different than a star. It doesn't blink or twinkle. It just stays in constant light with constant motion, streaming across the sky."

"Okay. So, you just look for one?" She asked.

"Yes, it's like looking for a shooting star, but it's much easier and much more likely."

She giggled, "Okay. Will you help me, though?"

"Yes, baby. Of course." I grabbed her hand as a laid my seat back.

I pointed out stars and planets while keeping an eye out for the satellite.

"What about that one?" She asked.

"No, baby, that one is a plan. See how the light flashes?"

"Oh, okay. I see."

She was so perfect. I watched her scan the sky. I couldn't have asked for a more perfect woman.

"What about... that one?" She asked pointing as a young child would.

"Which one?" I asked, following her finger.

"Umm... I don't know." She waited. "I think I lost it."

I chuckled. "It's okay baby... Let's look a little more."

We waited in perfect silence.

"There's one, right? That's one?" She sat up pointing frantically.

I looked and saw what she was seeing. "Yes, baby, that's it. That's a satellite. See how constant it is? Never changing speeds?"

"Yes, wow." She was captivated.

We watched. "It's like our love," I whispered.

"Constant and never changing." She answered.

I leaned in and kissed her. Slow and beautiful.

She parted back, "I love you."

"I love you too, darling."

She looked back towards the sky, keeping track of the satellite before it escaped our sight. "What made you ever want to look for satellites?" She asked me quietly.

"My mom," I answered. "I did this with her when I was worried about her, during the cancer treatments. I would get very scared and anxious at nights, wondering if I had her for one more week or month." My voice filled with emotion. "When I couldn't sleep, she would take me outside, and she would ask me to help her look for satellites. She taught me how to spot them. I would be so focus on finding them that I would forget that I was worried about her cancer. Most times when I was in deep concentration, she would come from behind and whisper in my ear. She would tell me "look for the constant light when I'm gone, Micheal... And just like those satellites, I will be in the sky constantly keeping an eye on you and shining my light Remember me when you look at the dark sky for that constant shining light."

"Oh, Michael." Rella choked her tears flowing. "That's the most beautiful thing."

"Yes," I couldn't help the tear fall, reminding me of my mom.

We sat in silence. My mom would have loved Rella. She would have gotten along with her so well. She would love our relationship and admire the purity of it. My heart was calmed.

"Rella, I have something to tell you." The satellite helped me keep my heart at a slow pace.

"Okay." She sensed my seriousness.

"I'm a virgin." I waited, trying to measure her response. There was a moment of silence. I couldn't speak.

"You are?" She almost whispered.

"Yes. I... I've always wanted to wait until I found the woman I truly loved. I want to wait until marriage." I forced my words out, gazing her way.

She had tears rolling down her check. "What's wrong, darling?" I couldn't help but notice the influx of emotion.

"Oh, Michael." She sobbed, putting her hands up to her eyes. "I..."

"Rella, it's okay. What's wrong, tell me."

"Nothing... It's just a relief." She choked.

"Relief?" I asked.

"Yes... because... well, I'm a virgin too."

"You are?" I tried not to sound too shocked even though I was.

"Yes, and I've been so worried you could tell. By my kissing. You're my first kiss, Michael."

"What?" I was now in full shock.

"Yes, and I thought I was bad at it. I thought that was why you were running away from me every time we kissed."

"Oh, Rella." I couldn't imagine the odds.

"Yes, and so, I felt like I just needed to get better... And I thought well, I thought you would want more from me, so I was pushing myself to give it to you. I love you. You're perfect, and so I just thought.... Well, it would be okay if I didn't... that's why tonight, I was acting all... well, you know."

"Rella," I wiped her tears. "Were you scared that I'd leave you for not having sex with me?"

She sobbed now, answering my question.

"Shhh, it's okay." I soothed her. "It's okay."

"I just didn't want you to think I didn't love you. But, I wanted to wait. And, I was scared. I've never really dated anyone before. I never thought.... I never thought I would ever fall in love."

I smiled at her, "But you have?" I questioned.

"Yes, yes. I have. I love you... I can't believe that you..." She receded in thought.

I answered her unspoken question. "I never went that far, because I never felt a connection too. I'm not the purest, but..." I slowed down, not knowing what to say.

"Oh, Michael." She leaped over to me and kissed me hard. "I love you; I love you."

"I love you too, baby."

"We'll wait together, huh?" She asked.

"Yes. We'll wait for marriage." I sounded more confident now than ever.

"You're going to marry me?" I felt her emotion bubbling back up.

"If it's the last thing I do," I said sternly.

"Oh, Michael." She kissed me again and then stopped suddenly. "So, am I a good kisser?"

"You're an amazing kisser, darling," I assured her. My pure Rella.

She kissed me again and then just cried into my shoulder.

"Shhhh, it's okay." I soothed her. She kissed me again, but the bright lights made us both pull back. Dad was here. On time, for the first time.

His truck slowed, as he got out. Rella quickly hurried back to her seat, embarrassed.

"What are Y'all kids doing..." Dad teased. "I can come back if you need me to."

"Dad..." I scolded him.

He laughed. "I'm just saying... you too looked busy." He taunted.

Boy did he just have no idea. "No Dad, it's not what you think."

"I know... I know my boy." He patted me on the back. "Rella, how are you doing? Are you okay? He noticed her tears.

"Yes, James." She smiled full of confidence. "We are. We're both virgins, and we're going to wait until marriage."

Dad and I were both in shock now. I didn't expect it. She was so calm and collected, full of relief. I didn't realize what a burden she had on her shoulders as well... I turned to see my Dad's expression. I was the one chuckling now. Dad never looked so shocked as to how Rella just blurted all of that out.

"Well..." He said in a reserved tone, "I'm proud of you both. Now, let me get the gas can."

She smiled. "I just wanted him to know, baby? Is that okay? I want everyone to know!" She was so childlike in the most endearing way.

"Okay, baby. He can know... He just wasn't expecting it." I laughed.

Dad came back and filled up the gas tank.

"That ought to do it." He said.

"Thanks, Dad." I put my hand on his shoulder.

"No problem. Nice to see that you can't plan for everything," He teased. Rella giggled.

"I'm never going to live this down with you two, am I?" I asked rhetorically.

"Nope." They both echoed.

On the drive back, Rella and I just held hands. We were both at peace. It had been such an emotional evening. But, how ironic. My lack of planning helped my plan. I felt the weight of the whole situation come off my shoulders. Rella's heart had been exposed to me in such a beautiful way. I loved her more for it. We were perfect together. Regardless of our virginity, we both had been waiting for the other without ever really knowing it.

There are so many stars sometimes; so many twinkling distractions of the world when it comes to dating and relationships. But in more ways than one, I had found my satellite in Rella. My constant love. She would never go out of my view, nor out of my heart. She calmed me and soothed me. I waited for her. I watched for her. And now, I turned to see the brightest light in all my life.

CHAPTER 8

About a month had passed since Rella, and I disclosed our virginity to one another. Ironically, ever since we've felt a whole new level of intimacy between each other. I sometimes think the world gets a little to caught up in physical attraction, and we neglect the emotional attraction between one another; like the intimacy of our hearts. Due to the physicality of the situation, or lack thereof, Rella and I were forced to relish in emotional intimacy. By doing that, it took our love to a level that I feel most couples don't reach until they've grown old together. We were able to see each other in a new way, in a new light and the past few weeks proved to be beautiful.

Also, I felt an enormous weight lifted off my chest since the night of Satellites. (That's what we called it.) I didn't like keeping anything from Rella, and since that night, I promised her that I never would again. In such a short time, I felt like I had known her all of my life and at this point, I couldn't imagine living without her.

Though marriage was certainly on both of our minds, I planned on asking her at the six-month mark. I wanted to date more and get to know more of the little things about her; the things you only come to know by spending time with that person. I figured that six months would be sufficient enough. She had already talked about her plans for the wedding, and it was very simple. I liked that. It didn't seem like it would be too much work to pull it all together. Plus, we were both getting busy with our jobs. The word about our gallery was traveling far and attracting new artists and Rella had been getting a ton of new clients. Word traveled fast, at her talent of being a great interior designer. She had even given us a few suggestions for the gallery, which made a huge difference, but that was another thing to love about Rella. Put her in a room and somehow, in more ways than one, she'd change it for the better.

This morning Rella called to let me know that she had a surprise for me. Saturdays we would spend all day together, and this one was no different. Most times, I made the plans since I knew the area the best, but she insisted. She said she was showing me a secret place of hers. I had no idea what she had in mind, so I was certain this day would be full of adventure.

I was up and ready by nine, even though she said to pick her up at ten till eleven. The woman slept in a little too much on Saturdays. I knew even if I did get there at eleven she wouldn't be ready still. I was never a "sleeping in type" though there were days I wished I was. Even now, it was just too out of the ordinary for me and too much lack of structure. So to pass the time, I decided I would do a little shopping.

I liked to surprise Rella with gifts. Around 10:30, I strolled out to my Jeep and headed for this small gift shop on 9th named Sweet Lil Things. Ms. Margaret always had beautiful jewelry, and I had wanted to get Rella a necklace of some sort. Nothing too fancy, because I knew she wouldn't like that. Just something beautiful, sweet and delicate as she was.

I knew I could count on Ms. Margaret to point me in the right direction. You wouldn't find a more generous soul in all of Michigan. She was the kindest person all around. She and her husband had lived here all their life. I couldn't tell you how long their little boutique had been open... It was longer than I could remember. I recall going as a young boy and helping my Dad pick out something for my mom. Ms. Margaret usually guided us on the best choice then, and I knew she'd do the same now for me.

I walked into the tiny little shop, and the decor was as it had always been. Little trinkets and tokens everywhere, it seemed. There was an array of wallpaper on every wall with floral designs. The chairs were lined with a bright fabric of pinks, purples, and yellows. Nothing matched, but somehow it all seemed to come together. Ultimately, I suppose you could say that it was a dollhouse for people. Everything was colored and wrapped in feminine beauty. As was always, Mrs. Margaret.

"Well, good morning Michael dear. How are you, child?" She asked. I was still a child to her. I'm sure she was around her mid eighty's by now, but you wouldn't know it by the way she moved around the shop. Mrs. Margret's memory was a little spotted, but she never seemed to forget a name or face. It was the most recent things that she seemed to have trouble with, but no one ever held her accountable for it. She was as sweet as they come.

"Good morning, Mrs. Margaret. I'm doing well. How about yourself?"

"Oh, darling, I am always well because I am always blessed." She smiled.

"Yes, ma'am." I nodded. "Well, do you think you could help me today?"

"Well, of course, I can!" She grinned. More than anything, Mrs. Margret loved to help. "What do you need?"

"Well, I am looking for a necklace for Rella, my girlfriend. I wanted something delicate but meaningful."

"Those are the best gifts. Let's see what we have. Come over here." She motioned as she walked around the counter on my left side.

I followed her and went to look in the glass display. Man, did I have the decision to make. The case was filled with beautiful necklaces.

"Mrs. Margaret, it looks like there is lot's of decision-making this morning," I stated in a teasing tone.

"Oh, well, it is easy to narrow down once you tell me about this girl." She smiled with a twinkle in her eye.

I smiled, "Yes, of course." Where to begin? Rella meant so much to me; it was hard to find a simple description of her.

"Well... she is beautiful, smart... she's everything to me. The descriptions of everything beautiful comes to mind..." I felt my voice shake a little bit.

"True love, is it?" Mrs. Margaret reasoned.

"Yes." I smiled.

"Oh, that's wonderful. I just love, love." She cooed. "It sounds like you two will tie the knot soon..."

"I hope so." I blushed a little.

"Every good man, needs a good woman... Just like a ship needs and anchor." Mrs. Margaret sounded. "It seems like this girl is your anchor?" she suggested.

"What? Like an old ball and chain?" I asked jokingly.

Mrs. Margaret laughed and said "No child. An anchor is what keeps your vessel from drifting and getting lost through the storms. It holds strong through the darkest of nights in your life. An anchor is trustworthy and faithful. She holds strong to you, does she not? Not your vessel... but the very strings of your heart?"

I was stunned by her description. Yes. That was my Rella. "Yes," I whispered.

Mrs. Margaret smiled knowingly. "Well, then, look at these."

I turned to the back corner, and I saw little necklaces with small anchors on them. Gold, silver, and some with small diamonds.

"That's perfect!" I shared in awe.

"Ok. Well, which one reminds you the most of her?"

I scanned them looking and searching... There were many choices. I felt like she would love any of them, but I wanted to pick the very best. As I scanned through the selections, my eyes kept coming back to one.

"Mrs. Margaret, can you pull that one out for me?" It was a little anchor, dangling at the end of the chain. However, there was an infinity sign, which it went through, kind of like a loop knot. It was so unique and beautiful as Rella was. The sign and the anchor to me symbolized timeless love. That's what Rella and I had. Timeless love.

As she pulled it out of the case, I couldn't help but smile. This was it. The gold color was perfect. Rella usually wore gold jewelry, rather than silver.

"Mrs. Margaret, that's the one," I said with complete confidence.

"You're sure this is it?" She asked, teasingly. "Sure didn't take you long to make the decision."

"The best decisions are sometimes the easiest." I smiled.

"Mr. Michael Harvey, I'd say you're correct on that one. Did you know my husband and I got married two weeks after we got met?"

Ms. Margaret always told her story of her love every time I was in. No matter how many times I heard it, I always pretended that this was the first time.

"Two weeks?" I asked knowingly as I followed her to the counter to check out.

"Yes, sir. We were in love as much as we were stubborn. So, we got married. Despite every body's say so. I thought my Daddy was gonna kill us both." She went on. "But, you know, look at us now! We're in as much love, as we once were as much stubborn!"

I chuckled. She had to be the cutest old lady I had ever seen. "Yes, ma'am! Well, I can't thank you enough for all of your help." She continued ringing me up.

"Of course, honey but you sure didn't need all that much." She winked. "Sounds like you know what you have and know that you want it."

I smiled. "Yes ma'am, I do."

She smiled back with a grin full of wisdom.

"Have a good day Mrs. Margaret."

"Yes sir, but don't you be a stranger, young man!" She called out.

"No, ma'am." I was so excited about the gift. I was sure Rella would love it.

It was just past eleven. I checked my cell... No sign from Rella. She was still getting ready; I could count on it. Her apartment wasn't far away, and I knew she'd need a coffee before we headed out on our little venture. I decided just to keep my jeep parked and walk to her place. She wouldn't mind the morning stroll.

Turning down ninth, I had about a 15-minute walk. I didn't want to make her feel awful for not waking up because I loved that about her. It was just who she was. The town square was filled with people doing some shopping. There was a local florist right on the corner before I turned towards her street.

I decided to pick up some flowers for Rella. I didn't know her favorite, so I decided to get a beautiful arrangement full of sunflowers, lilies, and hydrangeas. The colors were bright and vibrant, just as she. But the bouquet was as full as I knew my heart was.

I made my way past the crowds and morning shoppers. There was a business that was enriched with excitement. I too felt a jolly in my step that wasn't there before. Before I knew it, I was at Rella's door. My heart fluttered with the anticipation of seeing her beautiful face.

"Knock, knock," I said as I knocked on her door.

"Michael, is that you? Come in!" She sounded.

I opened the door, surprised that it was unlocked. "Rella, baby, yes it's me, but what if it wasn't? Baby, don't keep your door unlocked because what if..."

"Oh, Michael, it's alright." She turned the corner to face me. "Flowers? Aw, you got me flowers? They are beautiful."

My attention shifted immediately. "Oh, yeah, I did. Do you like them? "I handed them to her with a hopeful smile.

"Oh yes! Sunflowers are my favorite! How did you know?" She asked surprised.

"Well, I didn't. I just thought of what would remind me of you."

"Oh Michael, that is so sweet. You are so romantic. Let me put them in a vase." She headed towards the kitchen.

I couldn't help but noticed her wardrobe. I don't think I had ever seen her so... casual. She was dressed in jeans and a light blue t-shirt. Her hair was in a messy ponytail, and she had light make-up on her face. It begged my next question.

"So, where are we headed to?" I tried to hide my curiosity.

I noticed her smile immediately. "You'll see. It's a surprise."

"Can I have a hint?" I walked towards her.

"No hints, Mr. Harvey."

"Okay... but not even one?" I begged.

"No, sir." She said. I knew she wasn't going to budge.

"Okay then... well, if I can't have a hint, can I at least have a kiss?"

She smiled. "Of course you can... but only after I finish up with the flowers." She was just teasing me now.

I wanted to kiss her from the moment I walked in. I could never escape my desire for her. I watched as she pulled out a vase and cut the stems, pulling back some of the leaves.

"You're going to love today. It's going to be so exciting! I am so happy that the weather is nice. The high is going to be in the upper 70s. It's perfect for what we're going to do! I'm so excited; I can't wait!"

She went on as I watched her. I didn't say much... There was no need too. Sometimes I felt like I could listen to her talk all day long, and never grow tired of it.

She washed her hands and then put the vase on her table. "Okay, all done. Now you can have your kiss."

"Well, since you made me wait, you're going to have to pay me some interest."

"Interest?" She questioned, but before I answered, I put my hand on the small of her back and pulled her in close. Before she could respond, I was already kissing her hard. I could tell by her surrender that she was taken aback.

Her taste was perfect. She was perfect. I couldn't help but want to keep going. So, I did. As I kissed her, I could tell that it would take her to be the one that stopped us this time, and she did.

"Michael," she murmured as she pulled back. "I don't have the wedding planned for the surprise." She said softly.

"I didn't figure you did." I agreed. "We'd better get going."

* * *

Before I knew it, we were about 30 minutes outside of town. I couldn't imagine where we were going. Needless to say, I was on edge. Rella was driving, and well, she wasn't all that good.

"Slow down, honey." I coached concerned, and she roughly shifted the gears of my jeep.

"Oh Michael, you're a nervous wreck. Calm down."

I didn't say anything as I tried to take her advice. She was right. I needed to keep my cool. I needed to get my mind off the situation.

She followed the highway and then turned on an old dirt road, then on another. We were quickly getting to nowhere, it seemed. I had the little jewelry box in my back pocket. I meant to have given it to her back at the apartment, but we left pretty quickly after the sumptuous kiss. I would have to find time to give it to her today, and I was hoping for the perfect moment. I couldn't imagine finding it out here.

"Okay, we are almost there." Rella interrupted my thoughts. "We're about 10 minutes away. But, here is the thing. You can't go to my secret place a mess of nerves, so we are going to go sailing first."

"Sailing?" I asked suspiciously.

"Yes." She said with all of the confidence in the world as she pulled over to the side of the road. "Sailing."

"Baby, I don't know if you know, but... The beach is that way, west. We're heading North East."

"We are?" She asked sarcastically. "Well, what do you know?"

I couldn't follow her. She giggled. "Michael. Lighten up. It's not regular sailing, but car sailing."

She said it as if it was something that everyone knows of.

"Car sailing?" I asked hesitantly.

"Yes." She smiled. "It will get rid of all of those nerves you have. Now, let me explain." She continued. "So, This is what you do. You roll all of the windows down, and you play some good music. The kind that calms and stirs up your emotions all at the same time. I like to listen to Death Cab for Cutie while I sail.

You see? She pulled out her iPhone and plugged it into the aux option. The band started to play.

"Okay," I said. I had no idea where this was going.

"Okay." She agreed. "So then, you find a straight lonely road and drive about 20 miles per hour. You don't want to be dangerous."

"Dangerous?" I was worried as to where this was headed.

"Yes, you can't be dangerous. So, once you hit 20, you put the car in neutral and coast it until you come to a stop. The passengers then lean out the window while grabbing on to the ski railing on top, of course. Then close your eyes and let go of every worry or pain and visualize you sailing away from it all! If you do it right, it will feel like you are sailing, and the only thing you will hear is the wind and music... no, thoughts... no, regrets!"

I was in complete shock. This sounded insane. "Rella, baby... are you serious?" I couldn't help hide my concern.

"Yes, of course, I'm serious! It's part of the whole experience." She sounded hurt. "Michael, don't worry. Look, there is no one out here. We haven't passed anyone since we left."

"Rella, I just don't want you... us, to get hurt. What if we crash?"

"Into what?" She asked as she motioned around. There isn't anything that could be hazardous to us. "Even if we did lose control, which I won't, you simply hit the brakes and come back inside. It's not a big deal. I've done this a thousand times."

"Rella..." I wasn't buying it.

"Oh Michael, please. Just for me. You said I could plan this day. Just do it with me once. One time, then I'll never ask again."

The look in her eyes was that of a puppy's; one you couldn't say no too.

"Okay. But on one condition." I said. "You have to let me drive."

She paused for a minute. "Okay, but the driver doesn't sail. That would be unsafe. So, if you drive, I'll be sailing."

"Never mind," I said quickly. Seeing my beautiful love hang out of a window of a moving car was far beyond what I was willing to do for today. "I'll go first." She grinned, knowing all to well that was going to be my answer.

"Okay. I will tell you when to close your eyes. Go head and lean out and hold on to the top rail. Make sure you have a good grip. And don't let go!" The excitement in her voice was tangible. "Then, when I say "sail" close your eyes, okay?"

"Okay." I tried to hide my nerves, but there was no point. This was a little bit crazy.

"Don't knock it until you try it, Michael. Live a little!"

"Okay." I stood in the seat and took my place on the window edge. I leaned up over the top of my jeep and grabbed my luggage rails. Rella had called them ski rails. She was so cute.

"Do you have a good grip?" She shouted.

"As good as I'll ever have," I said sardonically. I could hear her laugh right before I heard her music blaring. The jeep was in gear, and we were moving forward. As we picked up speed, I couldn't help but grip the bar tighter, when before I didn't think I could have. The breeze became colder and colder as we gained speed. I couldn't help but think this would be the best in summer. As much as I didn't want to admit, it did feel... indescribable. A few minutes later, I heard my love.

"Okay, sail!!" She shouted.

I hesitated then closed my eyes. I could feel me breathe in the deepest of breaths I had ever taken. I felt so weightless that I lifted up my other arm as if I were spreading my wings to fly. She was right. Completely right. I felt like I was going to soar right out of the car. The exuberance of the wind was just enough to push all of my worries aside. The song she played "Passenger Seat" by Death Cab For Cutie was sufficient enough to calm every nerve I had in my entire soul. The feeling of car sailing was invigorating, and I soaked it in. I felt as though, I was sailing in the winds, and nothing could bring me down.

I don't know how long we were going because that's just the thing; this experience was like an hourglass without the sand. I'd lost track of time at that moment, and that's something, I wasn't used to, but I opened my eyes as I felt the car slow to a stop. For a second, I almost forgot where I was. That's how powerful it was. As I sunk back in the car, I was speechless. There was nothing to say because there was nothing to be said. It was a liberating and weightless experience like I never felt before.

"Well, what do you think?"

"I... I... it was..."

"Infinite." She ended my sentence.

"Infinite," I said with a question in my tone.

"Infinite. It's what the best moments are. That's what my grandmother used to always say." She said calmly.

"Infinite. Yes, it was infinite." I smiled. "Rella, I am sorry for..." I felt the need to apologize for discouraging her.

"Don't apologize Michael." She laughed. "I knew I would have to talk you into it."

I smiled gratefully. As much as I knew her, she knew me.

"Did you want to go now? I can drive?"

She laughed, "No, I want to head to our final destination. This was just part of the journey too. Besides, I've been sailing thousands of times. That's what my friends and did in college when finals were getting the best of us. My friend, Ally showed us but then, we decided it was just fun, so we started doing it all the time. It's my favorite thing. The only thing is; you need at least one other person with you. Last week, I thought of showing you and planned it on the way, here."

Her attention shifted forward. In the distance, I could see what appeared to be an old house and from what I could tell, it was a very fragile house as well. Looks like sailing wasn't the only dangerous thing my girl and me would be getting into today.

As we pulled up the old dirt road, I realized it was worse than I thought. The house looked to be 100 years old, but I could tell that back in its day, it was beautiful.

"Here we are. This is my secret place. I come here to talk to God." She said it with a certain zeal.

"God's in there?" I asked jokingly. "I figured He'd pick something more... I don't know... new."

She laughed. "Oh, Michael. God is everywhere." She got out of the jeep. "Come on."

I got out as we headed towards the door. "Rella, are you sure this isn't private property?"

"No, I am sure it is, but who cares? No one comes here anyway? Just look at it."

I didn't bother to reason with her. One thing I had learned over time about Rella was that there was no talking her out of something she wanted to do. Not even by the best persuasion.

We headed to the front door if you want to call it that. Really, it was just an old piece of wood barely hanging on the hinges. I wondered how many people it had welcomed home.

The house looked to be about three stories tall. Well, it looked like it was two stories, but you could tell that they later converted the attic into the third floor. Everything was old and dusty. Most of the furniture was still here. It was like someone just got up and left with nothing but a suitcase. I always wondered what kind of tragedy would cause someone to do that.

We looked around at everything, admiring it.

"Isn't it neat?" Rella asked. "Look at all of this!"

"Rella, how did you find this?"

"Well, one day I was just bored, and I started driving. A client canceled and you were busy with meetings. But look! Look what I found. It's beautiful, isn't it?"

"I wouldn't say beautiful, but it is neat. Aren't you scared to be here alone?"

"No... Well, at first I was, but I just prayed. Then, I felt The Lord. Like you know, how your spirit knows He's listening. Come with me upstairs, I'll show you!!"

We cautiously climbed the stairs. I looked for termite damage along the way; ready to tell her she couldn't come back if I found it. Oddly enough, though, it wasn't there. The staircase was sturdy. The only thing that was horrible was the front door. Everything else seemed to be preserved somehow.

As we reached the top of the stairs, there was a long hallway. There was something about it too. The way the golden light crept in from the dusty bedroom windows… it was exquisite to any eye thirsty for beauty.

"The back room," she pointed. "It's the prettiest in there."

I could see the French doors at the end of the hall. I then realized that this house in its prime was a masterpiece. I looked again at the floors. Mahogany. That's why it was in such condition. This house was built by a wealthy person.

Opening the French doors, Rella led the way. The light poured in the room as we entered. She was right. This was the most beautiful of all rooms. As we looked around it was as if it was the office of God. Everything was in fine mahogany, with gold accents. The furniture was leather, with plastic tarps over it, which I knew Rella had removed. Walking in, the back wall was a bookshelf, filled with old books. In front was an office desk with a leather chair with buttons on it. The most beautiful part of the room was the multi-colored stain glass windows and the way the light beamed right through them. It was posed as if it sat the highest authority. The only thing that told of its age was the dust in the room.

"Wow." I uttered.

"I told you. Isn't it wonderful." She said wistfully as if she were in a castle.

"Yes. It's stunning in here. I wonder why no one is living here?"

"I don't know… but I sure love to pray here."

"Why?" I couldn't help but wonder aloud.

"I don't know… Like I said. My spirit just senses The Lord." She explained.

"Like, at church?" I tried to understand, but I wasn't sure what she was talking about.

"Well, not necessarily. I've been to a lot of churches where I didn't feel God. It goes past religion… It's… relationship, I guess. I just sense that He is here."

I didn't say anything because I wasn't sure what I felt. I was in awe of the beauty, of course, but I never… had "felt" God as

Rella explained. I watched her head over to the big bay window. She bathed in the sunlight that the window was letting in. For a moment, it looked as if she were glowing. The light had a way of making her auburn hair look golden. Her eyes closed, her head was tilted up, I saw her as the angel she was. It looked as though God was embracing her and welcoming her. As I watched, I grew uncomfortable. Jealous even. The thought of God having her scared me. He had my mom; He couldn't have her.

I walked over and touched her hand. I didn't want to interrupt, but I felt I had to. "You're beautiful."

"Michael." She smiled.

"You are. You're the most beautiful thing I have ever seen."

"Thank you." She blushed and walked towards the desk. "Look at all of these books!"

I followed her towards the bookshelf. There had to be thousands as the shelves went all the way up to the vaulted ceiling.

"I wonder which one the owner read the most?" She asked aloud.

"Umm... I don't know." I was growing curious looking to the desk. I wondered if there would be something with a name? I couldn't help but wonder who's house this was.

I opened the top drawer and pulled out some papers. Most of them were handwritten notes. Like, Bible verses and personal memos. A black book was in there as well.

Rella turned. "What's that?" She asked.

"I don't know." I wiped my hand across the front. The gold letters appeared, "HOLY BIBLE."

"Wow." She said. "Can I see?"

"Sure." I handed the Bible to her. She took it and found the scarlet thread that served as a bookmark and opened it to that page.

"Oh, my," She sighed breathlessly.

"What is it?" I asked concerned.

"It's marked to my favorite Bible story."

"Wow! Really?" I asked. "What a coincidence."

"No, Michael." She corrected me. "There is no such thing as coincidence. When you see things that look like it, it is only God showing you something."

"Oh..." I didn't know what to say to that. I paused as I watched her caress the Bible. "Which story is it marked to?" I asked.

"The one of the scarlet thread." She smiled subtly.

"What one is that?"

She smiled, "Someone has forgotten their Sunday school lessons."

"Look, I only went for the snacks," I admitted.

She laughed. "Of course you did." She shook her head. "It's the story where Joshua was getting ready to enter into the promise land, but it appeared as it was already occupied. So, he sent two spies to go seek out the land and get information. When the two spies got there, they found a prostitute named Rehab. The king of Jericho, the land that they were in, discovered that two spies were in the city, so he send guards to find them and kill them. But Rehab had heard of The God of Israel and how their army had defeated everyone before them. She let the spies into her house and hid them in her roof."

"That sounds very traitor like." I sounded.

"Yes, but she knew she was soon to die when the land was overtaken. She had heard all of the stories and miracles that God performed through Moses. So, eventually the king's guards came to look for the spies but Rehab told them that she never let them enter her home. She detoured the guards saying that they went towards the city gate, and she told them that they needed to hurry to catch up. When they left, she bargained with the two spies on account of her kindness to them. They agreed that when they invaded the city, they would spare her and her family's life if she had the scarlet cord in her window that she let them escape out of. And so... as it came, Joshua did overtake the land. But as the spies promised, Rehab was spared by the Scarlett thread that was placed in her window."

"Wow." I didn't know what to say, but I was captivated by Rella's passion in telling the story.

"Yes. It's quite incredible. I remember my grandmother telling me the story when I was little she always said, 'All you need is a Scarlett thread of a chance.' The story and saying stuck with me. I remind myself of it when I need a little hope." Rella seemed to be distracted by her thoughts.

I watched her as she headed back towards the window. I knew she missed her grandmother, but I didn't want to push her. I had yet to hear the story of how she passed away, but I knew in time, she would share. She would bring it up when she was ready. I went back to the door of the office. I waited until she told me she wanted to go.

A few moments later, she turned towards me, and I could tell she had let a few tears go. I understood what loss was... I also understood that you didn't want to talk about it every time you cried about it.

"You ready baby?" I asked quietly.

"Yes." She said softly as we left the house.

The day had been emotional so far, for both of us. Sailing for me. The Scarlett Thread for her and memories of her grandmother had left us both pretty drained.

Driving back to town I asked, "Hey, how about an early dinner?"

She smiled, "Yes. I am starving."

"Me too," I said. I could tell the mood was lightening up a bit. "Hey look!" I pointed. "A FedEx truck... Looks like I will have good luck today!"

"What?" She asked quizzically.

"My Dad taught me when I was little, that if you see three FedEx trucks in one day, it means you will have good luck!" I winked.

She laughed. We went to the local deli and got something to eat. After, we drove around stopping here and there for the rest of the day. We weren't doing much, but just that is what we wanted to do. It was fun and casual. We both were just worried about being ourselves.

Rella did a little bit of shopping, which was my first experience shopping with a woman. Boy, was it a task. I never knew how complex it could be to pick out a shirt. Rella seemed to be very particular about her clothes. I always loved the way she dressed, but I had no idea the effort that went into it. We went to three stores, and it seemed like it took three days, but I was happy. Just to be with her, made me happy. She would ask my opinion, and I'd give her my most honest answer. Sometimes she agreed, at times; she didn't but, it was enjoyable nonetheless.

Not long after, then evening had arrived. Rella had volunteered to help the church with an early morning baking sale, so we called it an early night. I walked her to her door and remembered this morning; it triggered the memory of the gift in my back pocket. I had forgotten to give it to her.

"Oh hey, before we say goodnight, I forgot something. I got you a gift." I reached in my pocket. "I meant to give it to you this morning, but we rushed out of here pretty quick." I winked as she blushed.

"Another gift? Michael!" She seemed excited.

"Hey, I can get the woman of my dreams a gift, can't I?"

"I suppose. What is it?" She was already anxious for it.

I pulled the box out of my back pocket. "This reminded me of you."

She took the box from me and opened it slowly. "Oh, Michael." She gasped. "It's beautiful."

"You are my anchor..." I whispered. I looked at the necklace and saw the infinity sign. What were the odds? She said earlier the best of memories are infinite.

"Oh, and the infinity sign... Michael, how did you know?" She was begging the question.

"Honesty, I didn't." Shocked myself, I didn't know what to say. "I just picked that one out, because you are my timeless love."

"You're my infinite love." She corrected and leaned in for a kiss. "It's so beautiful. It's perfect. Thank you. And look, the anchor is like for sailing!"

"Yes, you're right." I was impressed with myself for a brief moment. I couldn't have been so lucky. I felt like this all happened on purpose.

“Thank you, thank you.” She said, glowing with a smile.

“You’re welcome. Let me put it one for you.” I suggested.

“Okay.” She turned, and I took the small necklace and placed it around her neck, delicately clasping it together.

“Perfect,” I said.

“I love you, Michael.” She said it in a way that brought heat to my blood.

“I love you too, my darling Rella.” I kissed her on the check and slowly eased back. This was always the testing point.

“Goodnight.” I offered her the subtle invitation inside.

She took it. “Goodnight. I’ll see you tomorrow.”

“See you.” I turned and walked down the stairs. “My beautiful Rella,” I thought. She was everything I could have ever imagined. I loved her more than I knew I could love. Everything seemed so perfect. So planned. So wonderful. It was like Rella had said earlier today... Coincidence is always God talking to you by trying to show you the way. Today, I wondered if He was doing that. Proving that Rella and I were meant to be. The sailing, infinite, the scarlet thread, it all seemed to merge into one theme. Rella and I. As I headed home, I couldn’t help but hope on that scarlet thread, that this day, our lives together would be infinite.

2 Months Later

CHAPTER 9

"MORNING DAD," I SAID, STROLLING through the gallery.

"Morning Son.... Running a little late." He said with a smirk.

"Yeah, I know. Rella and I were up a little late last night. We went to see a movie and got caught up talking."

"As always..."

"Yes..." I couldn't tell if he was upset with me. I'd been late more times over the past month than I think I'd ever been in my whole life. "I'm sorry, Dad."

He turned in his chair, "Son, don't apologize. It's good to see that you're not keeping time." Smiling, he turned back around in his chair.

I didn't know how to respond, so I decided to change the subject. "Well, the big show is tomorrow night, huh? Everything in place?"

"I think so. Stephanie said that she was going to be dropping off the paintings this afternoon."

"Okay, great. I'll be on the look out for her then." I said as I headed to my office.

Stephanie Mendoza was one of our new artists, and we were showcasing her tomorrow night. Her art was spectacular. She had an old soul of Van Gogh about her that had a way of just catching your eye and capturing your soul. She came in about a month back, and Dad and I were impressed. She was exceptional. We booked her right away.

All painters aren't the same and Dad, and I had an eye for the good ones. "We better book her while we can," Dad had said when she left after our first meeting. He was right. She was exceptional, and we knew she wouldn't last for long in the small galleries. Her talent was too big for her to stay in the small art gallery world. Give her a few years and she'd be a New York sensation. However, we were certainly glad to help her along the way.

The day would be pretty filled with preparation. I needed to call the caterer and talk to the local winery. We wanted to pick a different selection. For whatever reason, I was just in the mood to mix things up. Old Man Salvador presented us some new designs last week and to Dad's surprise, I said yes to all of them. There was just newness in the air for me. A change and Rella was to blame for that.

She was going to come by later tonight. We were going to set up the art together. With her interior design technique, she had the ability to give our gallery a face-lift. There were a few times we reached out and asked for her help. She did so well; Dad and I decided to pay her as a consultant. She hated the idea at first, but I insisted. I told her that this family business and she was now a part of it. Having said that, everyone gets a paycheck. Finally, she agreed. Plus, I got to see her a lot more. That was the very best part of the deal, in my opinion, of course, and it helped her a lot too. When customers came to us, we could point them to her and vice versa. It was an easy decision for all of us.

Life couldn't be smoother. Happier. Even Dad loved having Rella around. She just added life to things. There was this light about her presence that you just missed when she wasn't around.

Already it was noon. The day was going by so fast. I still needed to run to the winery and taste some of the new wines they proposed.

"Hey Dad, I'm going to head to the winery, okay?"

"Yeah, would ya bring me back some lunch, though?" He asked.

"Sure, what sounds good?"

“Ugh... How about one of those California Clubs from the deli?”

“Okay. Mayo?”

“That’s my boy.”

“Alright. I should be back in about an hour and a half.”

“Sounds good. See ya.”

Walking out I grabbed my keys, and I couldn’t help but be in a bit of a rush. I had a few errands to run as well. Ever since I bought Rella flowers that Saturday morning, I never stopped. Every week, I made sure to get her a new bouquet. Rella always appreciated the new flowers. It was the simple things that caught her attention most, and that’s what I loved about her.

Plus, I needed to pick up some dry cleaning. I needed to finalize everything today. Ms. Mendoza would probably arrive around 4:00 this afternoon.

* * *

I probably checked my watch more times in the past two hours than I had in the past two months combined. The business of the town was picking up as summer was drawing near and with that so was the pedestrian traffic. People walked about as if they had no place to be. While, sometimes I was one of them, I was not today. I picked up the dry cleaning and put it in the back as I hurried to catch the light that would lead to the vineyard.

Divine Winery was an old business, but the original owners’ son, Scott had made the place new and fresh. Over the past ten years, since he was put in control of the business, it seemed to flourish. Arriving I was excited and honestly, I could have used a glass of wine.

Walking in, I was graciously received by Scott himself. He always added the personal touch, which made me proud. Around here, local businesses were paramount, and all of us appreciated the sincerity behind it. We walked to a showing room, where he had me taste a few new wines. They were beyond excellent.

I approved the list without hesitation. They were vamping up their product, along with their business. Soon, Divine Winery would be one of the best.

With that, the meeting was very short. I needed to get back to the gallery, and I needed to get something to eat. I was nowhere near buzzed, but I needed something in my stomach. However, the grumbles turned to butterflies as I pulled out my phone. My Rella was giving me a call.

"Hey honey, what are you doing?" She asked in her sweet little voice, as I answered.

"Hey, baby. I'm good. Just heading back from the vineyard going to pick up some lunch for Dad then head back to the gallery."

"Oh, okay. Well, I was about to head that way. Would you like me to grab lunch? I'm right by the deli?"

"Oh babe, you'd be a lifesaver. You don't mind?" I asked.

"Not at all. Two California Clubs with mayo, right?" I could tell she was smiling.

"Yes, ma'am."

"Okay, see ya in a bit. I love you."

"I love you too."

"Bye." She hung up.

Every time I heard her say those words, it made me breathless. How could I have been so lucky?

About 10 minutes later I was pulling up to the gallery, just in time to see her stumbling in with two bags and a drink holder. She is as petite as they come; it was a little humorous watching her try to carry her weight in sandwiches.

"Let me get that," I jumped out the jeep with a smile. Easily, I grabbed all of it.

"Show off." She teased.

I couldn't help but smile. "Dad, we're here."

"Good grief, I'm starving." I could hear him get up and hurry to the front.

"What in the hel---- hello Rella." He was shocked to see her. "How are you?" he side glanced me as a "thanks for letting me know she was here" kind of look.

"I'm good James. Thank you. I brought us all some sandwiches. I'm pretty hungry myself."

"Oh, well, okay, then. Let's head to the back kitchen area." He was slightly embarrassed. It took me a bit too long at the vineyards. Dad always got a little cranky when he was hungry.

We all went to the back and enjoyed. Rella was so good with my Dad. She just fit in. My Dad was a private guy, and he's just really not one for the company in his personal time, but with Rella, he didn't seem to mind at all.

"Rella, how's the interior thing going?" He asked.

"Dad, thing?" I tried to correct him. He never remembered the names of things.

Rella laughed, "It's going good James. Business is well for me." She answered politely.

"Well, good. Glad to hear it. Are you with us for the rest of the day?" He asked.

"Yes, sir. And, I went ahead and took tomorrow off so I could be of extra help."

"Wonderful. We'll need it. This girl's art is amazing. We want to showcase it right, huh Michael?"

"Yes, we do. Wait till you see it Rella. She is very gifted."

"So I've heard. I'm excited to see."

We were caught in conversation as the doorbell rang.

"I'll bet that's her," Dad said. "I'll get it." He got up to go to the door. I could hear him, "Good afternoon Ms. Mendoza."

"Afternoon! I have a truck full of paintings for Y'all."

"Sounds good. My son will be out here in just a minute, and we'll start unloading them."

"I think that's your cue," Rella suggested.

I laughed, "Yep, it sure is. Come with me?" I offered my hand to her.

"I thought you'd never ask." She said jokingly.

We walked out together. "Hello Ms. Mendoza, how are you?"

"Great, Michael. Good to see you. I'm well, thanks."

"Yes, well, good. Um, this is Rella Allan my girlfriend and our interior designer. She's going to be helping us set you all up."

"Wonderful," Stephanie said. "A fellow woman's touch is always welcome." She smiled genuinely at Rella. I couldn't help but be exceedingly grateful that she wasn't a Charlotte Cruz.

"Thank you," Rella said. "I can't wait to see your work."

From that point, we started to unload her truck. Stephanie wasn't kidding when she said she had a truck full. There were at least 35-40 paintings. Rella started sorting them out.

"Ms. Mendoza, you are welcome to stay here and help us, or you can head out. I'm sure you are tired from the drive. Your choice. Don't feel obligated to stay." Dad said.

"Oh, okay. Well..." She glanced at Rella and saw the room she was setting up. A subtle smile crossed her face. By that, I knew she trusted her enough to leave. "You know what, I'll take that offer. I have a lot to get done before tomorrow night."

"Yes, of course. No worries at all. We'll see you tomorrow at around 6:00. The show will start at 7:00." Dad assured her.

"Perfect." She took another look at what Rella was up to. "Perfect." She said again, in a way that was a compliment. "I'll see you then."

"Alright. Call us if you need anything." I assured her.

"Yes, sir. Thank you both so much for the opportunity."

"The opportunity is all ours," Dad complimented.

"Thank you. Goodbye." Ms. Mendoza walked out. I felt like she was thankful for the time, but I knew she only left because she trusted Rella. Like I said... Everything she touched turned to gold.

We worked for hours sorting through the paintings and frames. None of us expected her to bring as many as she did, but it was all right. We had space for them, and I was confident that most, if not all of them would sell. They were spectacular.

"Dad, will you come with me to get the frames from the back? We'll need the rest of them."

"Sure, will do. Rella, we're going to the back for just a minute. I'll lock the front door. Besides, it's almost closing time."

"Okay," Rella said. "I'll be alright here."

Dad and I walked to the back. "Man, what a collection huh?" Dad asked.

"Man, I know. It's a good thing we had Salvador get all of those frames done. I think we'll sell most of them."

"Yeah, sure will. We better book her as much as we can." Dad warned.

"I agree. And did you see how she loved Rella? Dad, she wouldn't have left if Rella wouldn't have been here."

"I know son. She's a great addition to our team. She's like..." He broke off. I knew he was going to say she was like mom, but I knew he couldn't admit to that yet.

"Mom would have loved her, huh Dad?" I patted him on the back.

"Yes." He said bleakly.

We finished getting the rest of the frames. It took us a good 20 minutes to pull them all of storage. We needed a solution for the back room mess.

As we came hauling them back on a dolly, I was shocked to find my sweet Rella crying.

"Rella, baby, what is it? What's wrong?" I begged of her, as I gently put down the frames and rushed to her side. "Baby, what's wrong?"

She was sobbing. She just pointed to a painting in front of her.

It was a painting of a man on this, what looked like to be an abandoned beach due to the cold weather. The man stood with an old medium size looking dog. The clouds were gray in a way how the sky looks when the winter months are overstaying their welcome. However, if you looked closely, one could see they were losing the battle. The sun was setting and casting shadows everywhere, throwing warm golden tones as it tried its hardest to bring the warmth of spring. The beach looked quiet, peaceful, and empty. There was an old dead looking tree in the foreground that stood all alone on a small rocky hill that overlooked the rest of the beach. The painting held sadness and hope all at the same time.

"This painting..." She finally murmured. "It reminds me..." She broke into tears again.

"Shhhh," I soothed her as I took her in my arms. "It's okay. Shhhh." Slowly, she calmed down.

"Can I buy it, Michael? I know it's for the showing, but please. I need it."

"No, baby. You don't have to buy it. It's yours okay? It's all yours." I had never seen her this upset. I glanced at Dad. We were both a little concerned. I had no idea what memory the painting had evoked.

She continued crying.

"Rella, let's call it a night, okay? We can finish this tomorrow. Let's get you home."

Dad had already started closing shop. Rella's tears were too much for him to bear as well.

"Dad, I'm gonna..." I motioned towards the door.

"Go ahead, son. Take care of her." He insisted as he handed me my keys from the front desk.

"Come on baby. Let's go." She was still so upset... Like, emotional, I guess. I'd never seen her this way. "Come with me, darling."

We walked outside. The sun was fading, and there was a breeze. I was so worried about her. We got in the car, and she didn't say a word. I arrived at her apartment in all of 2 minutes. I didn't know how to proceed.

"Can I walk you in?" I asked cautiously.

She only nodded yes.

We walked in quietly. She was so shaken up; she couldn't even unlock her door. I grabbed her keys gently, and eased the door open and walked her over to the couch.

"Here baby, sit down." I took off her shoes. It beats me how she walked in those heels of hers. "Let me get you some water, okay?"

Again, she just nodded. There was no way I was leaving until I got some words out of her. I grabbed a blanket along with a cold glass.

"Here you go." I tucked her in and handed her the glass. "It's okay." I sat with her.

She didn't say a word for about ten minutes. I knew that the painting had evoked some extreme painful memory. I had a feeling it had to do with her grandmother. We still hadn't discussed what happened. Slowly, her tears calmed.

"Thank you." She whispered. "For taking care of me... And for the painting."

"Of course, Rella. That's what I'm here for. Okay?"

She nodded again and hesitated as if she were trying to decide to tell me what got her so upset.

She began. "My grandmother was... my best friend. My Mom and Dad were a little too young for children. My mom got pregnant with me right after she turned 19. My parents got married soon after. They fell hard and fast... But unfortunately, it wasn't love. It was lust. That's why I was so nervous about you and I... remembering?"

I nodded my head yes. She continued.

"They weren't great parents. Not even before I was a year old, my Dad started cheating on my mom. She was naïve. She loved me but, she was naïve as to what it takes to be a mom. She was more concerned with being in love at the time. So anyways, I spent most of my time with my grandmother. My parents went back and forth being together and apart. One minute they were happy, the next they were a hot mess. Usually the latter. My grandmother was my constant. I remember learning from her. She would give me lessons of life in the perfect way. I'd burn cookies, and she'd make a moral story out of it. She introduced me to church and Jesus. I suppose that's why I'm spiritual. She was so sweet, and I admired everything she did. When I was around 11, my parents were back together, even though I pretty much lived with my grandmother. My mom lived in an apartment complex, but my grandma's house was down the street. I preferred to be there and honestly, I think grandmother preferred the same. But, she was getting older, so I tried not to be a burden, however, I didn't see my parents as a Mom and Dad. They were more like my friends."

"Anyway, so when I was about eleven, my mom came home and found my Dad with another woman... one like Charlotte Cruz. It was her last straw. We moved out and officially moved in with my grandmother. I never saw my Dad again. Honestly, I didn't care too. He was a selfish Casanova. My mom was heartbroken, but when he was gone, she finally noticed me. We lived with my grandma for three years. We were the 3 Pink Ladies" as grandmother would say. We all became close. I finally developed a relationship with my mom. It was all because of my grandmother that we have a relationship now. It all seemed perfect, but then.... my grandmother..." She choked up.

"It's okay, Rella. Take your time."

"She got sick. She started just... wasting away. The doctors couldn't name the disease. Like, she got ill and a year later." She inhaled. "She was... gone."

"I was heartbroken. Both my mom and I were... But, more so, me. I sunk into a deep depression. I was 14 and already struggling with a teenage girl's life, but I lost me... my grandmother. I stopped eating and honestly, I stopped living. My mom tried everything, but none of it worked. Finally, one day, she just made me get in the car. She packed up our clothes, and we just started driving. I remember asking, "Where are we going." My mom would say, 'I'll know when we get there." So, on we went. We ended up clear on the other side of the country. I grew up in Kansas." She added. I had no idea.

"We stopped at what looked like the edge of the earth. I remember getting out and going to the beach. The waves were beautiful, and the sunlight was bright. It was what both mom and I needed... light in our lives. My mom probably had it the worst. She lost her mom, and only half way had her daughter since. I look back now, and I can see her desperation. I remember though being drawn to the water. It was refreshing somehow. I loved it. I felt like my grandmother would have loved it too. I remember walking along and stumbling across this old dead tree that sat on a rocky hill that overlooked the entire beach. I was shocked by its size and beauty that I called my mom to come and look at it. She was amazed as well. Then, I remember going back down to the shoreline and got lost in thought as I watched the endless body of water. I was standing there taking it all in when all of a sudden, I felt something ram my leg. It was a puppy, and as I bent down to get a better look, it jumped into my arms and started licking me. I couldn't help but laugh. It was licking me all over." She smiled at the thought.

"I remember my mom turning toward me because she recognized my laughter. It was the first time I had laughed since my grandmother had passed away. Honestly, it was the first sign of life... after experiencing my first heartbreak. I was shown then, that life was still within me and that it was okay to be happy without my grandmother. I remember playing with that puppy and the joy that it brought me. My mom was so glad to see me laugh. She quickly pulled out her camera to take a photo of it from where she stood. I still have it. I'll show you someday. If you look closely, you can see the owners of the puppy in the background, chasing after their him on the left side of me. You could see the old tree I was talking about, on my left as well in the foreground. I remember it so clearly; because it was the moment I started breathing again. The painting..." She teared up again. "It is just so similar to that place..."

She stopped waiting for my response. "It's okay, Rella. Don't cry." I soothed her. "Thank you for telling me." I didn't know what else to say.

"Thank you for getting the painting for me... seeing it... It was like it was from my grandmother. It reminded me of her... Like, she's still watching over me... It showed up in your gallery. Like... I think it's a sign, you know?" She was eager now for my approval.

"Yes, it very well could be..." I agreed. "So... you think she approves of me?" I asked it a scared tone. It made her laugh.

"Yes," Rella chuckled. "I think she does."

I hugged her close. My sweet Rella.

* * *

I stayed with Rella until she fell asleep. I left her a note confessing my love. It was so hard to go. Never had I seen her with tears like that. It broke my heart. I knew soon, I would ask her to marry me, but it had to be the perfect moment. The perfect time. I tried to sleep, but I couldn't. Being away from her, was beginning to be too much.

The next morning came, and I was already wide-awake. There was too much to handle to be late to work. I was up at the gallery early, at five, sorting through everything. I got Rella's painting and stored it in my office. When Old Man Salvador came by, I would ask him to frame it up nice.

The painting was, truly beautiful. Rella was right there was something special about it, even to me. Like, it was like my heart recognized the picture somehow or maybe the feeling it brought. However, an eerie feeling accompanied that. Why? I didn't know. Maybe it was just the emotion running high around here. My Dad arrived soon, as did Old Man Salvador. We went about getting the paintings in the frames. We planned to wait for Rella to determine where to hang them.

I couldn't help but wonder when she'd show. I knew she had to be exhausted. Nothing like an emotional evening to put you to sleep. We all went about our work when I heard the front door open.

"Happy Birthday!" Rella exclaimed as she walked in with a handful of balloons. I couldn't have been more surprised.

"You knew?" I asked shocked. I didn't remember if I had told her my specific day.

She glanced at Dad, "I had a little help." She smiled.

I laughed, "Well, are you sure you want to date an Old Man?" I teased.

"Of course I do. I like a little gray hair." She said.

"What?" I panicked turning towards a mirror. "Where?"

Both she and Dad broke in laughter. "Kidding, Michael, dear." She joked. "You don't have any gray hairs... yet."

I turned giving her a fake evil eye. "Yet?" I asked.

"Yet." She challenged. "Well, are you ready for your gift, Old Man?"

"Awe, you got me a gift?" Of course, she did... She was always so thoughtful.

"Yes. It's from your Dad and I. We partnered up."

"You did?" I looked at Dad. I was pleased to know that they were closer than I thought.

"Yes. Here it is." She pulled a small box from her purse.

In my heart, I was suspect. I had a feeling, as I tore open the wrapping paper... The box gave it away. I opened it to find a brand new Rolex.

"No, way," I said in shock.

"We both thought you needed a new one." Dad offered.

"Oh my gosh!" I was in shock. It was beautiful. It made my old one look like a fake.

"Read the back." Rella couldn't tame her excitement.

I flipped the watch over. It read, Timeless love." I teared up. It was perfect.

"Now, every time you check the time, you'll have to think of those who love you, first." She explained.

"Rella... Dad, this is beautiful... I can't believe." I was stunned. I imagined the price to be at least $15,000... I was shocked.

"You're worth it, son. Happy Birthday." He smiled.

"Thank you both." I couldn't help but be a little choked up. This was more than I expected.

"Put it on!" Rella insisted. "Let's see it!"

I took it out of the box and put my old one in. I slipped the new one out and slid it on my left wrist. "Perfect fit. How did..."

Rella interrupted, "I counted the links... Remember when I asked to borrow your watch to..."

"Yes, to keep me from looking at the time..." I remember the day in the park.

She laughed. "It was all part of the plot."

I couldn't help but feel loved. It was such an incredible gift, from two incredible people. The day went by quickly after that.

After the celebrating we all got back to work. We all put in a hard day to ensure a perfect evening, and that's what we got.

The show was exceptional. I was so happy that Rella was there to help. We couldn't write the tickets fast enough. Periodically, though, I couldn't help but look at my watch... It was a symbol of my timeless love. Ironically, part of me didn't want the clock to tick. As I looked around the room, Rella, and my Dad were talking and helping the customers with their choices. Everything was perfect or as Rella would say, infinite. I couldn't have asked for more. My life had been so dull. So mundane, until she came into it. It was like, I didn't know what was missing. I think that's why I counted the minutes of every day... I didn't care for them to go but now, everything had changed. There was a whole new frame that I was peering into. I suppose it's just as Dad had said the day before... for the first time in my life, I wasn't living by the watch.

1 Month Later

CHAPTER 10

TODAY WAS A BIG DAY. The six-month mark and, the day I planned to propose. Though the time went by so quickly, it seemed to lag at the same time. Rella was anxious. I could tell over the past few weeks that she was hinting around. We discussed when we were first starting dating that we would date for at least six months before making any big decisions.

Now, to think to wait any longer was pointless. We knew then, and we knew now. She was the one for me. I spent all yesterday at the local jeweler looking for the perfect ring. I wanted one that was as spectacular as she. No, budget. I walked out a mortgage down payment later. The gold base with the sparkling white 3k diamond was perfect. I wanted Rella to have the very best. Nothing less. She was worth it.

I had the whole evening planned out. I was going to take her to DC's on B Street where our first date was. I was going to walk with her all the way down main after, where a horse-drawn carriage would be waiting. Then, I would take her to a street I had named after her. "Rella Lane," our near where her secret place was. I had the whole speech prepared. She always talked about signs, and I was going to say, "here is mine."

I was worried it was a bit cheesy, but Rella loved stuff like that. She was like her mom in the 'hopeless romantic' aspect that I always teased her about.

I planned to pick her up at 6:00. She usually was getting off work by then. I hadn't said anything about this particular night because I wanted her to be completely surprised. Oddly enough,

I hadn't heard from her all day. As much as I wanted to call, I was worried I would let a hint out. I couldn't afford a slip, and I certainly didn't want her to catch on. This was all going to be perfect. I spent about two hours getting ready. I was so nervous I took two showers because I was sweating so much after the first. My heart was pounding. I picked out one of my nicest suits and placed the little blue box in my pocket. I remembered not long ago of giving her the necklace. She had worn it every day since. It warmed my heart to imagine that from every day from now on, she would wear this piece of jewelry as well.

I fixed my tie in the foyer as I headed out to her Jeep. I would arrive back home a man spoken for. I couldn't have been any more elated at the thought.

The sun was still in the sky and wouldn't start to set for about two hours. That was perfect because Rella loved sunsets. I wanted to propose to her with the sky painted in a beautiful display. As I got closer to her street, I became more excited. Before I knew it, I was knocking at her door.

"Good evening, baby. It's me." I sounded so she wouldn't be nervous as to who was there. I waited for a moment and knocked again. "Baby, are you home? Hello?"

"Go away, Michael." She seemed to yell from the other side.

"What?" I said shocked.

"I said, 'GO AWAY!'" She yelled.

"What did I do?" I thought. "Baby, what's wrong?" I asked.

"I'm in no mood. Just go." She said in an icy tone. Man was I confused and concerned.

"Rella, I wanted to take you out to dinner." I pleaded.

"Dinner? Dinner! That's all we ever have is dinner!" She screamed.

"Ugh..." I didn't know what to say... I couldn't imagine what was bothering her. "What's wrong with dinner?" I asked.

"Nothing is wrong. Michael. Nothing." She said coolly through the door.

Clearly, something was wrong. Girls always said nothing was wrong when definitely, something was wrong. "Can we talk about it?" I asked humbly.

"No!" She yelled.

"Rella, this isn't very civilized. Please, let me in." I begged quietly. She waited. "Rella, I will sit out here all night. You know I will. Please, let me in." I begged again.

"Fine!" She opened the door. I was shocked by what I saw. It looked like she had been sobbing. The black mascara streamed down her face making her seem a little scary. The angry scowl didn't help.

"Hey, baby... You look... beautiful." I offered.

"Oh, you're ridiculous. Of course, I don't." She stormed over to the couch and flopped down in an angry pout.

For a brief moment, I secretly wished I hadn't come in. I watched her sulk on the sofa before I approached cautiously.

"What's wrong Rella?" She hesitated. "Please tell me," I encouraged.

"I'm going to die an old maid!" She turned her head and sobbed into the pillow.

"What?" I thought. Why would she believe that?

"Rella..." I turned her head back up." Why would you say that? Are we okay?" My mind started panicking. Why would she think such a thing?

"Susie... A friend that I help with designs told me... She keeps asking why you haven't proposed. She says that if we are so in love, we would be getting married. She said that I was just like my mom!" She turned her head, sobbing again into the pillow.

Ugh... If she only knew what was in my pocket. "Rella, it isn't so... Don't listen to Sally."

"Susie." She corrected, her voice muffled by the cushion.

"Susie, Sally, whatever." I continued. "Who knows our love better than we do? Huh?" I lifted her up. "You can't let this upset you... You know how much I love you, don't you?" I asked in a pleading voice.

"Yes," she cried. "But we will get married one day, right? Like.. Soon, you'll ask?" She was sobbing like a little girl with hurt feelings.

I couldn't help but smile. "Sooner than you think but only if you have dinner with me."

She didn't pick up the hint. "Oh, Michael. Let's order in. I don't want to go out tonight."

"But Rella, I already made reservations..." This couldn't be more difficult. Couldn't she see the way I was dressed?

"It'll be fine to cancel, Michael. Please, don't make me."

And with that, I knew dinner was out... I had to think of something quick. "Okay, we don't have to go to dinner..." I stalled... "But, will you at least come with me to pick something up?" That was the only way I was going to get her out of the house.

"I don't know," She debated. "I look a hot mess."

"I'll agree you're hot, but not a mess. Just go wash the... Ugh... war paint off, and we'll go get something."

She finally let out a small laugh. "Okay. Thank you for not making me go inside anywhere."

"Sure baby." She got up and went to the bathroom. I hurried and texted the horse carriage driver, "Change of plans. Get there now." Fortunately, I hired him for the whole night, so he was at my beck and call. Boy was I thankful for that decision.

She came out wearing a t-shirt and sweats. No makeup and hair in a bun thing on the top of her head. Beautiful as ever, though.

"Okay, let's go." I hurried. Now or never. As we walked out, I noticed the clouds appear out of nowhere. You've got to me kidding me. There wasn't an ounce of rain in the forecast this morning, and now, it looked like Seattle. That was one thing about living near water; a storm could pop up at any minute.

"Oh look! It's going to rain!" Rella was so easily soothed.

"Yep..." This couldn't get any worse. Maybe I should wait. All of this seemed to be falling more apart by the second. I considered the thought and then considered again. "You know what. No." I thought to myself as I hurried to the Jeep. I've waited my whole life for her. Isn't that what timeless love is all about anyways?

"Rella, get in. Hurry." I motioned as I opened her door.

She gave me a strange look. "What's going on? Are you okay?" She asked concerned.

"Yes. I'm fine. Just get in." I motioned.

She got in, and I followed on the driver's side.

"Look, if you're upset about dinner, I'm sorry. I just don't feel like it." She said in a sassy tone.

"I'm not upset, Rella. We just have somewhere to be." I stated as I hit the gas in reverse and back into drive heading towards the park where I planned to meet the carriage. However, before I was even full speed, the rain started coming down. I was five minutes away from the park. This could all work, I just needed to get there now.

"Michael, you're going fast..." Rella warned. "Slow down."

For the first time, I ignored her. I took the turn to the park. I searched for the carriage and didn't see it. Instantly, I heard the alert on my phone. I reached down and looked it over. I slowed to read the message saying, "Sorry man. The rain ruins the carriage. We'll have to reschedule, or you can have a refund for the remainder of the evening."

"Grr." I let out a low growl. It would be about a 10-minute drive to get to the street.

"Michael, are you okay?"

"Yes, I'm all right. We're okay." I coached rhetorically as I rushed past the park.

"Michael, I think you need to slow down... and calm down," Rella suggested.

"No, Rella. I have to get there before the street floods too. Or before Noah builds another Ark. Okay? Just trust me." This couldn't be happening. All the planning... It was all supposed to be romantic. My inner speech was taking over, orating my emotion.

"Way to plan, Michael. Isn't this going to be romantic," It sounded. "Thank you, God. Way to pull a rain storm out of your hat..." Ridiculous.

"The street?" she asked confused. "What street?"

"Stop Rella. Just trust me."

"Michael, I think we should go back home. You're being rude, and I'm in no mood."

"No," I said sternly.

"Michael! Have you lost your mind? It's pouring. Turn around."

"No!" I gassed it.

"Michael!"

"Just trust me!" I accelerated. I could see the sign up ahead. We were almost there.

"Oh my gosh, we're hydroplaning!" Rella screamed.

Crap. We were. I tried to steer into it, but it wasn't working. The Jeep was going fast. Nothing to do but turn 2 miles ahead.

"Michael!" Rella screamed, scared for her life.

"It's okay. I love you!" I shouted.

I steered, silently wishing I wouldn't' have just accused The Lord of a hat trick. Please help I asked humbly in my mind.

All of a sudden, I felt the wheels hit the pavement... I quickly started to slow... Right before the turn towards the lane I was trying to reach, we came to a stop.

"Are you freaking crazy!"? Rella screamed. "I am walking!" She got out of the car.

"What?" I was shocked. "Rella, do not get out of this car." She was unbuckling the seatbelt and opening the door. "Rella, don't!"

"Don't tell me what to do!" She screamed. The small hint of red in her hair was shining through.

Before I knew it, she was walking on the road... Rella Lane... And she didn't even know it.

"Rella," I said, going after her. "Rella wait!"

"Michael, you are so inconsiderate! Don't you see what a day I've had! Then you drag me out of my apartment and threaten our lives by driving reckless in the rain!" She screamed past the droplets falling.

"Rella, I'm sorry. But... well, I had plans this evening and..."

"Plans?" She said sarcastically. "Plans?" She waved her hands in the air. "Well, I am so sorry my bad day ruined your perfect "plans" she emphasized dramatically.

"Rella, it's not like that!" I tried to explain through the rain. We were both soaked. Man, I better just get this out quick.

"What is it like Michael? Please tell me! What is it like?" She demanded.

"I love you Dad-gummit, you stubborn woman. Marry me!" I yelled.

"What?" She seemed shocked standing there, her hair was soaked, along with her clothes. Quickly, I closed the gap between us, reaching for the magic box in my back blazer. I lifted it up so she could see.

Her face paraded shock, remorse and surprise as I opened it revealing the striking diamond.

"This was my plan... Well, it was better.. But..." I motioned towards the sky." Well, you see..." I got down on one knee. "Cindy Rella Allan, Will you marry me?"

Her hand covered her mouth. She was shocked.

"Oh my, gosh," she mouthed. "Yes!" She screamed. "Yes, yes, yes!"

I quickly stood. The unpaved road now had my knees down covered in mud. "You'll marry me?" I yelled through the rain.

"Yes!"

I laughed as I pulled her into a kiss. There is nothing like a kiss in the rain. We pulled apart.

"Here, let me get this ring on you before it gets washed away!" I grabbed it and put it on her left ring finger.

"I love you!" She screamed.

"I love you too, my sweet love!" I echoed. "Now, can we go back to the car?"

She laughed and shook her head yes.

Holding hands we ran back. I went to her side and helped her in, and followed to mine, after.

"Michael Harvey! I cannot believe you just proposed!" She was in shock.

"Well, I can't believe how this just turned out," I said relieved.

"What... were your plans?" She asked full of curiosity.

"Look at the street sign, right there." I pointed.

She turned and read, "Rella Lane. Oh my gosh! Rella lane! You named a street after me?"

"Well, you're always talking about signs... I wanted to give you one, as a symbol of my love." I smiled slightly. Man, was she a sight to see.

"Michael!" She was crying now. "You are the most romantic man ever. I can't believe how I acted. I ruined it, didn't I?"

"No, baby... That's what I get for planning. It was perfect, don't you think?"

"Yes... But, I just have one complaint." She acted all proper.

"Oh yeah, and what's that?" I challenged her humor.

"What took you forever?" The look in her eyes was priceless. I never heard such sincerity from someone. I knew the way she meant it. I should have asked sooner. Both of us knew that I should have asked the first night we met... Forever. Well, that's how long it seemed.

"You're right." I grabbed her hand and looked deep into her eyes. "So, let me make it up to you." I offered.

She looked at me, as vulnerable as ever.

"Since I took forever... Can I just promise you forever, instead?"

The tears flowed as my voice choked out the sentence.

"Oh, Michael. Yes." She leaned in for a kiss.

I savored it... I knew, this same moment would occur again soon. A "yes". An "I Do." And "A kiss..." This was the plan. No matter the rain, storms or unexpected winds, we would always be together. Till death do us part. Our plan was to love one another, protect one another, and cherish one another. To live happily ever after and well, as far as plans go, I'd say, that's the best one to have.

2 Months Later

CHAPTER 11

I WOKE UP TO MY doorbell and a loud yelling of my name in Rella's voice. The past few weeks had been quite exhaustive. After our engagement, Rella explained that she didn't want to wait to get married. She felt like she could get everything planned in two months. At the time that I agreed, I had no idea the amount of pressure that would come with that.

"Coming..." I almost groaned as I rolled out of bed and headed downstairs. "Coming," I said again, as to soothe her knocks and persistent rings of the doorbell.

I opened the door. "Since when did you become an earlier riser?" I said while rubbing my eyes.

"Since I said yes to marrying you, silly!" She sounded, "What are you doing still in bed? Honey, we get married a week from today, and we have so much to do!"

She walked right past me and headed towards the kitchen. "I'll make you some coffee. We have a meeting with the wedding planner at 8:00. You better hurry!" She insisted.

Never had I seen my Rella so focused and determined. It was Saturday, and I remember when I'd have to pull her out of bed. She had been working day and night on all these plans. She had been working on the little details involving the cakes, photographers, reservations, food, everything. Little did I know that so much went into a wedding. I was a best man once, for one of my friends in high school, but honestly, I just threw him a party and showed up on the day. For some reason, when I agreed to the two-month time frame, that's what I had in mind. Boy was I wrong.

"Okay, baby... But aren't you going to give me a morning kiss?" I asked her as I headed over toward the kitchen opening.

She smiled. "Not with that morning breath of yours..." She winked at me.

I laughed and blew some of my morning breath at her. She let out her cute little scream and covered her nose. I could hear her giggling as I went up the stairs to get dressed. This day was starting whether I liked it, or not.

* * *

Only a few hours later and we had been through 3 meetings; one with the wedding planner, one with the DJ, and one with Scott from the local Vineyard. Though we were planning on a simple wedding, there were still many details to work out.

"Man, can you imagine if were planning an elaborate one?" I asked dryly.

"You would have never made it through." Rella teased. She knew that I hated this kind of thing. When we had art showings, I left most of the details up to those I hired. I figured that when you hire the right people, you can trust them to their opinion. I always trusted Scott with what wines to showcase... I always trusted Mr. and Mrs. Williams with what cheese and meats to serve and what little pastries would go along with them. Regardless, I knew the quality would always be there because it always was. However, Rella wanted to ensure everything was perfect, and that meant meeting with everyone several times.

"My mom is coming on Wednesday," Rella said over lunch. We chose a nice Italian place. It was the first break we'd had all morning.

"She is?" I asked.

"Yes." Rella's face turned. "She said she was bringing a boyfriend along," Rella said.

"Really?" I was a little concerned. "Are you okay with that?"

"No... But that's my mom. Oh well..." Rella sighed. "I'm sure it'll be fine... But..."

"But what?" I asked.

"I should warn you about my mother... She's a little... eccentric."

"Eccentric?"

"Yes..." Rella searched for the words to explain. "Just, don't take anything she says too seriously."

"Rella... How worried should I be?" Honestly, I was already nervous.

"Not too worried... Just don't be too serious." She laughed slightly.

I had a feeling that I was going to be the one in the awkward position.

Everything seemed to be falling together. I thought it was going to be hard to... well, keep our commitment to purity, to each other. Sometimes the engagement ring can serve as an excuse but really, that wasn't the case. We were busy, I honestly felt like I had hardly seen Rella. We would have dates, but most of our conversation centered around the wedding plans. I felt the whole thing a little ironic. In planning a ceremony for officiating coming together, caused us more time apart.

"It's just how weddings go," Dad had said, "it'll all pass soon enough. The day will go by so quickly... "Keep telling yourself to remember..." His advice still rang in my ears from the week before. More than anything, I just wanted to say "I do." I wanted to promise my Rella forever, as I promised her I would.

The day flew by, and I knew the ones after that would go just the same... Never have I felt the need to spring the clock forward, as I did now. Saturday had come to an end before we knew it. Rella still had a list of things to accomplish for the rest of the week. We would be very busy.

Fortunately, Dad also saw this one coming. He blacked our schedule so that we wouldn't have any showings. A month ago, I thought it unnecessary but now, I was entirely grateful. Just as fast as it seems, the day ended just as it started. Before I knew it, I was back in bed, anticipating the next day.

* * *

"Good morning," I said as I hopped into Rella's tiny car. I couldn't imagine how she drove this thing. It was so small. Little sports cars just made me a little claustrophobic. But, with the top down, the autumn air soothed me. She didn't drive her little Saturn Sky much, but when she did, it was done with style.

"Morning, honey. I brought you a coffee." She chimed as I climbed in.

I graciously accepted it. "So what's on the agenda for today?" I asked rhetorically.

"Michael! You don't remember?" She gave me a look.

"Err.... I.... No." I gave up. No point in trying to fake my way through this one.

"We have to pick up my mom! Remember? At 9:00 this morning?"

I looked at the clock. It was eight. I felt the nervousness billow up in me...

"Oh, yes," I assured her. "We have plenty of time. It's 30 minutes out. If we leave now, we'll make it there on time. We don't want your mother waiting." I saw Rella immediately tense up then relax. Her mother made her nervous for some reason but, I still could see too, that Rella was excited to see her. I felt more that she was nervous about me meeting her and what I would think.

"It doesn't matter, Rella nothing will change my mind about loving you." I had told her earlier this week at the cafe we always went to. I had come to cherish our time there together because it was the only alone time we had before the busy day of various plans started. Every morning, it served as a little vacation from it all. I loved that Rella would sit facing west... Because as the sun rose from the east, she would be highlighted in golden hues. She had no idea how beautiful she was, especially glowing in the sunlight. She looked every bit the angel that she was. We talked about various things. I tried my hardest to steer the conversation away from planning the wedding, to life after the wedding. We made plans... Places we'd go, things we'd see... It was a way of dreaming together. It was a way of ensuring each other that we would never leave the other. I reflected on it now, with such warmth in my heart. I didn't realize I was staring at her.

"Michael? Are you okay?" She asked with a smile as she followed the highway. "Why are you looking at me like that?"

"Because you're the most beautiful woman in the world. I'm the luckiest because I get to marry you in 3 more days." I said with confidence.

"Michael, don't say lucky... Say 'blessed.' That's the more appropriate term." She corrected me. "Luck is change. Blessed is from God."

"Fine. Blessed. I'm the most blessed." I smiled again, receiving the small scolding.

The ride to the airport was pleasant. We listened to a great playlist of Indie music to just calm us both down. I was starting to get nervous because Rella was.

"Well, are you ready? We're almost there, I think." She pointed. "That's it, right?"

"Yes, that's it!" I agreed.

Rella checked her watch. Little did she know that in the past few weeks, she was checking hers more than I was checking mine. Pulling up to the airport, we both took a deep breath.

"Here goes," she said in a cautious tone, following the signs that said "Pick Up."

"It'll be fine, love," I said, downing the last bit of coffee in my cup.

"There she is," Rella pointed as I followed.

I spotted the woman, who was her mom. She had fiery red hair down to her shoulders. She was built much like Rella. Tall and slender. Her wardrobe was different. It was dazzling and well, as Rella said, eccentric.

Rella rolled down the window. "Mom!" She waved as we were pulling up.

Quickly, she parked in the 30-minute time slot. Putting her car in gear, I gave a quick glance to Rella and told her it was going to be okay. She only halfway listened as she stepped out, and I followed.

"Hi, Momma." She said in a sweet tone.

"Oh, darling, darling! There's my sweet girl! Look how incredible you look!" Her mom's voice was a little on the high pitched side. However, it could have been just because of her excitement.

"Thank you, Momma." She gave her mom a hug and turned out to of it. "This is my Michael."

"Hello, Michael!" Her mom looked at me with her bright blue eyes. "It's so nice to meet you!" She looked at Rella, "Oh honey, he's the cutest. You did well. Momma approves."

"Mom!" Rella whined as flush filled her checks and mine.

"Thank you ma'am." I didn't know what else to say.

"Oh, don't you call me ma'am. That makes me sound like I'm an old hag. Call me 'Loretta' like everyone else.

"Loretta, then" I echoed. It dawned on me this was the first I learned her name... Rella always just called her 'momma.'

"Come on, momma. Let's get you and your luggage."

"Boy, if I haven't heard that all my life," Loretta said dramatically, "Me and my luggage." She laughed loudly.

"Mom..." Rella said in an annoyed tone.

I just smiled and winked at Rella so her mom could see.

Rella said, "See mom, you just egg him on." She punched me lightly in the arm. "So where is..." she looked around... "The boyfriend?"

"Oh, well, he is a surgeon, and he couldn't make it just yet but he'll be flying on Friday."

"Uh-huh..." Rella said.

"Oh, don't 'uh-huh me' Cindy Rella."

Rella just rolled her eyes.

I couldn't help but chuckle. Seeing the two of them together was quite humorous. Never would I tell her, but Rella was much like her mother... Over the next few days, I saw and understood more of Rella than I ever had. I think that's why they didn't get along at times because they were so much alike. Rella wasn't as loud or as blunt, but they had many similarities. I favored my new mother-in-law. It was all a part of making Rella, my bride.

* * *

The Big Day

I woke up ready. Ready to marry her. Ready to say 'I do' and prepared to spend the rest of my life with the woman of my dreams… but, I would have to wait just a little longer. The wedding was a 4:00 in the afternoon. We were having the wedding outside of an old country church. Rella wanted to be married near the house of God, but she still wanted to be outside. The fall air would be cool, but not unpleasant.

The old church was beautiful. We had the ceremony set up behind the church so the stained glass of the cross would be glimmering in the evening sun as the backdrop for our ceremony. Pastor Jake was wonderful to let us do that, and to agree to marry us outside. The church's only requirement for Rella and I was that we do four sessions of Premarital counseling. We did and honestly, it was a breeze. Rella and I answered the questions easily. Our time of courting had set a foundation of friendship for our marriage to stand on. Pastor Jake didn't have to say how rare that was, we had already known. He complimented Rella and Me a lot and at the end, agreed to marry us. We couldn't have been more grateful.

I was anxiously awaiting my Dad at the house. He was planning to pick me up and grab lunch. Rella was off with her mom getting their nails, hair, and all the frilly stuff done. Dad and I just didn't need to worry about any of that. Nothing but a comb and a little hairspray for my hair and I was all set. Rella and I decided to have a small service. We had good friends, but none close enough to feel like we needed to call them for our wedding. So, we decided that our parents would stand up with us. Her mom was the Matron of Honor, and my Dad was my best man. He always had been. We had a small girl, a volunteer from the church, to be our flower girl. The decorations and everything were simple and elegant. Just like my Rella was.

My suit was a light tan with golden yellow accessories. Those were the colors my Rella picked. Golden yellow, orange, and reds in line with the fall season. It was truly exquisite. I was thankful she didn't go with hot pink or something crazy. All of the flowers were of autumn tints that complemented the subtle gold accents. The wedding reception was at the same place of the ceremony, set up in a fancy tent behind us. There weren't going to be a lot of people there. Probably around 50 or so. We invited some of Rella's clients and close acquaintances she had made since living here. For me, Old Man Salvador, Mrs. Margaret, the Williams' of course, and a few others who had put up with me my whole life. Even though I told Rella we could have the works... the biggest ceremony in Michigan, if she wanted, but she said no. I couldn't help but be thankful. I didn't want a bunch of strangers at our wedding. The count was just enough.

We decided not to have a sit-down dinner either. We didn't want things to be that formal. So, we went with fine wine, and snacks from the local deli. It was the same thing we ordered for our showcases, but I wouldn't tell Rella that. She had spent so much time researching wines, cheeses, and all that would be served. I couldn't help but smile. She cared about all of the details. I knew today would run smoothly because of it.

Dad showed up around noon. I was dressed in jeans, loafers, and a polo. Even though I was nervous, I was ready to eat.

"Well son, are you ready?" He sounded as we rode in his old Chevy truck.

"As I'll ever be." I smiled.

"Nervous?" He turned to see my reaction to his question.

"No... Excited, though but not nervous... well maybe a little nervous. I don't like public speaking."

Dad laughed, "Public speaking? What does that have to do with anything?"

"The vow repetition. I'll be saying it in front of everyone, and don't I have to make a toast of some sort?"

Dad chuckled again. "Son, you just repeat after Pastor Jake. That's all. Don't worry about a toast. I'll handle that part, okay?"

I let out a sigh of relief, "Okay... Good. Okay." I instantly calmed down at what he had said. I was so nervous about speaking to crowds, even if they were full of people I knew.

"How about DC's for lunch?" Dad asked.

"That's perfect, Dad. I really could use a good meal."

"Okay. Sounds good." He took the turn on the right and headed towards my favorite restaurant.

Walking in, I saw Tony talking to a few customers when he saw us.

"Hey, aren't you getting married today?" he sounded in his loud Italian accent.

I smiled, "Yes sir. I could go for some good lunch before I go off saying vows."

"Well, you came to the right place, eh?" He nudged my Dad. "And er, it's on the house today! My wedding treat!"

"Tony, you don't I have to do that," I offered.

"I know, I know, but I want to, eh?" He shrugged his shoulders. "Eat what you like!"

"Okay, thanks, Tony. You're the best." Dad and I sat downed and gazed at the menu and ordered. Nothing like a good burger to make a man at ease.

"Hey, so I have something to ask ya." Dad changed into a serious tone.

"What's that?"

"Well," he reached into his back pocket. "I know women have that whole old, blue, new something or other, and I wondered if you wanted Rella to have this... It was your mothers."

He pulled out the bracelet that I hadn't seen since it was on my mom's wrist. It was gold, with diamonds and blue sapphires.

"Dad." I choked as my eyes filled up with tears. I couldn't believe he would offer it to me. I thought about asking him for mom's ring when I was going to propose, but I didn't have it in me. I knew Dad would give it to me, whether or not he was ready to, so I didn't want to put him in that position. But this... it was perfect for her.

"That way..." Dad swallowed hard as tears flowed, "a piece of your mom is with her..." he wiped his tears. "She'd want to be here Mic. She would've loved Rella to wear it."

By now, tears were rolling down my face. I could hardly find the words... "Thank you."

"Yeah.." Dad gently put the bracelet back in its box. "I was going to drop it off to her after I got you to the church. She is getting ready in the Sunday school building. I just wanted to check with you first."

"Dad." I tried to push back my emotions. "I can't tell you..."

"Don't." He stopped. "I'll start crying all over again. You'll make me look like a sissy in front of Chef Tony." He teased as he took a sip of water.

I couldn't imagine how hard that was for him... He'd never let go of my mom, and I couldn't expect that he would. All of her things remained untouched in our house. He never moved them, as if he was waiting for her to come back someday. The fact that he would offer me this... it was something special.

"Thank you, Dad."

"You're welcome, my boy..." he took another drink of water. I knew he was a little worked up. "I'm very proud of you."

"Dad..." My tears welled up again.

"I am... You're a good man. One I can be proud of."

"Thanks, Daddy." I hadn't called him that since I was a boy. The sound alone made his eyes light up with tears again.

"Dad gum... we need to get those cheeseburgers and get out of here." He tried to brush off the emotion.

I couldn't help but laugh at the gesture.

On cue, our burgers came. We ate fast, I think just to avoid any more emotional talk. Dad ordered us to go drinks as we wrapped up.

"Okay, so I'll take you back to the house so you can get dressed. I'll drop the gift off to Rella, and I'll meet you at the church no later than 3:00. Sound good?" Dad had it all planned out.

It was about 1:00 now. "Two hours to get dressed?" I asked him

"Well, take your time. Go for a run or something, but Rella will need this now. Ladies have to have their dress and stuff all planned."

"Okay. That's a good idea. I'm pretty... well, I'm starting to get nervous." I admitted.

Dad smiled. "You'll be fine. Let's go." He motioned towards the door!

"Yeah, but let me tell Tony thanks." I went over to the counter and asked for him. He came out of the back.

"How was it?" He asked with a smile.

"Best green chili cheeseburger I've ever had! Thanks, Tony. Will I see you tonight?" I asked

"Absolutely! I wouldn't miss it for the world!"

"Okay. Thanks again! See ya!" I grabbed a toothpick and met my Dad at the door.

I can't say I was thrilled to be heading home, but I was also relieved in a way. I think Dad was right about the run. I needed to calm myself down. It wasn't only the public speaking thing that had me nervous... it was... the honeymooning too. Though I wouldn't admit that to my Dad, I'm sure he knew. There was no way we were going to have the birds and the bees talk on my wedding day!

The mere thought of that made me antsy. Dad dropped me off, and I went and changed into workout clothes. I kept thinking of Rella... Since we started dating, I had never gone a whole day without seeing her. It was strange. I couldn't begin to imagine how beautiful she was going to look. I remembered proposing to her in her sweats and a t-shirt, and she was the most beautiful woman I had ever seen... I knew a white gown would suit her... my stomach grew anxious at the thought. Soon... I'd see her... in 3-2-1 hours from now...

* * *

Standing at the end of the aisle with my Dad was surreal. The cross was glowing in the background. For the first time in a long time, I found myself sincerely thanking God for creating such a beautiful day and giving me such a beautiful woman to marry. I couldn't have asked for more.

Not long after my prayer, the music began. The flower girl sprinkled white roses on the golden silk that served as the walkway. Her mother had come along too, dressed in a light champagne floor length gown. There was absolutely nothing that could have prepared me for the sight I beheld. Not even the most beautiful painting or the most poetic words could describe the pure and indescribable beauty that I witnessed.

"Rella.." I gasped as she turned and started walking down the aisle. She was dressed in white, with a dress that was slim and flowing. The neckline was fit around her shoulders, modest and beautiful. Her hair was slightly down, with some parts arranged in a beautiful design of curls. Her makeup was minimal, but her beautiful eyes lite up the place. I have never felt my heart be filled with so much joy. She smiled at me, and I had to fight myself not to go and get her.

As she drew closer, I noticed my mother's bracelet. It was the perfect touch. The gold matched the gold of her engagement ring. It was meant to be. She was a perfect vision of a bride. And... she was all mine.

Gracefully, I took her hand. She took it lightly, palms sweaty. I couldn't blame her, as mine were too.

"You are beautiful," I whispered.

"Thank you." She said through her smile. "You look so handsome."

I just smiled back. We both then turned to Pastor Jake, to take it away. I kept telling myself to remember this, remember this, but it was all happening so fast. She said her vows, I repeated mine. Then, before I knew it, I heard "kiss the bride."

In a way, it was like I was on autopilot. Rella was so beautiful; it was as if no one else was there. She captured my attention, just as she had captured my heart. It was hard to focus on anything but her.

We kissed and walked back down the aisle as husband and wife. I couldn't have felt more joy. The reception was excellent. Simple, tasteful and perfectly elegant. We were greeted by friends and family.

Rella and I danced and danced... She was a superb dancer. We cut and ate the cake. Posed for the pictures and laughed and enjoyed family. Her mom's boyfriend showed up, and he was a nice guy. He even asked to dance with Rella, in a sincere, fatherly way. I couldn't help but notice that Rella was impressed by it.

Dad looked happy too, but I knew it was hard for him. He missed my mother, and I knew he was thinking of her. That broke my heart for him, but there was nothing I could do except remember that she was circling the sky with a constant light on us.

By the end of the evening, I was just ready to be alone with her. I asked her if she was ready, and she just nodded yes with a sweet smile. Due to my last inconvenience with the horse drawn carriage, I was able to cash in on him coming and taking us to the local hotel before we went to our honeymoon destination the next morning. I had him waiting for a least an hour before the reception was over in case we wanted to sneak out early. Looks like this time, it served me well.

We alerted the crowd that we were leaving and thanked everyone for coming. Rella tossed her bouquet, and her mother caught it.

"You've got to be kidding me..." She said under her breath. I was laughing hysterically. It couldn't have been more poetic.

We both decided that rice wasn't the way we wanted to exit, and Rella had seen someone use little bells instead. So everyone rang them as well headed towards the carriage. I couldn't have asked for a more perfect picture... Truly, it was out of a fairy tale book. I suppose you could say, well, it was like I was the prince, and I had found my princess... Cindy Rella.

CHAPTER 12

Our first night together was indescribable. We were both nervous as we headed up to our hotel room. The hotel attendant asked if Rella wanted to sign her new name for the first time on the check-in slip.

'Rella Harvey" she said, as she signed it with a shaking hand. I loved the sound. She was forever mine and I, forever hers.

We got in the elevator, and I soothed her assuring her that we would be okay. We were both nervous and inexperienced, but I think that's how God intended it. We were vulnerable to each other. In a way, we had to depend on the other one more, and that made everything more intimate. I couldn't have imagined it to be any more beautiful that it was. We lost our virginity to each other, both giving an irreplaceable gift to one another. It was a gift we understood that we could never get back once given. We also knew it was a gift that nowadays, was hard to keep and quickly given away. I think, understanding that reality is what helped us keep our virginity until we found the one that was willing to say vows and promise to love us till death do us part. I mean... why would you give such an irreplaceable gift away to someone who is not willing to make that commitment? For us, it was worth the long wait. Rella fell asleep in my arms that night and at that moment, I swear I couldn't have asked for more. I felt infinite.

* * *

We decided the honeymoon would be at one of the U.S. Virgin Islands at a resort on St. Thomas. We were going to be there for two weeks. It was a longer honeymoon than most, but we felt as though we had a small wedding, we could have a more extravagant honeymoon, and we did. The island was beautiful. We stayed at a 5-star Marriott, and we were treated like celebrities. Couple massages, spa treatments, swimming, and some of the best food I've ever tasted. We walked onto the beach straight from our hotel room suite. It was beautiful. The past few days held more happiness than I could have ever dreamed of or even have wished.

"It's going to be hard to get back into a routine, isn't it?" I asked Rella as she was sunbathing on the beach chair next to mine.

"What routine?" She asked comically.

"Oh, right..." I laughed. She was so beautiful. "Well, are you excited to move in with me?"

"Oh yes, Michael. I'm thrilled. My mom and Steve, her boyfriend, had packed up my things before she left. Wasn't that sweet of them?"

"It was, baby. Very kind. So, all we need to move is boxes right?" You could hear the waves hitting against each other. It was hard to talk about going back to normal life, but we had to face it sooner or later.

"Yes... and furniture... but, I don't know if we'll need to move all of it. I might put some in storage or sell it."

"Why so?" I asked

"Well, I don't think it would match your house... My stuff is a little... brighter than your place," she said cautiously.

"Brighter? What's wrong with my place," I asked concerned. "You don't like it?"

"No, no, honey. It's not that... It's just a little... dull." She shrugged her shoulders with a perplexed look on her face, unsure how to continue.

"Dull... like... how?" I didn't understand. I thought everything was clean and crisp.

"Michael... It's a beautiful home. Really... I just think it could use a little more color. Aren't all of your walls... gray?"

"No, not gray...."

She gave me a look.

"Okay, they are gray, but I thought it looked good."

"For a bachelor." She suggested with a smirk.

I couldn't help but agree. "Okay, so, when we get back, we'll do some painting, all right?"

"Oh, you'll let me paint!" Rella jumped out of her lawn chair.

I smiled, "Of course honey. It's your house too."

"Oh, thank you, Michael." She leaned in and gave me a smoldering kiss.

"Well, if I'd known I would get a kiss like that, I would have told you a long time ago."

She laughed. "We'll have yellow walls... Or maybe a light purple. The master can be blue! What do you think!" She paced as she was thinking." So we can design it like, the ocean, to remind us of our honeymoon!"

"Whatever you want, my love." I would agree to anything to make her happy.

"Oh, Michael, thank you! I am so excited. I've never had my own home to decorate! I always decorate everyone else's, and now I get to do ours!" She couldn't have been more excited. "Oh, now I'm ready to go home!" She exclaimed.

I couldn't help but laugh. "Well, that was an excellent transition. What do you say we take one last swim in the crystal blue, go pack, get a massage, and get a good night's sleep before we leave tomorrow. Our flight leaves at 5:00 a.m."

"Michael Harvey... Are you scheduling our honeymoon?" She demanded jokingly. We had already made the agreement on our first day here that I wouldn't plan or 'schedule' anything.

"No.... It was all just... suggestion." I smiled.

She giggled while holding out her hand to me. "Let's go." She was the love of my life, and I couldn't help but be the beckon of her every call.

* * *

The plane ride back was exhausting. We switched planes three times and sat through 2, three-hour delays. By the time that we got home, we were exhausted. Dad picked us up from the airport, and I could tell he was so excited to see us. I was excited to see him too... The last time I'd been away without seeing him was probably in college. I couldn't have been happier to be home.

Home. With my Rella, of course. We had been back about two weeks and just finally, we got all her stuff moved in. I've never seen one person with so many clothes. The closet is filled to the max. She has been working on getting her things out of boxes, which, all in all, has been a task.

Along with that, Rella also has a different definition of clean than I do. Something neither of us could have truly understood until we were married. She doesn't mind things lying around, whereas it makes me a little tense. She's just more of a free spirit than I am, or as she says...

We've have gotten a good routine, though over the past few days. Usually, I leave in the morning before she does... My late little sleeper. I'm still an early riser, so a lot of times I go to the gallery first, and then when she wakes, we meet at our favorite coffee shop, The Daily Grind. After that, we go our separate ways. I usually go to the gallery, and she goes off and visits whatever client she needs or goes shopping. Sometimes I wonder if she does more shopping for herself than for her clients, but I don't mind. I love to indulge her as much as I can.

Speaking of, tomorrow I promised her that we would go paint shopping. I have coached myself to let her choose. She is the interior designer, not I, so I need to trust that. We've talked about designs enough, and she has shown me some great ideas and plans, so I'm just sitting back and letting her take the reigns.

This evening it's just nice to be home. For the past two Thursdays, we have had showings, which is good, but still exhausting. I feel like I was baptized by fire in that first week back to work. I've been looking forward to this Friday night ever since, simply because we don't have anything to do. Rella should be home any minute now. It's pizza and wine for dinner, and if you ask me, it just doesn't get any better than that.

"Honey..." She just arrived home.

"In here," I yelled from the kitchen. Just in time.

'Hey baby, what are you doing?" She asked all dressed up in a pencil skirt and long sleeved blouse. Her hair was pulled up in a bun thing, with a pen.

"Hey baby, you. You look like a sexy school teacher." I said with a wink.

She rolled her eyes, "Oh, Michael." She leaned down and started taking off her high heels. "What's for dinner?"

She had no idea how striking she was. "Pizza and wine?" I suggested hoping she'd agree.

"That sounds amazing. I'm starving!" She paired her shoes and hung them over her shoulder. "I'm going to take a hot bath while you order. Is that okay?"

"Yes, baby, that's fine. What kind of pizza do you want?"

"Ummm..." She hesitated. "Veggie thinly sliced."

"I thought you said you were hungry?" I asked comically.

"Hey, if you want me to keep this hot school teacher body, then veggie is what I need." She said with a cute little sass.

"Yes, ma'am." I winked at her again. She was truly adorable. "Love you."

She was heading upstairs, "I love you, too." I could hear her blow a kiss.

Soon, the pizza arrived. I was so hungry I could have eaten both by myself. Rella came back down out of the shower in sweats and a t-shirt. I couldn't help the emotion stir in me. The last time I had seen her like that, I proposed.

"Why are you looking at me like that?" She humbly asked.

"I like when you're in sweats," I admitted.

"Really? This over school teacher?" She questioned.

“Absolutely,” I said affirmatively while handing her a glass of fine Merlot.

“No, can you get me some water first? I feel dehydrated since my bath. I don’t want to spring on a headache.” She asked.

“Good idea... wine headaches are the worst.” I agreed.

“Thank you,” she said while looking around, “But where is that pizza?”

I laughed, “Right here, baby.”

“Mmmm, mmm.” She sounded as she took a bite. She had finished her first slice before I did.

“Man, you were hungry,” I said just swallowing.

“I told you! I had nothing but a granola bar because my client was difficult and annoying.” She waved her hand in the air.

“Annoying?” I asked.

“Yes. Very. She changes the design every time I’m over there. ‘Let’s do that’, or, ‘look at this.’ It’s like every home magazine she sees, she decides that’s the look she wants for our home. It’s driving me crazy!”

I could see her shoulders tense as she recalled the story. I went over to massage them... “It’s all in public service, honey,” I said.

“Well, public service sucks.” She said frankly.

I couldn’t help but chuckle. One minute she was prim as a princess, the next she was as bold as a bobcat.

“Oh, guess what we’re going to do tomorrow?” She said as it seemed to scroll across her mind. She turned and smiled.

“Paint shopping?” I guessed.

“Yes! Oh, I am so excited. We need to review the design plans tonight before we get samples tomorrow!” She grabbed another slice. “Let me get them!” She said while her mouth was half-full.

“Okay, but haven’t we gone over them already?” I just wanted to relax a bit.

“Yes, but we have to be sure!” I couldn’t help but hear the excitement in her voice.

“Alright, baby. Whatever you say.”

She brought the designs, and we looked at them for what seemed like hours. Around midnight, we headed for bed.

Rella was such a hard sleeper, and when she was ready for bed, she was ready. I almost had to drag her upstairs.

"Man, it's a good thing you didn't have wine after all," I suggested.

"I know... how ironic. I'm so tired; I'm drunk."

I laughed as I tucked her in. Oddly, as tired as I was, I didn't want to go to bed just yet. I wanted to go downstairs and wind down a little more.

She was so beautiful, especially when she was asleep. Innocent. Perfectly innocent. I couldn't have been a happier husband. I went downstairs to watch a little late night comedy. All those design plans had me nervous though I didn't want Rella to know that. I suppose I'm just... a little resistant to change. I'm set in my ways, sometimes. But, I knew it was time for a change. Rella changed me in so many ways; I don't know why I was so worried about a color pallet.

I thought the plans over. She chose light, pastel like colors. They seemed to be very elegant, but they just weren't something I was used to. Our bedroom was going to be the most drastic, from light cream to sea green. Man had I gotten myself into this, whether I liked it or not. I was thinking about it all when I heard Rella scream.

I couldn't run up the stairs fast enough! I walked into the bedroom and Rella was still asleep. She was kicking and punching, as though she was fighting. She was having a nightmare.

"Rella," I ran over to her. "Rella, wake up, baby. Wake up!" I shook her gently. "Wake up, honey. It's just a dream."

Slowly she opened her eyes. When she saw me and that it was just a dream she jumped into my arms and started crying.

"It's okay, baby. It was just a dream." I soothed her as I held her in my arms." I sat down on the bed with her. "Shhhhhh...."

Her crying slowed. "Oh, Michael. It was awful." She said through the last of the tears.

"Tell me."

"I had a dream... that... You... died." She started crying again. "In a car crash, you died." She said through the sobs.

Her words caught me off guard. I couldn't imagine such a thing. "Shhh, it's okay. I'm still here Rella. I'll never leave you. Shhhh..."

I couldn't believe the dream... What would spark such a thing? "It's okay baby, I'm here, just go back to sleep." I stood to lay her back down.

"Don't go..." She whined.

"I won't Rella..." I sat down beside her. "I'll never go... I'll always be right here with you."

At that, she eased back into her sleep... But, I, however, did not.

CHAPTER 13

THE NEXT DAY, I WAS tired. The nightmare that Rella had shook me up. I can't say why, I just know it had me nervous for some reason. Last night, I didn't go to bed until early in the morning, and even then, I didn't sleep well. Rella meant the world to me. I saw how upset she was from the dream, and it bothered me. I couldn't imagine ever leaving her and well, I couldn't imagine her ever leaving me. We were sewn together, somehow. She was like the blood in my veins and the air that I needed to breath. My heart was dependent on hers now. Everything was intertwined, woven, never to be apart again.

"What's wrong, Michael? You're quieter than a library this morning..." Rella commented as we sat at The Daily Grind.

"Nothing, baby, I'm okay." I tried to brush it off. I didn't want to talk about it ever again.

"You're sure?" She insisted.

"Yes. I'm fine." I transitioned to get off the subject. "So, are you ready to go get the paint?" I knew that would do the trick.

"Absolutely!" She pulled a small writing pad from her purse. "I have them all picked out... well, not the particular shades, but the look we're going for."

"Good, honey." I smiled as I took a sip of my coffee. I'd never seen anyone so passionate over paint. "You haven't taken a bite of your muffin."

"Oh, yeah..." I'm not hungry.

"Since when are you not hungry for a blueberry muffin?" I asked jokingly. It was her favorite morning choice.

"Since, I'm just not." She snapped.

I stopped at that. She'd been emotional ever since we got back from the honeymoon. I didn't know if it was the stress of moving or what, but I learned to settle back when necessary.

"I'm sorry. I didn't mean to snap." She interrupted my thoughts. "I'm just so excited; that's all."

"It's alright, babe. I don't want to force you to eat." I apologized too.

Rella and I never fought. It just wasn't in our nature. We would disagree over things, but never to the point of arguing about it. We figured why fight when we can just talk about it? Each was quick to correct themselves when they were in the wrong. That is the method that worked for us. Open and honest with each other and ourselves.

"Well, are you ready to go then," I asked as I took the last swig of my coffee.

She was already getting out of her chair. "More than ever!"

We headed to the local hardware store and told them what our project was. We got a basket and filled it with painter's tape, lots of covering plastic, brushes, rollers, the whole nine yards. Then, we went over to the color section are started to pick out the colors and glosses.

"Okay, so for the living room, I was thinking a light, grayish blue. I think it'll be beautiful. Which one do you like?"

"Errr. They all look the same." I commented as I looked at the three swatches she showed me.

"Michael!" She could help but roll her eyes with a smile. "No wonder all of my clients are women."

I just shrugged my shoulders apologetically. Picking colors was going to be harder than I thought. The Blues were hardly different from each other. Is it like white or white?

"Okay, the kitchen I think needs to be bright. Like, yellow!"

"Yellow?" I asked with a hint of fear... Oh man, I didn't know if I was going to be able to handle a yellow anything.

"Yes, yellow. You have white cabinets with cream walls. It blends too much. Light, golden yellow will bring warmth."

She pulled two color swatches. "Now, see, look at these two." She pointed, "and imagine them contrasted with your white cabinets are dark hardwood floor. It will look beautiful. With red accents... We can do like a rooster kind of theme. Honey."

Everything was blending in for me! Yellow, light, dark, I had no clue

"Michael?" She questioned. "Are you listening?"

"Yes. Rooster theme. That's great."

She chuckled. "Then why do you sound scared?"

"Because this is all very... girly. My love, I trust you. You pick what's best."

She was laughing now. "Okay, but let's go get the bathroom paint macho man. A lavender color, and then we'll get your bedroom paint."

We then picked out two shades, again; that were more similar to me than different. However, I will admit, seeing all of the color swatches together did look nice. I had faith in my girl. She was talented, and no matter my skeptics, I knew it would turn out great.

"Okay, so we have one more room to paint."

"We do?" All that was left was the guest bedroom.

"The guest room." She smiled.

"Babe, but no one will even be in there," I suggested. Why would I want to paint a room that I would hardly be in?

"You'll be in there more than you think... Plus, this one is an easy choice."

She went a grabbed two color swatches. "Pink... or blue?" She was smiling ear to ear.

"Babe, why would I want pi--- wait, what?"

She smiled wider now. "Let me rephrase then..." Tears wallowed in her eyes, "Girl or boy?" She was smiling ear to ear.

"Oh my gosh!" I raised my voice, "You're pregnant?" I left the cart and went to grab her hands. "Are you?"

She just shook her head yes, as the tears started to flow.

"Oh, baby!" I picked her up and spun her around! "Oh, we're having a baby!" I yelled at the top of my lungs, and everyone in the store turned to look.

She was laughing now. "Michael, put me down... I'm going to get morning sickness again."

"Oh," I put her down quickly. "That's why you didn't want your muffin!"

She smiled, "Yes."

"And that's why you didn't drink any wine!" I said as I was putting all of the pieces together.

Laughing, "Right... I was sure you'd figure me out with that one. Michael, 'too dehydrated'" she shook her head.

I smiled. "How long have you known?"

"Just since yesterday..." She put her hand gracefully on her tummy. "That's why I was late coming home. Ever since we got back, I was feeling nauseous, and emotional." She admitted. "I started crying at a client's house... and I thought it was PMS, but then I realized that I hadn't started my period. I had taken the test before I came home."

"Oh my gosh!" I was tearing up now. "We're having a baby!!" I half yelled again.

"Michael," Rella shushed me. "Not so loud. Everyone is staring at us."

"Fine, let them stare at my beautiful pregnant wife!" I said without a care in the world.

I picked her up again and kissed her hard. She was my sweet love, and we were having a baby!!! My baby was having my baby.

I couldn't have been a happier man!

* * *

After finding out Rella was pregnant, I refused to allow her to paint. I convinced her that we should hire someone and believe me, it took some convincing. She can be the most stubborn sometimes, but with a little shopping spree for new maternity clothes, I was able to win her over. It was hard, but I did it. I knew she was getting a little annoyed with me, though. I hardly let her do anything. I just wanted to be sure she was okay, but I could see that I was becoming a little obsessive about it.

"I'm a big girl, Michael," she'd tell me. "Being pregnant doesn't change my capability."

I knew it was true, but it was hard for me. She had been suffering pretty bad from morning sickness. Every day, at six in the morning, on the dot, she'd be in the bathroom. That made it harder for me to give her independence when I saw her in that state, but I knew I had to respect her boundaries. Rella was capable, and I had to acknowledge that.

We decided not to tell the family just yet. Rella and I wanted to tell her mom and my Dad at the same time. So, we decided to have a family dinner, but her mom wasn't able to make it until this Friday. Almost two weeks had gone by since the hardware store scene, and it was getting harder by the minute not to tell my Dad.

Dad was my Dad, he was my business partner, but he was also my best friend. I hadn't kept a secret from him since I was in my high school partying days. I think he kind of suspected something because, at work he kept asking me how Rella and I were doing... I knew what he was thinking, that marriage wasn't what it was made out to be. But, that just wasn't the case. Rella and I were perfectly happy. The pregnancy had brought along new stresses, but nothing we couldn't handle. Fortunately, we are financially set, so it wasn't like I was worried about being able to afford it. Honestly, my only worry was whether or not I was going to be a good Dad to he or she. I knew that my father was fantastic, and I could kind of, reference him, so to speak, but it's different you know? A child is now your responsibility...

Rella knew a lot more about the pregnancy, baby thing than I did. She even went to the bookstore and bought some pregnancy and first-year books for herself. There were so many facts; so many do's and do nots. It didn't take me long to realize how blessed I was with Rella being the mother of my child. She didn't seem nervous, and well, it was already quite becoming on her. She held a beautiful maternal glow that even I distinguished as different. I couldn't help but notice that now her hands were always caught resting at the base of her belly as if she were protecting our baby at all times. There were so many moments that I savored the past few days. I knew this time was something I would never forget.

Tonight was the big night of our dinner. Rella had the local baker make a cake that said, Congratulations Grandma and Grandpa. I thought it was brilliant. She was making her famous green chili chicken enchiladas. They were the very best.

My Dad had agreed to pick up Rella's mom so that I could get home earlier. We had a showing last night, so the day after, is always catch up day. I had so much to do. Stephanie Mendoza booked another show with us next week, so we immediately needed to get started with that. Especially if she chose to bring as many paintings as she did last time.

Around noon, Dad asked me to pay a visit to Old Man Salvador's shop. We needed to talk about some new designs, but also, we were in need of more storage. Dad and I had a plan to build frame shelving in one of our back rooms. Right now, everything was piled in there, and it couldn't have been more inefficient. On my way there, I called my pregnant wife to see how she was.

"Hello?"

"Hey, baby, what are you up to?" I'm eating cookies and ice cream... with potato chips." She said in a chipper tone.

"Ice cream and potato chips? For lunch?" I questioned.

"Hey, don't judge me. I'm pregnant."

I chuckled. "Yes, you are my love. I just wanted to call and see what you were up to. I'm heading to Old Man Salvador's place to talk business."

"Oh, okay, tell him I said 'hello.'" She paused, "Oh, and hey before you go, can you do something for me?"

"Anything baby."

"I need you to go to the store after you leave the gallery. I forgot the toppings for the enchiladas, so get sour cream, lettuce, tomato, and onion. I'm going to pick up the cake, and I'll meet you at the house. Dinner is at 7:30."

"Okay, sour cream, lettuce, tomato, and onion?" I asked to make sure I heard clearly.

"Perfect! Thanks, honey!"

"You're welcome baby. I love you, and I'll see you after a while."

"Okay! Love you! And the baby does too!" She hung up.

That was her new saying. Since we didn't know if it was a boy or girl yet, she just called it baby. She'd say, "baby is hungry, or baby is making mommy tired. Baby likes this..." It was a little comical, but I couldn't blame her... It was hard not to name the presence within her.

Pulling up to Mr. Salvador's shop, I could see he was hard at work, as he always was. He was such a good person.

Getting out, he spotted me. "Hey, there Michael. I'm just working on these frames of yours."

"Hey, Mr. Salvador! Sounds good. I came to bring you some more work."

"Well, I can't turn that down, now can I?" He smiled as he put down a chiseling too,l.

"I mean, you could, but I hope you won't," I suggested.

"Nah, I wouldn't. You and your Dad would never survive without me." He said in a joking tone.

"Now, there's more truth in that than you know."

He laughed. "So, what can I do for ya?"

"Well," I pulled out the piece of paper in my back pocket. It was an order form. "Dad and I need some more frames. Stephanie Mendoza is coming back, and we'll need to have a full stock."

"Yes, sir. Man, she's a great artist, isn't she?" Salvador said as he looked at the order of many different sizes.

"She sure is." I agreed.

"Okay, well, I will try to get all of these done by Wednesday. Is that alright?"

"Yes, that will be fine," I said... "Also, Dad and I were wanting to talk to you about another project?"

"Oh yeah? What about?" He asked.

"We need some shelving in our back room. It's a mess in there."

"Yes sir, you do. I've been telling your Dad for years now."

"Well, he's finally listened." I chuckled. "Do you mind?"

"No, sir, not at all. I'll get you a quote. What's that room? A 10x9?"

"I think so... You might measure just to be sure."

"Will do." He folded the order form and put it in his pocket. "So how are you and that pregnant wife of yours?" She said with a little smirk.

I tried to hide the shock on my face. "How did you..."?

He laughed out loud. "Son, you can spot a pregnant woman out of a crowd, easy. Especially Rella. She's glowing like she has been kissed by an angel."

I couldn't help but smile. You couldn't get anything past Mr. Salvador. "Yes, sir... We're telling Dad and her mom tonight at a surprise dinner."

"I'll be... How wonderful. How far along is she?" He asked.

"Just a few weeks." I smiled.

"I figured..." He paused. "I remember when my wife was pregnant about that much. She was eatin' some weird stuff... seemed to throw it up just as quick." He shook his head in disgust.

I snarled. "Rella just told me she had potato chips, cookies and ice cream for lunch."

He laughed, "Sounds about right."

"Mr. Salvador, I didn't know you had a child." He never spoke of it before.

"Oh..." he got quiet. "He's with his mother now, in heaven. He served in the army, as his old pop did... Vietnam" He stopped suddenly.

"I'm sorry to hear that." I didn't know what else to say.

"It's alright. I'll see them again someday." He assured me.

"You will." I was sure, with his character, that if anyone got to go to heaven it would be him.

"Well, I don't want to keep you here all day! You better get back so you can get that dinner started."

"Man, you're not kidding," I said... "Hey, would you mind.."

He cut me off. "Not saying a word." He smiled.

"Thanks, Mr. Salvador."

"You're welcome, Michael."

"Alright, well, I'll see you next week."

"Sounds good," he responded. "Tell your Dad I said 'hello.'"

"Will do!" I said as I turned to walk back to my truck. I was so shocked by what he said... A son? I don't know if anyone knew that about him. How sad. And how could anyone keep going after losing a wife and son... and still be a decent guy?

When I got back to the shop, I asked Dad if he knew that Old Man Salvador had lost his son. Dad didn't know. He said he didn't think anyone did, except me now. I don't think he meant to tell me; it must have just slipped. Dad asked me how it came up in conversation, and I soon realized that I needed to get out of the conversation.

"Oh, I don't remember exactly," I told the white lie. "He just was talking about his wife, then he mentioned it."

Dad seemed convinced. "Man, sad story." He paused. "So, dinner tonight, huh? At... 7:30?"

"Yes, sir," I said in a chipper tone.

"Alright... We'll you should try to get out of here a little early then..."

"I'm going to try, but I just want to make sure that we're caught up on everything first." I checked my watch. "I'm going to do some paperwork and make some phone calls, and then I'll see where I'm at."

"Sounds good," Dad said. "I'll handle all of the walk-ins that may come in, that way you can stay focused. But, I'll probably close down a little early. I still have to pick up Rella's mom."

"Oh, yeah." I hesitated. "Is it bad to say that I forgot?" I shrugged my shoulders slightly.

"To me," He tilted his head, "It's not bad but I'm not sure Rella would think the same."

I smiled. "You're probably right..." I thought for a moment. "Hey, what do you say we just close down at 4:00? It's Friday, I think it'll be alright."

“Yeah, you’re right. It’s our business, anyway?” He smiled as if he was giving himself permission.

“Sounds good. Well, I’m going to hop to it.” I transitioned back to my office. I needed to focus.

For the next 2 and a half hours, that’s what I did. I got so much done; I was almost impressed with myself. Almost. Things were set for next week, and everything seemed to be in place. It was about 4:15 and I was ready.

“Dad, I’m heading out. I’ll see you tonight, okay?”

“Sounds good. See ya.”

“Bye.” I waved as I headed outside to my Jeep. I needed to pick up my dry cleaning and go to the post office real quick to drop off a package for a client. I headed to the post office first, then to the dry cleaners. I was sure Rella would be home cooking by now. I wanted to hurry and get home to her to help. Enchiladas were a task, and I just didn’t feel right her being on her feet all evening.

My errands went smoothly. By 4:50, I was walking through our door. The house smelled like a spicy Mexican restaurant. I couldn’t help my mouth from watering. Man, could my woman cook.

“Hey baby, I’m home!” I shouted as I sat my clothes down and went into the kitchen. Rella looked beautiful in a sweet lavender dress that fit her loosely. I’m sure she didn’t want the slight weight gain to give her away.

“Hey, darling, in here!” I heard her yell from the kitchen. As I walked in, I tried not to be shocked by the mess. It looked like a tornado had struck the kitchen.

“How’s everything... going?” I asked with skepticism, as I looked around at what seemed a million dirty dishes scattered all over the place.

“Good,” she turned. “I’m just about to put them in the oven!” She sounded excited. I couldn’t help but smile.

“Rella, baby, you have a little sauce...” I pointed to the left side of her face.

She smiled, “Oh... Well, I was just really getting into it, that’s all.” She shrugged her shoulders with a bit of sass.

I chuckled, "I see that. How about I help you clean up."

I started gathering all of the dishes and putting them in the sink for rinsing.

"Michael..." She said in a 'your in trouble tone'.

"Yes?" I questioned.

"Where are my toppings?" Hands on her hips, I knew I was in for it.

"Oh, honey, I completely forgot!" I stopped what I was doing. "I'm sorry, I'll run and get them."

"No, Michael." She tried to hide her annoyance. "We need to clean the kitchen, and you still need to take a shower and get ready."

"I know, but let me..."

"Michael, I will go after we clean up a bit."

"Baby, I don't want you..."

"Michael! Do not say I can't go to the grocery store by myself! Trust me, I am fine! Just because I'm pregnant, doesn't mean I'm not capable."

I could tell she was fighting back tears of frustration. "I'm really sorry baby... You're right. We'll clean and then you can go, okay?" I went over to her and put both of my hands on her shoulders. "I'm sorry my love. I've just had a hectic day..." I shook my head, "I know it's not an excuse..."

She cut me off. "No, it's okay Michael. You're right. All of these hormones are making me snappy." She had tears rolling now, "I know you're just trying to take care of me... I'm sorry I'm such a bi..."

"Nope." I interrupted. "Don't you say that about yourself."

She stopped and looked embarrassed. "And not in front of the baby..." I smiled as I grabbed her stomach.

That had her laughing. "I don't think it has ears yet..." She looked down at her tummy.

"You never know...." I said convincingly.

We both laughed. I stood up and gave her a big kiss.

"I love you..." I murmured.

"I love you too..." She murmured back.

We washed dishes after that. Talking and laughing. Like I said before, we were never one to fight. Nothing is too complicated that a little communication can't solve. That was the number one rule in our relationship.

"Okay, well, I better get going." Rella went and grabbed her keys. "I'm sure it'll be a bit busy because of the evening traffic, so don't worry if it takes me too long, okay?" She gave me a look.

"Okay... But, I parked behind you. Go ahead and take the Jeep." I pulled out my keys from my pocket. "And please be careful and call me if you need anything," I replied.

"Okay, will do. I love you. Make sure you turn the oven off at 6:30, but keep them in there, so they'll stay warm. Six Thirty, Mr. Watch-man" she teased. "I love you, Michael. You are the best thing that has ever happened in my life." She came and gave me one last kiss.

"I love you too, Rella Harvey."

The flush instantly hit her cheeks when I said her name in that way... in that tone. I knew it made her feel flustered.

"Why do you do that to me..." She teased shyly as she nipped at my lips.

"I just want to make sure you know who you belong to," I said in a tease...

"Oh, I know, Mr. Harvey. I know who..." She kissed me. Hard.

"Dang, why don't we just move this dinner till tomorrow night," I said leaning in for another.

She gently pushed me away, "Oh no you don't... You've got us into enough trouble as it is..." She laughed as she put her hand on her tummy.

"Well, there's more where that came from," I said in a confident tone.

She laughed again, "Oh, I'm sure there is but not right now." She pointed at the kitchen. "Get to work so that I can go to the store!" She smiled. "You're distracting me."

"Okay, okay. But." I grabbed her hand once more. "I do love you."

"Love you too, baby." I kissed her hand, as she leaned away.

"I'll be right back my love." She smiled as she walked towards the door.

* * *

I finished putting away some of the dishes and washing the counters. Next, I need to shower up. I ran upstairs and quickly took a shower. I meant it to be faster, but I couldn't help but linger a little in the hot water. It was as soothing as a hot tub.

I got dressed in the light blue shirt that I picked up from the cleaners. Rella always liked me in blue, because she said it 'complimented my eyes' or something. She told me that when we were dating. Since then, I don't think I've ever bought so many new blue shirts in my life. The truth was, I wanted to flatter her, as she flattered me. There were times when I would be so caught off guard by her beauty; I was unsure of myself, and I wondered if I was good enough for her. She always assured me that I was, but I did my part to keep up, I guess.

The doorbell rang. The parents were early.

I ran downstairs and opened the door. "Hey, guys." I greeted Dad and Rella's mom. "Come on in."

"Hello, thank you." Said Loretta in her exuberant voice.

"Welcome..." She came in, "Dad?" He walked in behind her. "This is the earliest I've ever seen you be! A whole 30 minutes."

He laughed, "Well, I'm not one to be late for enchilada's."

We all laughed. Boy wasn't that the truth. My Dad was a sucker for Mexican food, and it was hard to find up north.

"Can I get you guys something to drink? Wine, tea?" I looked at them both.

"Oh, I'll take the wine!" Loretta said.

"Which kind? Red, white?" I asked.

"Any kind is a good kind." She said with a sly smile.

I chuckled. "Okay. Dad?"

"Iced tea will work for me."

"Okay, be right back."

"Where's Rella," Loretta asked.

"She went to the store to get a few things..." I explained.

"Oh, that's my girl, she's a little last minute sometimes." Loretta waved her hand.

"Well, it's my fault. I forgot to do what I was asked." I said in a self-condemning tone.

They both laughed at that.

"Let me get those drinks," I assured them.

I went to the kitchen and fixed them up. When I came back to the living room, Dad and Loretta were talking about fishing of all things. I handed them their drinks and sat, listening idly to their conversations.

I tried to stop myself from checking my watch. I was wondering where Rella was. "Stop." My mind told me. "She's just fine. Don't worry." I coaxed myself. I waited a little while longer, but the anxiety was growing... And the worry was creeping up. I went to the kitchen and took out the enchiladas. They smelled amazing. As soon as she arrived we'd be able to eat. Any minute now she'd be here. I checked my watch again. Where was she? I walked back to the living room, feeling more anxious than ever. Dad noticed.

"Michael? Where's Rella?" Dad asked, "You might want to give her a call. It's getting a little late."

Dad looked a little concerned, which made me even more nervous. "Yeah, will do."

I pulled my phone out of my back jean pocket and dialed her number. It went straight to voicemail.

I clicked. "She didn't answer," I told them.

We all paused. "I'm sure her phone died. The traffic is bad around this time. I'm sure she's okay." Dad shrugged. "She's probably fighting her way through traffic."

"Yeah, you're right." I agreed... But, I couldn't say that made me feel any better.

Loretta and Dad chatted a little more. I called Rella again and again.

"This is what she is talking about." My mind teased. "You being obsessive." No. No. I needed to stop. She was fine. She should be walking in at any minute now.

But, a few more minutes passed by. It was now 7:15. There was no reason she shouldn't be back. No good reason, anyway.

There was a silence at this point.

Dad stood up. "Michael. Perhaps call her one more time. If she doesn't answer, we'll go and look for her."

"Yeah, Yeah..." And Rella was notorious for letting her phone battery die. I called, and again it went to voicemail. At this point, everyone in the room was nervous.

"Let me get my keys." I said it just as the doorbell rang.

I turned and looked at my Dad... He looked back at me empty handed.

"I'll get it," I said calmly. Too calmly. As I walked to the door, I prayed it was my Rella. She just rang the doorbell because her hands were full. Everything was okay. She was just fine.

I reached the door and opened it to two officers.

"Mr. Harvey?" They asked.

I could fill my stomach sink... My heart started to beat so fast; it felt like it was about to stop. I shook my head yes...

The two looked at each other as if they were debating. Then, one stepped forward.

"There's been an accident."

CHAPTER 14

I JUST STOOD THERE. IN shock. Trying to absorb the word. Accident.

By then, Dad and Loretta had rushed over and brought the officers further into the entryway. Then, they started talking.

"Mr. Harvey... You're wife, Mrs. Harvey. Rella Harvey...."

They looked at me for confirmation, but I could give them none. I couldn't move. Fear had me frozen over. They looked at my Dad for their assurance. He shook his head yes.

"Mr. Harvey," they turned back to me. The officer swallowed hard as if he couldn't continue. The other officer stepped in.

"Mr. Harvey. There was a drunk driver. He hit your wife, head on while driving, into oncoming traffic. She was killed on impact."

The words pierced my heart like a dagger. I stood there as if I didn't hear him... As if it were all a dream.

"Mr. Harvey... Rella has passed." The other officer said due to my lack of response. "I'm so sorry for your loss."

It' couldn't be. I just saw her. She was just getting a few things from the grocery store. This was all wrong. I felt the panic rise in me. I couldn't breath. I was suffocating. The air itself was becoming heavy. It was a loud sound and deafening silence at the same time.

I heard Rella's mom scream in pain. I heard my Dad gasp in shock. But me... I was silent as if the air were pushing me down to the ground. It couldn't be... Not my Rella.

After a moment, my Dad asked the officer, "You're sure?"

"We are confident, but," he looked at me. "You'll have to come with us to identify the body."

I had slowly fallen to the ground, on my knees. I just stayed there... I couldn't move. I heard sobbing from Loretta. My Rella. Our Baby? Our baby?

"The baby..." I let out as a desperate attempt... If she... then the baby is...

Everyone looked at me with horror. My Dad had tears in his eyes now. He bent down.

"Michael? Did you say, baby?" He asked in a way that suggested sheer pain.

"Yes..." I teared up as I mumbled under my breath, "That's why you both are here..." I was losing it slowly. "She's pregnant."

"Oh my God," Loretta's mom screamed. "Oh, my God!" She began to wail uncontrollably.

The officers looked at each other in shock. Their training didn't prepare them for this. I'm not sure there was training for this kind of thing...

"Michael," My Dad said. "Michael."

I didn't give him my attention. I was frozen. A tear slowly streamed down my check.

"Michael, I know this is unbearable but come with me son. Let's sit down in the living room for a while."

He looked at the officers, silently asking for one of them to help me up. One grabbed my left side while my Dad grabbed my right. They walked me over to the nearest chair. I could barely move.

I felt myself slowly fade away... I couldn't be in this moment, so I fled to another.

"Anywhere but here..." I thought... "Go anywhere, but here." I felt myself slowly fade.

* * *

I don't know how long I sat there... it felt like hours. I heard people talking... Dad's voice... Loretta's voice... Officers... Phone calls... Voices... However, I just couldn't get over the fact that I would never hear my Rella's again.

"We need him to come with us." The officer reminded me and Dad, "To officially identify the body."

"He's in no condition. Look at him." I heard my Dad argue in the background.

"It's protocol, sir. We can't go without him."

I listened to their back and forth. He needs to; he doesn't need to. Part of me wanted to stay here, but another part of me wanted to go... Because maybe, it wasn't Rella. Maybe there had been some mistake. Maybe Rella just... Maybe it wasn't her.

"I'll go." I stood up all of a sudden, and everyone in the room looked at me. "Let's go," I said in a demanding tone.

Loretta and my Dad rode with me in the police SUV. It was a strange situation. So much of the unimaginable seemed to be happening. It appeared that they took the back way. I was sure to avoid the wreckage on the street... We made the long 20-minute drive, taking the extended route to the police station. We pulled around back to a Medical Examiners office. It looked cold on the outside, but I'm sure it was nothing compared to what it was going to be like on the inside.

My body was on autopilot. I didn't say anything. I didn't necessarily decide to get out of the car, I just did. I didn't want to walk in, but my legs forced me to. My body was reacting, as it should while my mind was trying desperately to catch up with what was happening.

Opening the door, I could only think one thing. "Please don't let it be her." The hall was long and cold. The walls were a light gray, but the florescent lighting gave them an eerie translucent appeal. The floors were old porcelain tile. The hall seemed to grow narrower by the moment. If one could picture a place in which you store death, this was it.

"This way." The officer pointed left.

We turned to a shorter hallway with a window at the end.

"Mr. Harvey, you can stand out here, or you can go in with me."

"I'll go in." I paused. "Alone." I didn't want Dad or Loretta to see her if it really was her, and to be distraught if it truly wasn't. Which, it wasn't, right? It couldn't be. This all had to be a misunderstanding.

The officer swallowed. "Ok. Through this door."

I walked in, and the chilling cold hit my skin immediately. I started to feel a little claustrophobic. My senses were violated, as I smelled strange smells that were anything but natural.

"Hello, I'm Dr. Williams." The young dark haired woman said solemnly. She looked down, "This way."

We walked to the edge of the room, furthest away from the appearing window. Everything was in slow motion now. It seemed like we were in outer space. Every detail could be captured, in the most vulgar of ways.

The doctor faced the adjacent metal wall that had stainless steel doors with handles. I watched her go to the one on the top left. I felt chills when I read the name 'Harvey'.

She looked at me in a silent way of asking if I was ready. I would never be. She grimaced slightly as she opened the door and pulled a body out.

I immediately recognized her. Her beautiful auburn hair pulled back. My tears were flowing now. My Rella.

My Rella, who was so full of life, lay there lifeless. Her lips were a cold tone of blue. Her eyes were closed. Her skin was cold and seemed to be dying more and more by the second.

"Rella..." I whispered as I touched her arm. I flinched at the coldness.... the stillness. "Rella?" I said in a whisper.... My tears were flowing now. "Rella... Rella, wake up. Rella wake up baby. Please come back to me." I couldn't help but ask her to come back... Inside I was praying to God for some kind of miracle.

"Mr. Harvey? Can we have your verbal consent? Is this Rella Allan Harvey?"

The sob escaped me as I tried to speak. I couldn't. I just shook my head yes as my heart screamed no. It was my Rella... but the life in her was gone.

I couldn't imagine her hurt, nonetheless gone... "Oh, Rella..." I cried... I turned to the doctor. "Did she feel pain?"

"No." She responded. "The impact was very strong. It broke her neck on impact. Her death was painless."

Painless... No.... Her death wasn't painless... Not to me... I held her hand and placed it with mine on her belly.

"The baby?" I couldn't help but ask, even though I knew the obvious answer.

The doctor just shook her head no. "There was no way it could have survived."

"Is there any way to know what it was?" I asked.

"No... Her pregnancy was too early."

The tears escaped freely... My Rella... My baby... How cold this be? "How could this be?" I asked. "How could this be?"

"How could this be?"

* * *

I vaguely remember being guided out into another little waiting room. The doctor came and handed me a bag. Inside was her beautiful lavender dress that just hours before hung from her body. Inside was another bag... that held her wedding ring, a little anchor necklace... and my mother's bracelet. The mere sight of those sapphires caused me to lose it all over again. They had been worn on the wrists of my two loves... and now, my three losses.

The cries had finally escaped. I had fallen to my knees, not caring if I ever rose again. She was gone, and so was every feeling of life in me. I began to be violently brought back into reality. I was a widower. My wife... My baby... They were gone. The moment was catastrophic. I literally could feel my heart breaking. This feeling... it goes past grief. It goes past depression. It barely could be held by utter despair. The emptiness surrounded me while loneliness watched. Sinking... I was slowing sinking into what felt like a bottomless pit. I heard the wailing of a man who sounded like life was being stripped from him in the most agonizing of ways... Then I realized, the man, was me.

CHAPTER 15

December 17th, 2009. I'll never forget that day; for it was the day I buried my heart. I remembered it too well; only three days after I left the morgue identifying that my Rella and future child were dead. Killed by a drunken semi driver, just passing through. They were killed on impact. Later on, I went to see my Jeep. It was completely crushed. Like my heart.

Rella hardly had a bruise on her body. Just a few scratches. The doctor said that the impact snapped her neck. She didn't feel a thing. How ironic; because I felt it. I was feeling it every day since.

The funeral was held at noon. I choose that time because that's when my Rella usually was stepping out into the world... For me, it was symbolic, that she was stepping into a new one now. I had never thought too much of heaven. I figured that my mother went there when she died but now, the idea was forced into a belief for me. What other place deserved such a beautiful woman, like Rella so soon? No other place than heaven. Rella was there. She had to be. It was nothing to do with God and everything to do with her and who she was.

I remember going to the cemetery and everyone was dressed in black. That too was symbolic for me because when you lose someone you love, the color of life is gone. You're only left with black and white. Rella was my color and my canvas and my brush all in one. Black would have to do from here on out.

I buried her in the lavender dress she was wearing because she was wearing it in celebration of happiness. I prayed that too was symbolic, that somewhere, some place, she was happy with our child. I picked out the grandest of flowers and stopped at no price to make everything appear pretty, as Rella always did. I asked Pastor Jake to do the ceremony. He agreed kindly though I knew it was hard for him too, as Rella and I became good friends to him. Little did he know that when he married us just a little over a month ago, so soon would death do us part.

Everyone told me how lovely the funeral was... But I couldn't understand that. There were so many feelings, and lovely wasn't one of them. I kept the coffin open as long as I could because that was one of the most unsatisfying parts of the whole thing. The coffin. How can one box be the measurement of the greatest love you have ever known? How can one box measure up to that? How could that be the representation of what I lost when I lost Rella? No. I wanted her face to be seen. I wanted everyone to see what God has stolen from me.

As it turns out, there was another funeral later that day too. The drunk that killed her. For me, it was a good thing, because if the crash didn't kill him, I probably would have. Turns out he was divorced. He had four adult children, only 1 appeared. There were maybe eight guests in attendance, including myself. I went not out of apology, but out of revenge. There were few things that could have made me feel better on that day. Seeing his cold dead body be put in the ground was one of them. I knew the feeling I had was an evil one, but I couldn't help it. I needed some sort of closure. Not that his funeral gave it to me, but it helped.

I don't remember much else of that day, other than the drive home. I picked up a bottle of whiskey and sat in my living room, drinking it straight out of the bottle. The next day, I got another... Then another. The drunkenness didn't take away the pain; it just put me in a state to where I didn't have to feel it as much.

I took a few weeks off from work. Of course, Dad understood but slowly, those weeks started to fade into months. I'd go in, but truly, I wasn't there. I couldn't be in this reality without my love. It was a total of nine months from the day of her death since we had first met; the first six of them were spent dating; Two were spent in engagement; 1 in marriage. They were all gone now, and as far as I was concerned there was nothing left. Time had all but stopped for me.

I still wore the watch Rella gave me, but I stopped it from ticking. I set it to the time that Rella left that day to the grocery store because that was the last second I could remember feeling happy. That's where it stayed, and when I could, that's where I went. As I said before, whiskey helped but when that didn't work, I'd force myself to sleep and beg my dreams to take me to a place where she was.

My life had changed dramatically. Everything I did before, I had a purpose, but now, everything I did was in a failed attempt to remember my life with Rella. Every week, Friday, at 6:30 I got all dressed up and bought fresh flowers and went and put them on Rella's grave.

Last week, the florist asked, "Who do you get these flowers for every week? She must be special."

I smiled coldly. "My wife." I responded as respectfully as I could.

"Well, you must have such a wonderful marriage. She's a lucky girl." She smiled. "I'll see you next week." She said as she went back to the back of the store.

"No. She isn't lucky." I wanted to tell her, but I refrained. It wasn't her fault. How could she expect that a man so young could be a widower? Still, it was hard.

Little reminders of Rella being gone destroyed me. I started to fear any subtle hint of her. So quickly they could send me over the edge, making me just want to run and hide. Ever since she was gone, I just wasn't myself. I had a temper now, and everything made me mad... But it was probably because I was already angry. I tried my best to stay in routine, but everything seemed to remind me of her. Sometimes, I just tried to trick myself. I would go to the coffee shop and order a latte for her. I'd drink my coffee and just pretend that she was running late... as usual. The uneaten blueberry muffin somehow would bring me solace... For a short time, at least. Most days, it worked. In those moments, I could find enough peace in my imagination that it helped soothe the dreadful reality I was in.

A lot of times, I felt that my memory would always flood back to that day and how I could have changed it. If, I would have just picked up the groceries she asked for. If I would have just pushed her to let me go instead. Dang enchilada toppings ended up costing me everything that mattered. I remembered the pain so easily. I always went back to that day... trying desperately to remember before, and wishing the after didn't happen.

My phone seemed always to be ringing. If it wasn't work, it was Dad. And if it wasn't Dad, it was Loretta, Rella's mom. Everyone was worried about me. Calling me. Checking to see if I was okay. How many times had I soothed them saying I was fine, when of course, I wasn't. How could I be?

I didn't have anything to say to them or anyone. No less, the phone rang tirelessly. One strange number was calling me relentlessly, though. Some telemarketer or something. After five calls in one day, I answered with hatred in my voice.

"Who is this?" I demanded.

"Hello, Mr. Harvey. My name is Tom, and I work for your cell phone company. Our records indicate that your second line, under... Rella Harvey hasn't been used for some time. We would be happy to discontinue that for you, to help you save some money on your monthly bill."

"No," I said in a firm tone.

"Okay, well, we're just trying to help you, Mr. Harvey. It looks like it would reduce your bill up to... $100.00 per month."

"I said... NO." My voice was full of fury. I regretted taking the call.

"Okay, sir." The guy quickly caught on. "Well, thank you for your time, Mr. Harvey. We are here to help you. Please feel free to fill out the survey at the end of the call and let us know if I was any help. Thank you. Goodbye."

"Goodbye." How many times I have had to digest the very word... Goodbye.

There was no way I could disconnect Rella's phone. Nor could I empty out her clothes. Dare not, did I touch her stuff. I couldn't handle anything that involved my loss of her or a reminder of it.

The time of the year didn't help anything either. November and December. The joys of the holiday cheer made me nauseous. I had become a Scrooge in my own right. I didn't have anything to be thankful for and nor did I rejoice anyone's birth after the life of Rella, and the birth of my son was stolen from me. I hated laughter... Happiness was all but gone from me. I didn't care anything about presents... Because my most precious one was gone... I was sure there wasn't anything that could bring me joy again. Not like the joy that Rella had brought to me... A season of cheer. As everyone seemed to celebrate, I sat in the background in utter despair.

The days all but drifted into the nights... They were all the same to me know as the sadness merged into my very being. Everything seemed to blur together with no end and no beginning... A tortuous prison, never ending... I would go home and watch the sun fade, and the moon creep across the sky with a subtle strength... It angered me every time I saw it. The moon. The very moon that Jesus looked at... The memory arose, and the thought of my first kiss with Rella took me aback... I couldn't help the emotion that flooded me.

"Why God? "Why, why, why?" I screamed it out into the night sky. "Why did she have to go?" My heart pleaded for the answer... "What did you them from me?"

* * *

2 Months Later

Time flew by, as I dragged along. I did everything the best I could, but I can't say it amounted to much. I strolled into work around 10:00 and I left as soon as Dad said I could. I'd pick up hard liquor on the way home, that no one knew about, of course, where I'd drink some or all, depending on the day.

The hardest thing to let go of was the guilt. The question of "what if" became a demon that terrorized me every night. "What if... What if you wouldn't have forgotten? What if you would have driven her? Or if you would have gone? What if it would have been a different dinner? What if? What if? What if it were you instead of her?"

I tried to coax myself into thinking that it wasn't my fault, but the truth was, is that I considered it to be. My stupid busyness allowed a mistake that lead to my tragedy. I couldn't let go of that, no matter how hard I tried.

Some nights, when it seemed to be the worst, I'd go through my phone voicemails. I had three messages saved from Rella. Short, 3 to 4 second messages.

One: "Hey, it's me. Call me! Love you!"

Two: "It's Rella, I'm running late." Laughing she said, "Sorry. I'm on my way."

Three: "Hey baby, I just wanted to tell you that I love you. I'll see you in a bit."

A total of ten seconds... I heard her. Sometimes, I could even feel her... I usually cried myself to sleep, missing her and begging my body to go to sleep so I could forget just for a while safe in the realms of the unconscious.

The best part of my day was waking up in the morning. There was always an 8-second drag before reality hit me. The part where I didn't remember she was gone. Seconds. I lived for the seconds I could remember her. Those seconds were like tiny air bubbles that I gasped for, but they were always barely enough to get me out of bed.

As the days went on, it seemed like even the seconds weren't enough. The pain in my heart was growing, like a virus it was taking over my heart. Today our baby would be 4 and half months old. I had an app on my phone, and I was keeping track of what would have been just so I wouldn't have to be, so to speak. During any down time at work, I'd look at the growth chart of the child I would never have. We would have learned today, whether it was a boy or girl.

"Michael," Dad said as he entered my office.

I looked up with attention, but my eyes held an empty stair.

He came and sat down in front of my desk. "Michael, son, I love you." He began, "But I'm worried about you. I know you've suffered a significant loss, but. You can't go on like this."

He waited for me to respond. I didn't.

"Michael. You look like a train wreck. You wore those clothes for the past two days. You haven't shaven in weeks and don't think I can't smell the whiskey that's on your breath from the night before."

I just sat there... What did I have to say?

"I know this is hard. I know losing Rella..."

"I didn't lose her!" I said in a firm tone. "She was taken from me. Stolen! Along with my child!"

Dad took in a sharp breath. I had never spoken to him in that tone. "I know son. I know, and I'm sorry... But you can't go on like this... When I lost, your mother... I..."

"No, don't go there Dad." I stood up. "Mom died from cancer, and at least you had a few years with her. You got a kid out of it. I had nine months. A dream of a baby, then like that" I snapped my fingers. "It's all gone." My voice was shaky from emotion.

Dad stood slowly. "Michael, I understand. I don't expect you just to forget about it, but I think you need to... talk to someone."

"Talk to someone? About what? Why?"

"You need to grieve... But there comes a time where you have to stand again. You have to... move forward. You may never move on, but you at least have to move forward." He walked towards the door. "There is a counselor on 3rd named Debbie Walters."

"I'm not going to some quack doctor." I snapped like a rebellious teenager.

"It's not a request son." My Dad looked at me in a way that I'd never experienced. "Don't come back to this place of business until you talk to her." He walked away.

I stood, shocked. Was he making me go? Forcing me? Part of me wanted to rebel and refuse... but there was something in me at the same time, asking, "What do you have to lose?"

"Nothing," I answered easily. I've already lost it all.

* * *

A week had passed before I succumbed to Dad's order. I tried to show up to work the next morning, and he changed the locks. When I called him, he said that he would be waiting for a call from Dr. Walters before he'd let me back in.

"You're in no state to do business, Michael. I am sorry." He had told me before he hung up. It was hard to hear my Dad talk to me that way. We were business partners, best friends, father, and son... For him to act this way, it made me realize that maybe I did need help.

I looked at myself in the mirror as I began to get ready for my appointment with Dr. Walters. I saw my reflection and paused. I looked... horrible. It appeared as though I had aged five years since... it happened. I had lost weight and muscle tone. My beard was scraggly and my hair too long. The picture of myself made me tear up. Not out of vanity, but out of sorrow. I couldn't help but think that Rella would be disappointed in me. The thought of that alone caused the tears to fall. I missed her so much...

Driving down 3rd in the new car, I was looking for the office. Everything was so different compared to the view from my jeep. That too was a struggle. My mangled Jeep was totaled in the accident, and it forced me to buy a new vehicle. For whatever reason, I chose a car instead. It was a BMW-1 series sports edition. I had never owned a car before, but it seemed like this was the time change for everything. I think I liked the idea of a sports car... I wanted to speed through the rest of my life.

Rella's car was still parked out in front of our house. I shuddered at the fact of her taking it instead of my Jeep that horrible day. The damage was already bad, I couldn't have imagined it being worse. The one good thing that happened that day was her not being able to find her keys. She would have felt so much pain with the semi hitting her in such a small vehicle... Her car reminded me of that every time I looked at it. She didn't feel any pain. But, ironically, it's presence sometimes brought me more...

"Turn right." The GPS sounded, interrupting my thoughts. I still wasn't used to all of the high tech business.

I turned and saw it. "Dr. Debbie Walters, Ph.D. of Clinical Psychology." I felt embarrassed as I got out of my car. I felt ashamed to have to get this kind of help, but... a quick reminder of my reflection this morning before I shaved pushed me through. Even I knew now that I did need help.

I walked in the door, as it chimed my entrance. There was a secretary to my right on the phone. She was blonde and Barbie-like, by all measures. Her chipper voice already had me annoyed as she hung up.

"Hi there, can I help you." She asked.

"Yes. I have an appointment."

"Okay... is it..."

"Michael Harvey," I answered for her.

"Oh, okay." She pulled out some papers. "If you'll just fill out these forms and Dr. Walters will be right with you."

I took them from her and sat down. I hated doing stuff like this. So many mundane questions further pushed my annoyance level even further. About 15 minutes later, I had them all complete.

"Here you go, ma'am," I said as I sharply handed them back.

"Thank you. You can go on back. Last door, down the hallway."

"Thanks." I turned, and I could feel the tension rising. I was nervous. What was she going to ask? How would I answer without breaking down? I could hardly even think of Rella before...

I steadied my pace and slowed as I approached the door. Part of me wanted to turn around and run, but I held my ground and knocked slightly on the door.

A Hispanic, dark-haired, middle-aged woman answered. She was about 5'7 and was wearing red-rimmed glasses, a white button up shirt and black skirt. I stood there a moment a little stunned... A hairy Old Man is what I expected.

"Mr. Harvey?" She asked expectantly.

"Ugh," I snapped myself out of it. "Yes."

"Come on in and take a seat." She walked back and motioned.

"Thank you."

"Well, I'm Dr. Walters, and I was just looking over some of your paperwork."

"Yes, ma'am." I looked around the office, and it was very cozy. It smelt like apple cinnamon, and that reminded me of autumn. I chose the leather chair and got comfortable. I could see how people would open up about an array of things in an office like this. There was a homey feel to it.

"So, your Dad called me initially and told me a little bit of what was going on. However, I want you to know that I'm not treating your father, nor is anyone forcing you to be here today. You may start or stop whenever you like. And, whatever you say here is confidential, just between us. Nothing will be shared."

"I understand." I wasn't surprised Dad called. I knew he was worried about me.

She nodded. "Well, Michael, why did you decide to come in today?"

"My Dad won't let me go back to work." I sounded.

"Does he have a reason not to?" She quickly countered.

"I..." I didn't know what to say... "Well, I..." I took a deep breath. "I lost the love of my life. My future baby, with her. And, I'm struggling... I don't know how to go on without them."

"I see." She said. "Can you tell me how you are struggling?"

"What do you mean?"

"I mean, what part of your behavior is different?" She explained.

"I'm not eating... sleeping... or functioning really... And I just can't believe...." I stopped because I was about to break.

"You can't believe?" Dr. Walters asked.

I waited... ... ... "I can't believe she is gone. And I don't know how to believe it. Or if I want to."

Dr. Walters just paused for a moment and seemed to take it all in.

"Mr. Harvey, I believe that I can help you, but I will need your participation. Are you willing to commit to coming here and working through this together?"

I shook my head yes...

"Okay. That's all I need. This is going to be hard. Harder than it is now. Processing grief doesn't happen overnight. But, sometimes it's the journey itself that leads to the healing."

"Yes, ma'am."

She smiled slightly. "Well, I want you to know that you can always tell me that you want to stop. You can always tell me when you don't feel comfortable or when you don't wish to do something. Okay?"

"Yes, ma'am."

"My specialty is known as Cognitive Behavioral Therapy. Its roots are in that we all have thoughts, good and bad, and we act on those thoughts. Unfortunately, though, when we have bad thoughts or maladaptive ones, we tend to make poor decisions because of them. So, what I am going to try to do is to help you locate those thoughts that are not healthy related to your wife's death. We will also try to replace them with ones that are easier to deal with because this will help lighten the load of emotional pressure. Therefore making this a smoother transition, does that make sense?"

"Yes, ma'am." It sounded reasonable.

"Good. Okay, so I am going to have to ask you a few questions about your daily activities and family and that sort of thing. Is that okay with you?"

"Sure."

"Since the death of your wife, who would you name as some important people? Family? Friends?"

"My Dad. He's my best friend and my business partner. I don't have a lot of other friends. Rella... she was my best friend."

"I see. And Rella, that was your wife's name?"

"Yes," I answered bleakly.

"Could you tell me about your daily life? What do you do?"

The questions were hard for me to answer because I was ashamed of them... Now looking at the way I lived for the past few months, I did seem crazy. Drinking and crying myself to sleep. Listening to voice messages. Going to her grave. Stopping my watch... But, I had to tell her... It was hard, but at the same time it was a relief to let someone know just how much I was hurting.

We talked for a good hour about what my life had been like since Rella had been taken away. Dr. Walters listened; truly listened without judgment. I kept going, and she didn't stop me. I couldn't remember the last time I had said so much.

"So, when you go home, and you drink, do you find yourself relieved? Does it make you feel better?" she asked.

"No. I mean, I suppose it makes me physically relaxed, but emotionally... I still know she's gone."

"I see. And when you sleep, do you dream of Rella?" She asked.

"A lot. I do... Not necessarily dreams, but I just see her face."

"Okay. Are they more like nightmares are just dreams?"

"Just dreams... The awake part is the nightmare." I said bleakly.

She closed her eyes and nodded.

We talked more about how I had been behaving and what had become my coping mechanisms. She took notes as I spoke.

"Okay, that's good Michael. Thank you for being so open and honest with me." She said as I knew this session was coming to an end. "How about we meet twice a week for now? Does that work for you?"

"Yes. It does." I agreed.

"Okay then, I will see you Wednesday."

"Yes, ma'am." I agreed as I stood. I shook her hand and left the office.

I was kind of shocked that I felt a little better... Not about Rella being gone, just about choosing to go in. I knew there was no getting Rella back... But, I just needed, a little bit of hope even if it was for me just to get back to where I was before I met her. I didn't want love again. I didn't want to be okay with her being gone... But listening to myself I realized that I was on the edge of being an alcoholic. I was drinking too much and not doing too much of anything else. The cold reality hit me that I was more like the drunk who killed my Rella, than the husband that lost her. I sat in my car hurting, assaulted by the thought, but I could not deny the truth.

I needed to get up. I just needed to be able to stand. Like my Dad had said. Since Rella's funeral, I had been sitting and wallowing in misery and pain, and as I sat there with Dr. Walters I realized just how asleep my life had become...

3 Months Later

CHAPTER 16

I DON'T KNOW IF MY grief had gotten better, or if I just had gotten better at hiding it. A week after I started attending therapy, Dad allowed me to come back to the gallery. I began to get back to my old speed and early morning routines. I began to shave again, on a regular basis, and I started not to drink as much. Started. Not finished.

The past few weeks had been a struggle. Not in dealing with the past, but in trying to figure out what to do with the future. One would think that it would be simple just to go back to the way things had been before Rella was in my life, but it wasn't that easy. It's like, you live your whole life with the lights dimmed. Then, all of a sudden, they are turned on to their full potential. You realize all that you didn't see and all that was dark... Rella was my light. She allowed me to see life in the brightest of ways and now, to go back to the dim. It was proving difficult and depressing.

The days seemed to go by, though. I stopped listening to the voicemails and buying an extra latte at the Daily Grind... But I still went and delivered flowers every week. I still had not started my watch up again... I couldn't for some reason. When I looked down and saw the time, I reminisced to a place where she was there. Every time I saw those little hands pointing steadily, there was a feeling of peace that came along with it. Little did Rella know when she said, "Now every time you think of that watch, you'll think of those who love you," that it would be every time I looked at the watch. Now every time looked at that watch; I remembered the one whom I loved the most. The watch helped me keep track of the days that had gone by since the accident. The crazy thing is, when I would calculate how many days I had lived without my sweet Rella, the pain would rush in like a wave from the realization. Though, no matter the pain, I couldn't stop counting and keeping track.

Some days were better than others. I started to overbook myself a little bit because I noticed that made the day go by faster. If I pushed myself hard enough, it was easy to go to sleep at night... at least, I wouldn't cry as much. I could balance the scale if it weren't tilted too much one way or the other.

Thursday we had another showing with a new up and coming artist, David Del Fierro. He was very talented. Dad and I were thrilled when we booked him. His expertise was abstract painting. Personally, I had never really been a fan until recently. I think it's because that's what I felt like inside. Abstract. No one to understand, but each has their interpretation. His work was soothing to me in some way because of it. I was anxious for his showing. Art was, always had a way of relaxing me. More than ever, I looked forward to our shows. I browsed the art more and pondered in a deeper way. Looking for meaning in the paintings sometimes brought understanding of myself. "A healthy coping mechanism," Dr. Walters called it, as I told her. Regardless, it was nice.

Dad came in right on time. He'd been that way since everything happened. I think he was still nervous that I wouldn't show up or that I'd have some kind of breakdown. Honestly, I couldn't blame the guy.

"Morning, Michael. I brought you a breakfast burrito." He walked in and handed it to me.

"Thanks, Dad."

"It's potato, egg, spinach, and cheese."

"Thanks." I sat it down. My appetite still wasn't fully back.

"So, how is everything?" He asked in a strange tone.

"Good. Why?" I knew he was baiting for something.

"No, reason." He shrugged.

However, I knew my father better than that. "Dad," I said in an inquisitive tone.

He sighed. "You weren't in church yesterday. You haven't been in a while. I was just wondering why..."

He was right. I stopped going shortly after Rella's death. "I don't know..." I responded.

"What do you mean you don't know? I think church could be helpful." He suggested in a forceful way.

It was enough to cause me to snap. "Which commandment says, 'Thou shalt not steal?'"

Dad confused said, "Ugh, I don't know... The 8th one, maybe? Why?"

"Well, I just find it ironic."

"What do you mean?" Dad asked confused.

"That God says not to steal when he stole from me."

"What?" Dad asked shocked.

"Rella. He stole Rella. So, I think He's a bit of a hypocrite."

"Michael!" Dad scolded.

"Hey, you asked me why I wasn't going to church. That's why." I stared at him point blank.

But, I didn't expect the tears in his eyes... "You'll see one day, Michael. God isn't the blame."

"Dad..." I wanted to say 'Yes He is!' and 'It's all His fault!' and 'He could have stopped it!' But I couldn't bring myself too...

My Dad just turned and walked out.

I didn't mean to make him upset, I just... I didn't need a lecture. Especially on God. I was angry with God. Mad as hell. It was just too much to go to church and sit and pretend everything was okay. Of course, I believed Rella was in heaven. Of course, she had wings and stuff. But what about those of us left down here in the step stool to hell, because we're living without the ones we love. No one answered that question and if I heard, "everything happens for a reason" one more time, I was sure I was going to pronounce myself an atheist.

The conversation made the day start off on a sour note, and it dragged on, after that. My Dad's feelings were hurt, and I was just ready to go home. I had an appointment with Dr. Walters in the early morning, and I needed rest before I embarked on that little journey, as well. Ever since I agreed to do work with her, she was correcting my thoughts and making me keep feeling journals, thought logs and everything in between. Though it was time-consuming, at least it gave me something to focus on rather than just sitting alone. But, I was behind this week and needed the extra time to catch up.

Before too long, the end of the day was near, and I decided to head to the grocery store before heading home. Lately, my diet had been the summation of fast food, and I needed something fresh and not fried.

"Dad, I'm going to head out. I'll see you tomorrow, but I won't be in till noon."

"Sounds good. Bye, Michael." His tone was solemn.

That was the most he said to me all day after our little discussion this morning. As much as I wanted to apologize, I couldn't. And ultimately, I wasn't sorry. I couldn't be... And why should one be sorry for how they feel? It's not like I could change that. I think honesty or "tell the truth" is in the book somewhere too, anyway.

"Buy," I walked out frustrated.

I decided to go ahead and go to the local grocery store to get some fruits and vegetables. It started out as a mundane task, but as I turned on the road... I almost had to pull over. I hadn't been to this particular market since Rella... This was the road where the accident happened.

"No." I coached myself. "Dr. Walters said not to personify everything in relation to Rella's death."

I kept driving. I didn't notice how tight I was gripping the steering wheel until I arrived at the store. My knuckles were white from the hold. My heart was beating a lot faster than normal. But I did it. I made it.

"You did it. See." My inner speech gave the courage I needed to get out of my vehicle.

By the time I entered the store, I felt a lot better. I had calmed down substantially, but my anxiety seemed to be up. I was nervous, for some reason. I grabbed a cart and walked towards the produce section. I almost turned around because my mind was taunting me again, but I made it to the apples.

"This was the last place she was... alive." I swallowed hard. It was true. Rella made it to the grocery store, but she didn't make it back.

"She probably stood right over there." My thoughts were loud. I felt my heart quicken again as I imagined her in the lavender dress.

"What if she would have just stayed a little longer... Or what if, you hadn't forgotten?"

"Stop," I said quietly aloud. I took a deep breath. "Stop living life in reflection of what could have been with Rella." I echoed Dr. Walters in my brain. "It's not your fault," I whispered aloud just to remind myself enough to get out of the store.

I took a step forward, furthering myself into the produce section. I grabbed bananas, apples, and diced pineapple. Now for the vegetables. I started to reach for the carrots when I was interrupted.

"Michael Harvey, fancy seeing you here." Mrs. Margaret's old little voice sounded.

I turned and faked a smile on my face. "Yes, ma'am. I got to keep healthy."

"Oh yes, of course." She agreed. "Well, I haven't seen you in a while. How's your Daddy?"

"He's good," I stated as I was secretly coaching myself not to go back where the last time I saw her... at our wedding.

"Good. Well, I'll need to drop by y'alls studio soon, to get some new art for the boutique."

"Yes, ma'am. Please do." I sounded professional.

"I will. Yes, and how's that beautiful wife of yours doing? My husband and I just loved the wedding. So beautiful and elegant wasn't it?"

I tried to slow my heartbeat again. She had to know what had happened. Rella's death had made the front-page news. I attempted to speak, but I couldn't. I just nodded. She must have forgotten... old age.

"She is so exquisite, Michael. You picked a winner. Did I ever tell you about my husband and I? You know, we got married two weeks after we got met?"

"Two weeks?" I asked in a shaky voice. I was about to lose it.

"Yes, sir. We were in love as much as we were stubborn. So, we got married. Despite every body's say so. I thought my Daddy was gonna kill us both dead." She went on. "But, you know, look at us now! We're in as much love, as we once were as much stubborn!"

"Yes, ma'am." I fought back the tears. I couldn't have a break down here.

"Well, you and that sweet little thing will be like that." She pointed her finger matter-of-factly. "I know it when I see it."

Again, I just nodded, begging my tears not to overflow. It wasn't Mrs. Margaret's fault. She was old, and everyone knew she forgot the most recent of things. And Rella's death was just that... recent.

"Now then, you better get home, ya hear? Take care of that sweet girl and come by my store to get her a gift soon. Girls love presents." She shook her head in a grandmotherly way.

"Yes ma'am" I fought it out.

"Okay, Bye now dear. Tell your Daddy I said 'hello'!" She pushed her squeaky cart away, as I stood there in shock. I couldn't move. I couldn't breath... There was no talking myself down this time. I needed help... my Dad.

* * *

It was early in the morning, and James Harvey was at his gallery. He'd been there for a few hours now, praying and wondering what to do to help his son Michael. The night before he had called him, falling apart. James hadn't seen his son like that... ever.

"God," he prayed, "I'm scared I'm going to lose him too... Help me help him. I know you love him more than I ever could." He prayed a version of that silently all night long. Something had to give. He recognized this. Michael was too young to remember when he was in this state after losing his wife, but he was much like Michael was now. Scared. Wondering how to go on. He drank. He cried, and he did everything he could to hide it from Michael. He was sure to this day that Michael never knew the state his father was once in... But, no less, James knew.

"I had Michael, to bring me back." He thought, "But Michael, has no reason to be brought back... An art studio isn't enough... Nor is my advice. He called Rella his anchor, and now that she was gone, he was like a wandering lost ship in the dark."

Keeping the truth from Michael about how I dealt with his mother's death seemed wrong now. Perhaps if he knew what I went through, he'd listen. Last night, he opened up, but I didn't have the right words. He needed more. He needed to hear from God.

"I know..." James thought. "Salvador. Salvador was the closest thing."

Early in the morning, he called.

"Tom?"

"Yeah," Old Man Salvador asked, "James, you okay? It's early."

"Yes. I'm okay, but it's... It's Michael. I need your help. Can you come by to talk before he comes in?"

"Sure. I'll be over in about 30 minutes."

"Okay, the front door of the gallery is unlocked," James, said

"I'll be there." Old Man Salvador agreed.

"Okay. Bye." James hung up.

Old Man Salvador did too. He got ready and headed that way.

"Lord, let this be what he needs." James prayed silently.

James paced, hoping that just as Salvador was coming in right before dawn, that hope would be coming to Michael's life the same.

* * *

"James?" Old Man Salvador asked as he walked into the dark gallery.

"Back here," James answered.

Old Man Salvador's boots echoed on the floor as he strode back to Dad's office. "Hey… you okay?" he asked James.

"Yeah… I just… I need to talk to you about Michael."

"Okay, what's going on?"

"Last night, he went to the grocery store. He ran into Mrs. Margaret. They got to talking, as Mrs. Margaret does, and well, she brought up Rella. She had forgotten that…"

"Oh gosh…" Old Man Salvador sighed. "Ugh…" he shook his head in disbelief.

"Salvador, Michael called me and sounded like a scared little boy with a monster under his bed. I rushed up there and found him in his car sobbing. He's been making so much progress… but this," his voice was quivering.

"No, James, I understand."

"He's mad at God Salvador. He told me that 'God stole from him'. I know he's going to therapy, and talking to Dr. Walters, but I can see through it… Because, I can see myself."

Old Man Salvador listened.

"When I lost Rachel, it was hard. I tried to hide it and attempted to cover it up… I looked the other way when people looked at me. I put on a good face but…" his voice cracked. He paused a moment… "I almost killed myself. I went home one evening and took Michael to one of his friends' homes. I had a pistol and…"

Mr. Salvador listened without judgment.

"I almost did… But Michael… I couldn't bare the thought of leaving him alone. God saved me as much as he did but, I'm worried because I see too much similarity in Michael's behavior. Only, he has taken God out of it, and there is no little boy at home needing him. In fact, it's just the opposite." James paused, trying to fight back the emotion. "I thank God he called me. A stunt like that at the grocery store could have thrown him over the edge."

"James, what do you need me to do?" He asked.

"Tom... I know that you're the only one... that knows what it's like to lose a wife and child. Michael respects you... He always has... Can you talk to him? I just don't know..."

"I'll talk to him, James."

Old Man Salvador knew what I was trying to say without me having to say it. "Thank you."

"But, I think it's best that we're alone when I do," Salvador reasoned. "How about you send him to the shop later. Okay? Just give him an order form, and I'll talk to him."

* * *

The two widowed men planned and rallied for the third one of their kind... Michael. A Father, a friend, and Dad, in the mist of an early morning, put out a search and rescue for the wondering ship lost in the sea of life. Little did Michael know, that even when one has lost an anchor, there is always a lighthouse, to guide you back to shore... you just have to be willing to look for that light.

CHAPTER 17

"MICHAEL, YOU SEEMED A LITTLE rattled this morning? How is everything?" Dr. Walters asked.

"I... I had an incident last night." I didn't know how to tell her what had happened the night before. I didn't want to come in today, but I made the promise to Dad that I would.

"Okay... Well, can you tell me what happened?" She asked.

"I went to the grocery store. The one Rella went to before... anyways, I was there. I coached myself like you taught me, you know. Like, not seeing things as representations of Rella's last moments here, you know? It was the first time I had been to the store; she last went to."

I continued. "Anyways, so it was already overwhelming. Then, I ran into Mrs. Margaret; she owns a local boutique, but she's old and has a poor memory. One minute she's asking me about my Dad... and the next, she started asking me about Rella. How she was, and that I needed to be a good."

My voice broke. The memory of last night came flooding back.

"It's okay, Michael. We're here now, right? In the present."

I shook my head. The memory of last night had hit a nerve deep inside me. I was sure now, I had reached rock bottom.

"So, what did you do, after that?" Dr. Walters asked.

"I called my Dad. I needed help. I knew that I would go home and down a bottle of liquor if I even made it out of the store."

"And your Dad came?" Dr. Walters asked.

"Yes... he always comes. He's always there for me." I said humbly, remembering the fight we had just the day before and how rude I had been.

"It's good that you can have someone to count on." Dr. Walters highlighted the positive, always.

"Yeah..." I agreed.

"So, what happened after your Dad came?" She asked.

"He drove me home and just stayed with me awhile."

"And did that help?"

"Yes... a lot."

"Michael, what made you call your Dad for help?"

I had taken a long pause before I answered. Part of me didn't want to be truthful as to why I called for help. Part of me was ashamed to tell her what I was thinking but by the same measure I was embarrassed by my thoughts the night before, I was scared of them also...

"I... I didn't know if... I'd find my way home..." I paused as I was trying to explain. "I had no concerns if I didn't make it home, that is."

* * *

Our session lasted longer, after that last remark. It wasn't that I was suicidal at that moment, with a plan or anything. It was just that... In that place, there was just an unwillingness to go on, and I knew that I needed someone to help me get through it. Today, talking about it all, I realized where "that moment" could have led and how thankful I was for my Dad. He was there when it counted the most. He always had been. Driving to the gallery, I wondered to myself, "who was there for him when he was suffering the loss of his wife... my mom?"

I walked into the gallery half past noon. "Hey Dad, sorry, I'm a little late."

"It's alright son. No worries." It was strange that he said that because he looked worried.

"Okay... Are you all right?" I asked.

"Sure am but I need to ask you a favor." He changed the subject.

"Okay. What's that?"

"I forgot to give this order slip to Old Man Salvador. I need you to run by his place and deliver it. And, I think he might have some frames ready for us."

"Ugh, okay." I took it from him. "He comes in tomorrow, do you just want to wait till then?"

"No, go ahead and get it to him, if you don't mind." He said with a slight 'non-negotiable' tone.

"Okay, will do Dad..." I paused, unsure how to thank him. "Dad... I wanted to thank you for.... being there for me last night..."

"Son," he grew serious. "I want you to know something... I am always there for you. I'm sorry about last night... you had a right to be upset, and there is nothing to be ashamed about, okay?

"Yes. I know." I grew quiet. I didn't know what else to say.

"Well, head over there, for me. Okay?" He suggested again.

"Alright." I'll see you in a bit. I agreed... As I turned and walked out, I felt a little antsy. The look on my Dad's face, it bothered me... it resembled something like fear... something like... a last chance. I didn't know...

* * *

As I pulled up to Salvador's place, I didn't see him in his shed, which seemed a little odd. That man was always working, but it was around lunchtime, so I was sure he stopped for a break.

I got out and checked the shed just to be sure, but he wasn't there. I ventured to try the front door. Before I made it up the porch steps, he opened the door.

"Hey, Michael. Just taking a little lunch break. Come on in." He opened the door for me.

"Yes, sir." I took it. "Thank you."

"Can I get you some iced tea?" He asked.

"You know, I think I could use a glass." I agreed.

"I can always use a glass of iced tea, you know what I mean?" He chuckled at his little joke. It was true, though. You'd usually catch Mr. Salvador with a glass of sweet tea around. He turned the corner, and I could hear him pour the ice in the glass.

"So, how have you been Michael?" he asked from the other room.

"I'm hanging in there..." It was a little strange to make small talk with Mr. Salvador. We regularly talked business.

"Hey, well, sometimes that's all you can do, you know?" He said as he came back in the room and handed me the class.

"Thank you," I said as I took a drink. "Man, that's pretty good." I complimented.

"Yes sir," he paused. "Well, why don't you come have a sit with me for a bit."

He motioned in a way that seemed suspect. As I walked over, I thought 'this had Dad written all over it.'

I sat on an old chair while he paused on the couch. I prepared for the lecture that I was sure was coming my way.

Old Man Salvador took a deep breath. "My wife, she was alive when we lost our son. He was, well, the light of my life. June, my wife, she had trouble getting pregnant at first. We tried for years, but you know... it didn't seem to take. She was upset and well; I'd be a liar to say I wasn't disappointed... But I just figured we'd have to make the best of it."

I'd never heard Mr. Salvador talk like this but there was something about it that made me hold on to every word.

"Then, you know, out of nowhere she was pregnant. I have never seen a woman so happy. It was as if she had won the lottery. When I saw Rella, it reminded me." He choked up a bit. "Anyhow, we had ourselves a boy, and we were a lot like you and your Dad, my son and I. Best friends. Ever since he was little, we worked on stuff, projects, building stuff all the way up through his high school days. When the war started, he wanted to defend the good from the bad, and I had to respect that. The last time I saw him, he was pulling out of this old driveway."

I continued to listen.

"For a while, Michael... I wasn't a very good man." He paused. "After my boy died... I started to drink. The truth of the matter was, is that I was angry. You know... I didn't know what to do with all that emotion. The last thing I wanted someone to say to me was that it was okay because it wasn't. My boy died in a war caused by another man. He was innocent, in every regard. It was hard to grapple, and well, I didn't do to well."

"You know some things tie your life together, June and my boy were my thread. The loss of my son hit me in a way that I never really had a chance to be prepared. For a while, I didn't treat June the best. I never hit her or anything like that, but I just wasn't present. I spent too many years like that... Before I knew it, she was sick. Cancer came in fast... I'd like to think it was a little bit of my fault. A broken heart get's sicker easier. She'd lost a son, and lost me, in a lot of respects, as a husband."

He paused. "When she was diagnosed, I shaped up. I straightened my act because I had something to fight for. I thought when I lost my boy, I lost everything, but the truth was, I still had someone who loved me and needed me. I regretted how I behaved and changed but not too long after, she died. Moreover, you know..." He took in a ragged breath... "There I was... pulling up in that old driveway, you know?"

I knew... Everything he was saying, I understood.

"A man... well, we're taught to be strong but I wasn't. How could I be strong when the threads of my life were pulled out from it, leaving nothing but tattered pieces on the floor? I was broken... And man... I was known as Grumpy Salvador. I was bitter and toxic like lye. I was mad at God... but mostly, I was mad at myself. I had a lot of guilt. What if I would have told my boy 'no' to going into the military? What if... when we lost him, I would have been better for June. My thoughts had created a prison for me, with loneliness and shame as the lock and key." He paused. "It wasn't till an old pastor got ahold of me that I changed."

"What did the pastor say?" I asked in an intrigued tone... It was hard to see Mr. Salvador the way he was describing.

"He told me how selfish I was."

"Selfish?" I asked with a little hint of outrage in my voice.

"Yes sir, and he was right." Old Man Salvador looked me square in the eye. "I was selfish."

"How?" I challenged. "You lost everything..."

"That's what I said to him. And he said, No. That was your wife. Your son. They lost everything; it's you, who still has something to loose. The breath you have in your body, you waste in vain. You take the very life that they lost, for granted. It's selfish.'"

We both paused... I felt a little conviction as his words cut deep, but I couldn't deny the truth in them.

"He was right, Michael... I hated God for taking life from them, and leaving me with this life all alone. All the meanwhile, the irony was ringing loud and clear. June and my boy are in heaven, and I'm sure they are happier than ever but when they were taken from this world, they lost the gift of life. The very thing most precious... was the very thing that I was taking in vain."

I knew what he said was right, but I was too prideful to admit it. "Well, it's easy for someone to say when you haven't been there..." I snapped to the pastor in Salvador's story.

"You'd think that, Michael... But I have been there... and I'm telling you the same thing."

I sat a little shocked by his words.

"I know you don't need to hear that some things happen for a reason... Because that's not always true. Sometimes bad things happen for no reason at all... It's life. But Michael, if you keep going down this road... You're going to end up all alone and in another kind of place that's far worse than this."

"But that's not good enough!" I stood raising my voice. "It's not good enough to know that God took Rella! It's not good enough that there is no reason. It isn't good enough to know that I'm selfish... I see her... every time I walk into that house.

Every time I see a child on the street, I see my kid... God has left me here in a personal hell." My tears started to well in my eyes. "You know, what's ironic?" I continued, "Rella had a dream a few weeks before the accident. She had a dream that I died! That it was me! Well, maybe it should have been, because this life... the breath that I have left, I don't necessarily want it." I was starting to pace now, as I lectured. "What's a gift that you don't want? Huh?"

"Well, looks like Rella's dream did come true then, didn't it?" He asked calmly.

"What do you mean?" I snapped.

"You are dead. Look at you. Wishing the gift of life away. That's as dead as it gets, son."

I paused, as I tried to fight back tears. The words... the truth... It was hard to take... I couldn't bare it. The emotion was too strong. Not even my hard shell could stand up to it.

"You're right..." I began to sob. "You're right..." I feel to my knees.

Old Man Salvador got up and met me down on my knees.

"Michael, my boy... They are gone... And it's too late to get them back... But it's not too late for you. You can be still happy."

"But how do I live without her? How?" I begged him for an answer.

"You live a new life, son. Not the old one with her, but a new one, without her."

"That's the hard part because I don't want to." I stiffened.

"And that's the part where The Lord comes in." he answered.

"But I hate Him."

Old Man Salvador smiled slightly. "He knows... That's okay... He also knows you love him too because hate cannot live without love, but they both cannot dwell in the same place. I'm talking about your heart son. Your emotions choose hate, but when the dust settles God knows you will want to choose love again. Be proud that you have the courage to admit it." He turned and sat beside me. "Most people don't... they just go on saying stuff like He isn't real. It takes a brave man to admit that he's upset with the Most High."

"But don't I get like.. Turned into a pillar of salt?"

He laughed. "You can if you handle it the wrong way... If you were angry with your Dad and took a knife after him, don't you think there'd be some consequences?"

I looked at him crazy... "Well, yes... But I wouldn't ever..."

He interrupted me, "Same way with God. He is God, but He's a Father first... just like your Dad is a man, but he chooses to be your Dad first. Treat Him like a Father, God will respond like one. Defy Him as God, and He'll respond to that too. I bet if you took that knife after your Dad, he give you a little smack to protect himself, right? A little discipline?"

"Yes." I contemplated.

"Well, if you go cursing The Lord, don't think He won't punish you. But, it doesn't mean He doesn't want you to be honest about how you feel, Michael. You can be mad, and you can 'not understand' something... But that doesn't mean He's going to smite you unless you go taking a knife after His name."

"I see." Old Man Salvador made God make more sense than anyone I knew.

"You need to find a new beginning, Michael." He looked towards the window. "I still drive down that same old road, but I have come to realize, that it's not going to lead to the same place that it once did... A home with a wife and child... It doesn't lead to that anymore. Once I let that go, I realized that it can lead me to something else... something different... something new."

"How did you find the new?"

"That my boy, I can't tell you... That's between you and The Lord but mainly, it's up to you. You have to choose what meets you at the end of the road. No one, not even God, will decide that for you."

I peered out the window towards the road.

"But I will tell you this, Michael..." He looked at me in the eyes." The road crossing, it isn't there forever. You keep going down the path you're on; you'll forget your way back home. Now is the time to turn it around. Not later. Now."

The warning sent chills down my spine. I understood what he meant. We sat there in silence for a while. It was soothing. I thought about all he had said.

"There isn't a purchase order, huh?" I asked him.

He smiled. "No."

"Dad set this up."

He smiled again, slightly. "Yes."

I turned and looked back out the window.

"Your Dad loves you, Michael... He asked me to speak to you..."

"Really?" I asked.

"When your Dad lost your mom... he was in a similar state..."

"I don't remember that."

"No, you wouldn't... Just like the common person now, they wouldn't know. A person can be good at hiding what they don't want someone else to see."

"I've tried hard... but... last night... I can't tell you how hard it was."

"I know, Michael. I'm proud of you for asking for help. Seeing the counselor and everything, it's good but... Sometimes a man just needs the hard truth from a person who's old like me."

I smiled ruefully... "So... what now?"

"Find a new end to your road, Michael. Get a new beginning. It's okay if you have to search for it. No reason not to start now..."

"And God? Do I need to make peace or something? Because, I'm still mad."

He laughed. "It's not a rule book son. It's a relationship. It might do you a little good to talk to Him, though."

"Talk to Him?" I questioned... Rella would say the same thing.

"In the secret place."

* * *

That's all Old Man Salvador had to say for me to know what to do next. I needed a secret place... and what better one, than Rella's?

I left his house and took the highway to get on that old dirt road... I can't say that I knew what to expect, I just felt like... maybe just going there, I would have some kind of epiphany or something. If one thing was true, I trusted Mr. Salvador and I trusted my Rella. She went there to be with God... Maybe He would meet me there too.

The old dirt road was filled with memories of my love... But, I wasn't as caught up in them now. I couldn't be... Salvador made me realize that in all of this, there was something else to loose. Myself.

From a distance, I spotted that old worn down house. It looked as old as ever but still strong as an ox. In a way, it was like Old Man Salvador. That made me smile... Maybe, as Rella would say, it was a sign. Man ever did I need one.

I pulled up and got out of the jeep. I looked around; to make sure no one was near... I strolled up to the door and stepped in. It was creepy to be here alone. I quickly imagined how many times Rella came here by herself. I remembered our discussion telling her that it wasn't safe. She argued, "I'm pretty sure if God is there it's safe," and how was I supposed to respond to that? I smiled at the memory as I turned for the stairs...

When I reached the top, the light was pouring in through the window. Last time, I didn't know if I noticed the small stain glass at the top, of a white dove... It was beautiful... Graceful. I stood there for a moment and gazed at it... So simple and so much beauty.

The light from the natural windows was bright. As the evening was drawing near, the golden tones of the sun were growing deeper in color. I walked down the hall and into the old office.

Almost instantly, walking in, I felt like I had a déjà vu. The familiarity of when I was here with Rella collided into now's reality. I couldn't help my eyes from welling up again. Her presence... I could almost feel it again in this place. I went over to the desk... grazing the top with my hand. As I looked down, I could see her footsteps etched in the dust, going to the window...

I followed her path... I remembered seeing what looked like God embracing her. Would He dare do the same for me? I walked to the bay window and closed my eyes, blinking out the tears.

"I don't know what to do," I admitted. "Please show me what to do." I fell to my knees in prayer position. "Please, just give me a sign." I kneeled sobbing when the light angled just right... as I had seen before and embraced me.

I opened my eyes and saw myself golden. It was the same way that Rella had been before. I looked amazed, as my eyes caught the sight of that little black book.

"Holy Bible." I read aloud. I opened it. The scarlet thread marked the story of the scarlet thread. The story of hope that Rella told me about... I looked up with all the expectancy and faith. "God, just give me a rope... I at least need a rope to get out of this pit of despair." I clutched on the bible... Silently wondering if maybe, this was just it.

CHAPTER 18

"HELLO?" MY DAD ANSWERED.

"Hey, Dad?" I had just left the old house and was driving down the old dirt road.

"Yeah, son?"

"I need to meet with you. Can I come by your place?" I never went back to the gallery that afternoon...

"Sure. Everything okay?" He asked.

I smiled at his concern. "It's getting there... I just need to talk to you."

"Okay, I'm just leaving the gallery now. I'll meet you there in about 15 minutes."

"Okay, but make it twenty for me." I was still a ways off.

"Ok. Bye." He hung up.

Driving down the road, I couldn't help but think of the analogy that Old Man Salvador presented... Realizing that there would be something different now, in my life, than what I had first anticipated. I understood, but I knew, that one thing was for certain, was that I needed to get away from the memories for a while. I mean, I lived in the house that my wife had newly decorated... Every day, I saw what could have been, and I wasn't strong enough for that... Not yet. I needed a new scene. A new sunset... I needed an unfamiliar place to clean my slate. In a way, I think I just needed to get away from myself.

A few minutes later, I pulled up to Dad's house. He was just pulling in too.

"Hey Dad," I said as I got out.

"Hey, son.." He came over and gave me a hug.

"Thank you," I said... I figured he had talked to Salvador.

"Yeah... come on in. I've ordered pizza."

"Ah, your finest dish." I teased.

"Hey, it always has been." He admitted.

We walked in and got settled in the kitchen.

"You said you needed to talk?" Dad inquired...

"Yeah... Dad... I know you talked to Salvador." He nodded as I went on. "Well, I did too... and I listened..." I was unsure how to continue. "I think I just need to get away for awhile... And, well, I believe I need to sell my house."

"What?" he sounded a little alarmed. "Sell it?"

"Yeah... Dad, I just can't live there... I know that Old Man Salvador still lives in his, but it's just not for me... When I'm there, I see two things... The old, lonely me or the married to Rella me and well, the truth is, is that I can't be either of those anymore. It's just too hard being surrounded by all her stuff and all the memories we had in that place..." I stopped.

"I understand... So, what did you have in mind?" He asked a little confused.

"I need to get away... I don't know where, or really for how long but would you mind packing up my things? I mean, I'll hire movers, but will you oversee all of it?"

He paused. "Michael... this seems... drastic..." He went to the fridge and grabbed a bottled coke.

"It is, Dad." I agreed. "But, what happened was drastic," I argued. "Please?"

He waited. "This is really what you need?"

"I wouldn't ask this much if I didn't."

He looked out the window. "Okay. Just, let's work out the details."

That's what we did for the rest of the evening. I made plans to call the movers and a realtor the next day, and I was going to let Dr. Walters know that I was leaving town. There was a lot to do, but I was motivated for change. Something had to change if I was going to.

* * *

I headed home late that night. Dad and I worked out just about everything. Even though I didn't know where, I was planning to be gone for about three weeks. This house would sell fast, we both knew, and I felt that it was enough time for me to get away, and then come back to something new.

When I got home, I started looking at places to go... I had no clue. I mean, it's not something you Google. "Where to go when your wife dies, and you're left all alone?" Yeah. Wasn't easy at all. I didn't want to leave the country or anything... I just needed a place. I needed a peaceful, happy place. California? No... Too many weird people. New York was too busy and crowded. I browsed for what seemed like hours before I decided to go to bed. Maybe I would dream of the place.

I was planning to leave as soon as tomorrow night to my yet known destination. I decided I better find a suitcase. I went to the closet where I kept them. When Rella moved in, she had pretty much taken it over our closet. Her shoes, purses, bags, were everywhere. I looked around at the top and spotted my old luggage back in the corner...

"Now, if I could only get to it..." I looked around for something to stand on. I found a storage box that would do. It would give me enough lift to grab the handle.

I pushed it up close and reached for it. When I did, everything quickly came tumbling down... Including me.

"Ugh..." I was flat on my back with stuff everywhere... Turns out that fast food had counted more than I thought. I sat up slowly and looked at the mess around me when it caught my eye.

The old leather book, with a string wrapped around it... 'Journal' it read... I couldn't imagine it... It had to be Rella's.

I reached for it and opened it to find it filled with her elegant handwriting. There were tons of entries, all starting when we started dating. I looked at the front. It was dated when we first me. It was a treasure. Our love story, written by my love.

I couldn't believe it! I had never seen her write before. I never even knew she kept a journal...

I sat back and fanned through the pages... The dates were marked when we first met... when we went sailing... the first time we kissed. I looked through, but there was a page bookmarked. I flipped to it and realized it was a picture.

I pulled it out and recognized it completely... The little girl, with the little puppy. The old dead tree. The beach. I remembered the day she told me about it, and how it helped her when she lost her grandmother. This place. The painting that hangs in our living room! It was all so similar. We got so caught up, that day and well, with life that I never saw the actual picture she talked about. I looked back at the journal skimming, reading what she wrote:

> December 13th, 2013
>
> I've thought long and hard about a surprise for Michael. He does so much for me; I couldn't help but want to do something for him. I plan on taking him to my beach... A place of pure, perfect peace. I think it will be good for him... The last time his feet touched the sandy banks in Michigan was before his mother, Rachel, passed away. I think in some ways, he still feels her loss... Just like I feel my grandmothers... The beach is a perfect place to let go... It's a place where you can't help but see a different picture of life. Our life was so different now. We are together and in love... expecting a baby... Sometimes life goes by so fast and makes so many twists and turns. I go to the Secret Place for guidance... but I like to go to the Safe Place for reflection. The crystal blue waters have always served as a mirror in which I can see my life through... The good and bad always appear in the speculum image it presents. I will take My Michael there... I wonder what reflections he will see?

Rella wrote this passage, the day before she passed. She was planning to take me there. She went on and told in detail how she was going to do it... A surprise trip. It was just something she would do. I turned and found a map to her place. Her beach, where she once found happiness again. A place of hope... A place of rest... That was the answer. I sighed with relief. Her words couldn't have been more telling of what I needed.

I knew this was where I was supposed to go.

* * *

I called Dad the next morning. I stayed up all night packing. I couldn't help but have a little bit of excitement. There was again, an expectancy that I couldn't name. As much as I wanted to Google the place, I decided not too. I wanted to be led by Rella; just like she planned. I would use her little map as my guide. She gave enough detail that I was sure I would know where it was. East of here, located at the tip of the thumb of Michigan. I figured that was why she ended up here in the first place. She must have paid a visit when she left Chicago and just kept driving.

"Port Austin," I told Dad the name of the town.

"She was planning to take you there?" He asked again.

"Yes," I told him the whole story.

"Okay... Well, you're sure that's where you want to go?" He seemed a little skeptical...

"It's not where I want to go; it's where I'm supposed to go."

"Okay, son. I trust you. Just be careful." He paused. "Have you called the realtor and moving company and everything?"

"Yes, I did. I let them know that you were in charge. The only thing is, is when the house sells; I'll need to sign. You can just FedEx the documents. I trust your judgment otherwise."

"Michael... You're sure about all of this." He still needed some convincing.

"Dad, I couldn't ask for a more blunt sign. I think she needs me to go there."

He paused. "Okay... I.... I love you son."

"I love you too, Dad." I paused. "I'm sorry to leave you like this. Is the gallery going to be okay?

"Of course, son. You don't worry about that."

"This is a lot to dump on you, Dad. I don't mean to..."

"No, it's fine. I would tell you if I couldn't handle it. We'll be okay here. Don't worry. Just make things right. However, you need too." He urged.

"Okay... Thank you for everything."

"You are my everything son. So, thank you for being my joy." He said solemnly. I could hear the tears in his eyes.

"Dad..." I choked.

"Keep in touch." He warned.

"Yes, sir. I'll call you when I get there."

"Good. Or you'll be grounded."

I laughed. "Well, we can't have that." I smiled. "Love you Dad. Talk to you soon. Bye."

"Bye."

I hung up. None of this was easy, but it was all already hard. I put the rest of my things in the suitcase. I packed lightly. Whatever I didn't have, I'd buy when I got there. I took a last look around the house as I headed towards the door. I couldn't stop the emotion welling upside me. There were so many memories of her, even though she only lived here a short while. The décor, the paint, the styling. Every day I saw these things, it reminded me of her absence every day, and I was brave enough to admit that was no way to live here now. I'd never move forward if I stayed here... And with that, I said goodbye to my house and the memories.. and closed the front door for the last time.

Rather than calling Dr. Walters, I decided I would go there first to talk to her and tell her what was going on. I didn't want her to worry or call out some alert on me, especially with the intensity of last session.

Pulling up, I grew a little nervous. I didn't know what her thoughts were going to be, or if she'd agree with me, but I knew in my heart, that I was already determined.

I walked in and again, was greeted by the blonde. She was flirtatious, but I always ignored. In no way was I even tempted by relationships.

"I'm sorry just to drop in, but I need to talk to Dr. Walters," I explained.

"Okay... I think she is eating lunch, but let me check, Mr. Harvey." She smiled.

"Thanks."

A few minutes later she came back with Dr. Walters.

"Mr. Harvey, we don't have an appointment today. Is everything alright?" She seemed concerned.

"Yes, I'm alright, but I do need to talk to you."

"Okay," she looked at the receptionist. "Please keep my schedule clear for the next half hour... My next appointment isn't until one, correct?"

"Yes, Dr. Walters."

"Okay." She looked at me. "Mr. Harvey, come on back."

I followed her to the office and grew more anxious... It was like I was quitting a job or something without resignation.

She opened the door and closed it behind. I sat on the couch that I always did. She sat in a chair across from me.

"So, Mr. Harvey, what brings you in?"

"Well..." I started, trying to find the words. "This is going to sound crazy, no pun intended."

She chuckled lightly.

"But, I am going to go away for awhile."

Immediately, I saw her tense up.

"Where to?" She asked.

"I'm not sure," I explained. "It's a place where somehow, I think Rella will be. I don't think here, is a good place for me anymore."

She took a long pause. "Mr. Harvey... I know things are difficult, but suicide is never the way out. I can help you through this."

"What?" I asked confused.

She gave me a blank stare, and I thought back to what I had just said... 'Leaving to a place where Rella was...." Not good.

"Oh, no Dr. Walters. I don't mean... I'm not going away like that!' I rushed an explanation. "I am taking a vacation. Literally, a road trip. Last night, I found one of Rella's journals, and there is a map to a beach she went to when she was little. I've decided to go there and get away for a little while."

Immediately, she looked relieved. "Oh, a real trip. Mr. Harvey, you had me worried there."

I laughed slightly under my breath. "I'm sorry Dr. Walters. I just came in to tell you, honestly. I think this is something I need to do."

She smiled. "Mr. Harvey, I'm not going to talk you out of it. I respect your decision to take a vacation. My only request is that when your there and if things begin to feel overwhelming, that you call my office."

I understood what she meant. "Yes, ma'am." I paused, wondering if I should go further.

"Is there something else?" She was able to read me very well.

"Yes," I waited... "I've also decided to sell my home. That's one of the reasons I am going away. I've hired movers, and my Dad is going to oversee everything. I know it seems rash, but honestly, Dr. Walters, being in that house has become a personal coffin for me, just a bigger one. I sit in a place where everything around me reminds me of Rella. I believe it's time to get a new beginning. I have come to realize that... well, I can't get my old life back, but I can start a new one from this point if I choose to. I don't know yet, how I'm going to do that, but I think getting away, clearing my head, will help."

She nodded and paused. "Mr. Harvey... it seems that you have had a breaking point... in a good way. All of the things that you are saying are very rash, but I believe you have logical reasoning behind them. May I ask what brought this about?"

I didn't know what to say. "My logical reasoning isn't necessarily based on logic."

She smiled. "Try me."

"Well... I don't know if you're a woman of faith, but Rella, she always talked about signs. I've received quite a few of them in the past 24 hours."

"That, Mr. Harvey, is something I can understand perfectly." She looked down for a moment. "Just promise me, that in all of this, truly, if something happens, you will help me, help you." She gave me a stern look.

"Yes, Dr. Walters. I will. I plan to be gone three weeks. I wouldn't mind calling the office to check in if you feel that's better."

"No, I trust your judgment. You call me if you need to." She arranged.

"Yes, ma'am. Well, thank you, Dr. Walters, for not thinking I'm nuts."

"I don't think anyone is nuts, Mr. Harvey. I think that people get lost in life sometimes through tragedy and heartbreak. I believe that the light is what helps people navigate those waters, so to speak. And, the light comes in many forms; therapists, doctors, friends, signs, and faith." She waited a moment. "I believe, Mr. Harvey, that light can finally be seen at the end of your tunnel... It's up to you, though, to follow it."

I had never heard Dr. Walters share such an opinion... It was a beautiful thing she said.

"Thanks again, for everything." I reached to shake her hand. "Thank you."

"Anytime, Mr. Harvey. The best of luck to you."

I smiled... Rella would have corrected the luck part, "Be blessed, Dr. Walters." I couldn't help but say it for her.

I turned and left the office. Part of me felt like that was all part of it. Closing the doors not only to Rella but grieving as well. I nodded at the receptionist as I left, and before I knew it, I was on the road, to a place I'd never been before.

I couldn't help the butterflies flutter in my stomach because I had never done anything so... random. Free spirited, so to speak, but I knew that there was a first time for everything. I wondered if maybe that's part of what tragedies are for. Not to bring you down, but to show you a different way. Losing Rella was the worst thing in my past but for the first time, I started to think about the future. I thought about the suitcase in my back seat... a tragedy had left me with nothing but a suitcase to start all over with. I had up and left everything, in search of something new... The whole scenario reminded me of what Dr. Walters said about the light, at the end of a tunnel. A beacon of hope guiding the lost back to the shore of life... That's what I was searching for.

CHAPTER 19

I AWOKE, NOT QUITE OPENING my eyes. My body ached from the day before the drive and long walk on the beach. The hotel bed was soft, but nothing compared to my bed back home.

I thought for a minute... The movers should be there right about now. I hoped Dad was managing everything okay. I started to drift back asleep, tired from the drive and the beach and... Pickles!

I jumped up, looking for the old dog I found. There he was, at the foot of my bed, waiting for me expectantly.

"Hey there, old guy," I mumbled rubbing the sleep from my eyes... "You did not chew anything up did you?" I started to look around... "If you did, the lady is going to kill me... It took all of my persuasion and a sizable deposit for her to let you stay."

I looked around carefully for any damage. There didn't seem to be any, yet. I looked up and found the dog waiting by the door. "Bathroom," I said my thought aloud. He wagged his tail eagerly.

"Okay, okay. Let me get dressed because I could use the bathroom myself."

I washed and groomed, putting on some jeans and a t-shirt. The weather was pleasant, but still a bit on the chilly side. I combed my hair, as normal. However, I didn't bother to shave.

"No one here cares if I look a bit scruffy, huh big guy?" I asked him rhetorically.

He barked in agreement.

"Alright, let's go!"

He followed me out the door and down to the lobby. They had an excellent coffee set-up, and so I grabbed a cup and headed out to the beach with Pickles.

"How about another walk, before I try to find your owner?"

We walked along the shore, as I had done the night previous... I couldn't believe I was here... I could not imagine that I found that old dead tree from Rella's picture. The whole situation seemed a bit surreal. The weird thing was that everything looked so similar to last night. The sunrise to the east only mirrored the sunset in the West that I saw the night before. I could understand why Rella would surprise me with coming here. The sheer beauty of the place was a present in and of itself.

Pickles and I walked awhile, passing the dead tree up on the cliff again and walking back. There was more peace on this beach than I could ever remember feeling when I was little... perhaps because when you're little, you have no need for peace. Everything in your little world goes minute by minute and your content. However, as an adult, boy how things changed. The past year and few months had been a roller coaster of emotion. If there was one thing that I needed, it was peace. The sun started to rise higher over the horizon, and I figured it was time to get Pickles back to his owner.

"Come on, boy!" I patted my leg to get his attention. He came obediently. "Let's get you home."

He followed me to my car. I was shocked by how well behaved. He listened to every command. Several times he had the chance to run away from me but choose not to. Maybe he understood what I was trying to do; bring him back to his owner? I typed the address into my GPS. It was strange how I navigated here without it. Rella's map was simple enough to lead the way. The journal was still on my dashboard. She was the only direction that I needed.

The home was only a few blocks away. It made since. 2701 Sunset Drive. I made the appropriate turns and headed that way. "Going to take you home, buddy," I said to Pickles as I turned towards the direction the GPS was taking me.

It was a very nice neighborhood. Everything was picture perfect. White picket fences, brick roads, beautiful, full-grown trees that shaded the streets, and established neighborhood. It was a place where any parent would want to raise their children. It was the American dream. I pulled up to the 2-story house.

"Here we are boy," I said to Pickles in the back seat. He barked and wagged his tail at the sight of his home.

As I got out, I noticed the for sale sign. I couldn't imagine why anyone would leave this place. Before I made it up to the front door, it opened.

"Hello, my name is Alicia, I am the realtor agent for this home," a woman with brunette hair and light brown eyes answered. "Are you here for the open house?" She asked cheerfully.

"Ugh, no ma'am... I am here to return this dog. This address is on his collar."

"Oh," she paused for a moment.

"Is the owner here?" I asked.

"No... I am sorry... It is a very tragic story. The owner has Alzheimer's disease. His wife died a few years back. He was moved to a residence... a nursing home a few days ago. His kids are overseas, and they've just arranged everything over the phone. I guess they forgot about the dog."

"Wow." I wasn't expecting that. "That's sad..." I didn't know what to do.

She looked at Pickles with pity and worry. "I don't think they would have any interest in him..." She put in the kindest way possible. "The children, I mean."

"Well, I figure not being that they handled their father over the phone," I said suggesting. To me, it sounded awful. I couldn't imagine doing something like that to my Dad.

"Yes...." She agreed with my silent insult. "Well, do you want him because the nursing home doesn't allow pets. If you say no, this dog has no home... I'd hate to see it in a dog pound. This neighborhood is uptight about loose dogs roaming around. It wouldn't take long for him to be caught."

"Ugh..." I looked down at him... Poor guy. He lost everything and didn't even know it, but I could relate.

"I don't know... I..." He looked at me as if he knew I was deciding his fate... How could I say no?

"Yeah... I'll take him, but I don't feel right just leaving with him. Can you give me the name of the guy at the residence center? I would feel better knowing I had his permission. Surely he'll remember his dog..."

"I am not supposed to give that information out... However, this is an extenuating circumstance and, you do not seem to be a serial killer..." She turned. "Let me get the address."

I couldn't help but laugh because I remembered when Rella told me the same thing, the first night I walked her home.

The agent came back with a small piece of paper. "Here you go... I hope it all works out. Sorry for the inconvenience."

"No, no, it's alright. Thanks for your help." I thanked her.

"It is so kind of you know..." She added. "To take him..."

"Awe, well..." I looked at Pickles... "You never know... I might need him more than he needs me."

She smiled.

"Have a good day, ma'am." I turned back towards the car.

"Thank you! You do the same!" She waved.

I got back in my car and typed in the new address. "Looks like it's going to be a day of seeking and finding, huh Pickles?"

He wagged his tail in approval. "Okay, here we go!" I took off...

I knew this was odd just to show up to someone's place, but, I just didn't have it in me to take a man's dog without his permission. Especially when it sounded like everything else had just been ripped from underneath him.

I pulled up to the very nice nursing home. By every means, it was a lovely place, but in no way was it in comparison to his neighborhood. I thought about my Dad again. I couldn't imagine ever putting him in a place like this. It seemed so cold and lacked life. I understood that sometimes things happened, but man, I already felt sorry for this guy. No man wants to be taken away from the place he calls home.

"Come on Pickles," he jumped out. "Hopefully I can persuade them to let you in."

At the front of the building, through the sliding glass, double doors a woman greeted me. "Hello, who are you here to see?"

Quickly, I pulled the piece of paper from my back pocket. "Thomas Jackson."

She said, "Okay..." while looking at the dog.

"I know you probably don't allow pets, but he has Alzheimer's and well, this is his dog. I found him on the beach yesterday, and I don't know... I'm willing to take him home, but I just want to be sure that Mr. Jackson doesn't... well, you know..."

She smiled. "Yes, I understand." She paused. "It's room 204. Just make it quick, my boss is out for the moment."

"Okay, will do. Thank you so much!" It was so nice of her to sneak us in.

"Yes, sir."

I started to walk down the hall with Pickles. "See, it's not so bad, is it?" I asked him.

We went to the elevator and took the ride up. The arrows pointed left for even numbered rooms. I walked down the hall a little more than nervous... I had no idea what to expect.

When I reached the door, I heard a baseball game on and knocked slightly.

"Come in." The old voice gave permission.

I walked in slowly, Pickles behind me. "Hello, Mr. Jackson?"

He turned. His eyes met mine. He was a small Old Man. Looked to be no more than 5'6". He looked tired and worn but certainly not gone yet.

"Hi there, how can I help you?" He asked. "If I don't remember you, I'm sorry." He warned.

I laughed. "No sir, you wouldn't remember me."

"Good, because I don't." He shrugged his shoulders. I could tell already that he was a character.

I smiled. He was a charming Old Man. "Well, Mr. Jackson, I just..." I didn't know how to begin... I didn't want to cause this man any grief.

"Hey, what do you got there?" He interrupted, noticing Pickles. "Come here boy..."

Pickles instantly came, and Mr. Jackson petted him. I sat and waited. Here it comes. He'll ask me what I'm doing with his dog.

"This is a good dog you have," Mr. Jackson said. "I had a dog like this once."

Oh, no. "You did?" I tried to keep my cool.

"Yeah, I did once... I think." He continued to pet Pickles. "Dogs are good, you know? Sometimes they are just the friends you need."

"Yes sir," I agreed. I was waiting for any sign that he recognized him.

"What's his name?" he asked.

"Pickles." I just knew that would jog his memory.

"Gosh, that's a strange name, son. Why the heck would you call a dog Pickles?" He said matter-of-factly. "Sounds like something my wife would have named a dog." He reasoned.

"Yeah..." I was starting to get choked up. You could tell that Pickles loved this man because he never stopped wagging his tail or wanting him to pet him. It was as if Pickles was begging him to remember who he was. However, old Mr. Jackson couldn't remember his best friend. Pickles was whimpering at him as if he was crying out loud "remember me. Remember all our memories. Remember me, please, please remember me. I'm yours, let's go home." I turned my head... I had to look away or else I too would plead for Mr. Jackson to remember.

"Well, what brings you here?" He asked as he tried to calm Pickles down from making all that noise. "I'd ask your name, but I'll forget it." He laughed.

I hesitated... There was no way I could break this news... "Well, I need your advice, Mr. Jackson." Asking this question was the only way I could get his permission.

"On what?" He asked cheerfully. I wondered how many things he got asked about now, rather than just told.

"You see, I found this dog on the beach, and I think the owner... well, something happened to him. It's really sad, and well, I wanted to take Pickles for my own, but... I don't feel right... taking a man's dog, you see?" I tried to frame it the best I could.

"Well..." he paused... "Sounds to me like that owner would be thankful. Seeing that someone took his dog, when he couldn't. I think it is important that a dog is well taken care of and loved. I don't think you need permission to be kind, young man."

"Yeah." My voice cracked because I knew he had no clue what he was doing. He was giving away his dog. "You know, you're right..." I walked over to the window. "You're right, Mr. Jackson." I looked down at pictures that were on the shelf below the window.

There were photos of who must have been his wife and kids. From all scenes of life, it seemed, there was a picture to account for it. I teared up when I saw some with Pickles in them... It was him, sure enough. This had to be the saddest thing I'd ever seen.

I walked alongside the window and looked at all of the photos.

"Those are nice, aren't they?" Mr. Jackson offered. "The only face I seem to remember is my wife's..." He paused. "But love like that... you don't forget."

"Yeah, I can agree with that." I faced away from him. He couldn't know the emotion that was stirring in me.

I continued looking at the photos.

"Have you been in love?" He asked.

"Yes, sir." I kept my answers short.

"Did you hold on to her?" He questioned.

"The best I could..." Tears were falling now. "But some people, they are just meant for better places than this old world huh?" I turned to face him now.

"If that isn't the truth, my boy." His eyes were misty. "If that isn't' the truth..." He whispered.

I turned back... It was time to go. I never expected all of this to be so emotional. I took one last glance at the pictures when I spotted a familiar scene.

"Have you lived here in Port Austin, always?" I didn't know if he'd remember.

"Sure have. That's something else I can't seem to forget."

I bend down to get a better look... It couldn't be...

The photo was taken at a beach. There was Rella's dead tree sitting high on a rocky hill on the far side of the photo... You could see a woman standing beneath the tree with her camera out. There was also a little girl and a puppy at the beach... No.... It couldn't be...

I pulled out my wallet. Rella's precious picture was in there. I flipped it open to compare the two... My heart all but stopped. I looked between the both... It was the same scene just taken at different angles. Rella's picture was of her, playing with the puppy with what now, made since as Mr. Jackson and his wife in the background. This photo was of Mr. Jackson and his wife. Pickles as a puppy... with a little girl, smiling in the background. My Rella... Pickles was the dog! The little puppy that brought her joy that made her laugh again. My love had held him.

My tears were hitting the ground so hard. I couldn't believe it... This was not a coincidence... it was a miracle.

"You okay?" Mr. Jackson asked. I'm sure he heard me sobbing by now.

"Yes, sir." I wiped my tears... "These pictures are just beautiful." I tried to gather myself.

"Thank you..." Mr. Jackson seemed a little confused. He stammered then asked, "Hello, who are you?"

I stood silently. I could see instantly, that the man forgot everything he'd just experienced.

"I'm an old friend...." I choked. "Someone you knew and once gave excellent advice."

"Well, that's good." Mr. Jackson looked more confused than ever. He spotted Pickles lying at his feet. "Hey... look here at this dog... is this your dog?"

With that, I knew, it was time to go… "Yeah, it is?" I walked over towards Pickles.

"Yeah…" He paused a moment. "Well, it looks like you have a good dog here son. You make sure you keep taking good care of him you understand? Sometimes they are just the friend you need."

"They are… He is…" I looked at him. "Come on boy…" He slowly got up and inched his way to me. He looked at his owner one last time, and I swear he knew that the Old Man… the man he knew, was gone. All his efforts to try to get him to remember him had failed and failed for the last time.

"Bye Mr. Jackson… thanks for your help."

"Bye…" He seemed confused, but I made my exit… Not half way down the hall, I got on one knee with Pickles. My love for him had grown exponentially in the past few minutes. I couldn't believe it… That little puppy from the picture that once was with my Rella stood with me now. It was unfathomable.

The odds were out of the park… I petted him. "I'm sorry boy…" he seemed sad as his head hung low. "But you know what… I could sure use you as a friend." He looked up at me as if he knew what I was saying…

He was old and gray. His eyes looked tired. Now, doing the math, he had to be at least twelve years old. He looked sad.

"It's okay my boy…" I fought back the tears again… "Sometimes an ending brings a new beginning…"

He looked back at me knowingly. "Let's go, boy."

He walked with me… Just like a friend would. On the path to new beginning…

CHAPTER 20

TODAY HAD BEEN THE LONGEST day and ranked top ten in most emotional. After Pickles and I had left the nursing home, I didn't know where else to go, but back to the beach. We stopped at a local restaurant and got sandwiches. I bought him one too because it was such a rough day for the both of us. I quickly found out that Pickles is not a fan of olives.

After that, we just walked in the cold. I had many thoughts running through my brain. What happened with Pickles and Mr. Jackson was beyond remarkable. The fact that I found the beach where Rella had once been was a gift, but to find the puppy that helped Rella, now as an old dog. Well, it changed my view of God. We weren't on the best of terms but this... He had proved something to me today. There was a sense of sovereignty. It reminded me what Old Man Salvador said just the other day about how God is a God, but He chooses to be a Father. I wasn't sure if this was Him showing the former, the latter, or both. With the miracle of it all, I was sticking with both.

Pickles stopped hanging his head down low sometime during our walk and started sniffing me and licking me a lot. I think this was his way of getting to know me. There was a peace about walking along the beach with Pickles. I could tell that he had done this a million of times and enjoyed every second of it. There was no other feeling of small than standing beside a large body of water. It humbles you in a way. That mid-afternoon I felt like we bonded in a way that we both needed. But also, I felt like I bonded with God once again... The anger in my heart was starting to fade... With everything that happened today, one thing I was sure of was that God had a plan in all of this. I was just going to have to wait and find out what it was...

After our walk, Pickles and I sat on a wooden bench, to admire the view from a further distance; as we soaked up what warmth we could get from the sun that was shining. It was getting to be around six o'clock and honestly, I was ready to surrender to the cold. The hotel had a restaurant, and that would be good enough, not to mention it was warm. Before I got to leave, I saw that the moon was out already starting to show. I couldn't help but remember what Rella told me about the moon. I did feel closer to Jesus knowing that he too once looked at that same moon. I couldn't help but smile as I said "Amen." Maybe God wasn't so bad after all.

We went back to the hotel, and I washed up. When I got out of the shower, I found Pickles snoring as he slept at the foot of the bed. I realized just how much he had done, for how old he was... I worried that I pushed him too hard. Tomorrow, I need make sure the day wouldn't be so physically demanding.

I went downstairs to the bar. If there was any day to this trip that was going to end in a drink, it was this one.

"Scotch, on the rocks," I told the bartender.

There was a man about my age who walked in. "I'll have whatever he's having." He told the bartender.

"Scotch on the rocks?" the man responded.

He nodded and turned to me, "Man, you've had the kind of day I've had." He sat down next to me.

I didn't know what to do or say other than just nod.

"Jack Rite... Rite the wrong way." He laughed at his joke that he must have told a million times. "Nice to meet you." He extended his hand.

"Ugh, Michael Harvey." I shook his hand. "Nice to meet you too."

"So, what brings you to the tip of the thumb of Michigan?" He asked as the bartender served our drinks.

I wasn't one for small talk and honestly, I didn't want to speak at all, especially after today... However, there was no reason to be rude. "Ugh... It's a long story... Just taking a vacation."

"Oh... I see."

"You?" I asked respectfully.

"Oh, I'm from here..." He paused. "I just got kicked out of my house... by my wife." He sounded ashamed.

"Oh... Sorry..." What could I say to that?

"No, don't be. It was my fault. I cheated on her..." He downed the drink and motioned to the bartender for another one. "Like I said, I've had a rough day."

I didn't know what to say. I could never understand why people cheated in a relationship. If you love someone, it should mean something. I think cheating was such a selfish act. I couldn't imagine having ever cheated on Rella. I suppose my silence, though, came across as judgmental.

"I know what you're thinking." He turned to me. "What kind of guy cheats on his wife?" He looked at me, searching to see if I was asking that question.

Might as well admit it. "Actually, yeah, I was." I shrugged my shoulders slightly.

He looked down. "We've been married for seven years. Right out of high school. Both of us have changed a lot... well..." he reconsidered. "I've pretty much stayed the same, but she... she's changed a lot. She's gone to school, got the fancy degrees, and well... now she's in a whole different class. Me, I'm still the quarterback with the barely passing grades. I have grown to be not good enough for her, and I've known it for a while. When someone needs you to be someone your not, you grow apart. Then, others seem to fill the gap."

I nodded again. Again, what was I supposed to say?

"It's my fault... but it's her fault too... we both let the love die."

"My wife said it always takes two." I blurted out before I could reason. Rella always said that no problem is ever one sided.

"Yeah?" Jack nodded. "I'd say she's a smart woman. You're a lucky guy."

"Was." I shifted... "She passed away a few months ago. We were married for just over a month, so... well, I'm no expert. I have no room to judge." I felt a little guilty. I felt on my heart that I was accusing this man of being selfish... Old Man Salvador's words echoed in my mind... "You're selfish." To judge means to be judged. The words echoed in my brain.

"Dang... man... Never mind." The bartender sat his drink in front of him, but he slid it to me. "This one's on me... you need it."

I sat and looked at the drink. "I once thought I did... but that's why I'm here. I'm trying to move on." I pushed the drink back. "Only one for me tonight." I smiled slightly.

He nodded. "Why here?"

"She was planning to take me here. I found her journal after she died." I didn't want to go into all of the details.

"Man, I'm sorry. Any idea why she wanted to take you here?" He dug.

"She came here when she lost someone, and she found joy on that beach out there..."

"And you're trying to do the same?" He asked.

"Something like that... I guess..." I paused... "I'm trying to figure out how to lead a different life. The joy I had with her is irreplaceable... So it's not going to be the same joy.... it'll be of a different sort." I tried to reason.

"I understand." He nodded. "Well, I'll be here for the next few weeks. I can't get an apartment until two weeks from now. If you need a friend."

I paused. Maybe this was Rella too. "You know what, I could use a good friend." I smiled.

From then on, we talked sports. Both of us were Redsox fans, and we were excited about the upcoming season. That topic alone gave us enough to chat until it was time to go to bed. When I went back to the room, I realized how thankful I was for the mindless chatter. It was nice to talk about something other than loss. I realized that maybe I needed to be a little more open to people. Who knew what it might bring?

* * *

1 Week Later

A week passed, and it seemed that I had found a relaxing routine. Pickles and I would wake up whenever our bodies decided to, and we walked the beach until whenever we decided to stop or when we got too cold. We'd go to local shops and explore here and there, but other than that, we just were living a peaceful time, which was what I was looking for. In a way, we were leaning on each other to get through the day.

I can't say that I found the epiphany that I was hoping for yet, but I just decided that everything would happen in due time. Every evening Jack and I met at the bar. I limited myself to one scotch on the rocks, whereas he... had a little more. Regardless, though, we talked like old friends, and it was again, just nice and normal. I couldn't remember the last time I felt normal. It seemed I had been drowning these last few months. Now, I was keeping my head up. I can't say I was swimming anywhere, but I was at least able to tread the water below, and that was enough for me right now.

Pickles seemed to love the beach so much. I figured he'd grown up with it as part of his routine, so that was no surprise. I enjoyed his company. His presence was comforting. Ever since losing Rella, if there was one paramount feeling over all of the others, it was loneliness. With Pickles by my side, I knew wasn't alone.

"Zzzz, zzzz, zzzz, zzzz" My phone vibrated. It was Dad.

"Hello?" I asked.

"Hey, Michael. It's me. I just wanted to let you know that you have an offer on your house. It's... It's the asking price we talked about. What do you say?"

"Seriously? Dad, is all my stuff even out?" I couldn't believe it.

"No. We're still working on it. Michael, I put the sign out this morning. There have been three calls, one with the asking price. We could get into a complicated bidding situation soon. It's your call."

"Ugh..." I didn't know what to say. I couldn't believe it was all happening so fast. "Well," I paused.

"If you're not ready to sell son, it's okay. We almost have everything packed, though... I had Rella's things put in storage. I packed your belongings separately. It's just your furniture that's left."

"No..." I waited. This was one of those moments. The kind that you can't go back on. "Dad, ask for each person to give their best offer. Take the best one."

"You're sure son?"

"Yes. I'm sure." I needed to do this. There was no going back.

"Okay, I'll call the agency. Is everything okay over there?"

"It's great Dad. It's a much-needed break."

"Good. I just want you to be okay, Michael."

"I know Dad... I can't thank you enough for all that you've done. I don't know how I would have made it through without you."

"Son, you'd do it for me and in a way, you already have. I love you."

"I love you too Dad."

"Okay. Well, I'll call you in a few hours so keep your phone on you. I'll have to fax the papers for your signatures."

"Yes, sir."

"Bye."

"Bye, Dad." I hung up. I then took a very deep breath as if I was going to jump into the abyss. The moment I had long feared had finally arrived... The moment of change. I liked how my life's portrait looked with Rella in it, but the time had come to make it a blank canvas once more and start over. It was the unknown that brought so much fear to me because I felt like I was willingly stepping into the darkness. I couldn't see what was around the next corner or what my next step would hold. I just knew I needed to face my fears and walk blindly into the dark having the faith that maybe one day I would find another light like the one Rella brought to my life. Though I knew what I needed to do, I couldn't help but feel relieved, happy, nervous and scared all at the same time. This moment was a decision I would either thank myself or hate myself for, later on. It was a risk that I was willing to take.

Pickles and I continued to relax on the beach. Dad called again, a few hours later and it was a done deal. I got ten thousand over the asking price, so in the financial measure, it was a win. The evening rolled around soon enough, and I missed my Rella. I missed her voice and her laughter. The house was a reminder of her death, but it was also a memory of her alive. I was conflicted, and I couldn't help but to miss her. Part of me worried that no matter what I did, I would always painfully miss her. I don't think I would ever want the pain of missing her to stop; I just would want to be immune to it.

* * *

"You look like hell. The beach have some intense waves today?" Jack asked as I sat down at the bar.

"You could say that." I agreed.

"What's wrong with the surf?"

"I sold my house today."

"Is that good news?" He inquired.

"Yes... Maybe... I think so." I didn't know.

"You miss her, and she was there... So you feel like you've lost a piece of her existence." Jack summarized.

He had a way about him. He reminded me of a crazy redneck you'd see in a movie, but he had this ability just to see between the lines. "Yeah."

"I understand. It's how I feel about the divorce papers."

"What?" I asked.

"I got served today." He lifted them up for me to see.

"Man, I'm sorry."

"No... It was a long time coming, but I feel maybe it is for the best. I will say, though now that the time has come... I can't say that I feel at peace with it. I have mixed emotions, and I feel like maybe I could have tried harder to change my bad ways that crippled our marriage. Don't I know whether to move on like she is willing or to fight for her? Should I let go of everything, including selling the house we built our life around or should I try to hold onto everything? You know?"

"Do you love her?" I asked.

"What... Yeah, sure I do." He answered.

"No, do you love her Jack?" I replied.

"Yes... Yes, I love her." He responded

"How much?" I asked.

"What?"

"How much do you love her, Jack? How much is everything worth? Is it worth letting go or holding on? How much does your love to her cost? Is there a price tag on it or is it priceless? The answer to those questions will tell you whether or not to sell or sign those divorce papers. The selling of my house was essential. It was foreclosed on when I lost Rella. You're not in the same boat."

"Well, darn man." He drank the shot of whiskey.

"That's the truth Jack, and it's the question you'll have to ask yourself. Knowing you could get her back, would you let her go? Or are you willing to let her go because you're scared not to get her back? Either way, there's a battle."

"Isn't that the story of life?" He agreed.

* * *

That night, I didn't sleep. I battled in this war of emotion against myself. With everything that I had been shown, I knew I was supposed to come here. I felt like I was validated in my decisions when the whole thing with Pickles happened. Everything was falling into place, but I had this empty feeling. I was letting go of the grief, but this empty spot was forming in its place. My heart begged the question... now what? What does one do in the middle of one book ending and another beginning? As much as I felt found... I felt lost.

* * *

The morning sun had just lifted itself over the horizon, as Pickles and I watched it wake. I had a warm cup of coffee in my hand that I was using as a hand warmer more than something to drink. I had been here a little over two weeks, and I only had a few days left. I felt an anxiousness in me start to rise. I knew when I returned home that everything would be different. My house was sold and all of my things packed. I felt like it was the same way in my heart. I had all of the emotion, the anger, the worry, the hurt, all of it seemed to be packed up, but with nowhere to go.

There was a sense of a different life coming about and that maybe this weird feeling was the in-between state. As I petted Pickles, I tried to imagine the future. What it would be like, what I would do, how would I feel. However, I couldn't. Not because grief, not because Rella wasn't there, it was just like I couldn't see that far ahead. I had a vision that was only capable of seeing the right now. Each day, I took it as it came. I began to realize that maybe that was the new way of life. Maybe that was the lesson that I was trying to learn.

"Maybe it's a way to lean completely on God." The words appeared boldly on my heart.

As I looked at the horizon, I couldn't help but think of God. God. I still didn't understand Him. The rules, the regulations, the reasons. I did not understand any of it and, well, I didn't figure I ever would. As I saw the sun, it was like He was there with me. A slow, steady hand, lifting the light gradually, with everything around it, emerging out of darkness. I wondered too if that was symbolic. Maybe that was my heart. I remembered the first night asking the questions of maybe. Maybe this scene was my cold hardened heart, wakened by the warming of the sun. Perhaps I needed to be completely defrosted, so to speak, to be able to take the next step.

* * *

"Hey, mind if I come with you?" Jack asked as Pickles, and I was walking out for our evening walk.

"No, not at all." I agreed. We hadn't seen each other since we last talked at the bar and whether or not Jack was going to move on with the divorce.

"Thanks... sure is beautiful out here." He stated.

"Yeah... So where have you been? I haven't seen you in a while?" I asked.

"You sound like my wife." He warned jokingly.

We both laughed. "Sorry." I laughed again.

"No... We're ugh... well, we're talking." He sounded happy.

"I'm glad to hear that." I agreed.

"Yeah... that's why I came here, to thank you."

"For what?" I was confused.

We continued to walk down the beach. "You... Your story, about losing your wife. It has got me thinking," he paused not knowing how to say what he wanted to say.

"Thinking?" I asked.

"Well, I thought about what would happen if anything ever happened to Audree." He stopped for a moment. His voice choked slightly. "Man, it got to me, and I found myself thinking over the past few days. 'What if I lost her,' and I realize that someone doesn't have to pass to lose them, you know?"

I nodded.

"So... I asked myself the other question, you asked me. How much is my house worth? How much do I have to lose to... I don't know... live again?" He waited... "How much is my house worth, Michael?"

I waited for his response.

"It's priceless." He stopped and looked at me. "I wouldn't have figured that out, without you."

I smiled. "Thank you for that, Jack... I pray it..." I was shocked by my use of the term pray... "It all works out."

He smiled. "Thank you... But Michael?" He asked.

"Yeah?"

"I know that you came here looking for answers and, well, I don't know if you've found any yet." He turned and looked at me dead in the eye. "I know that your house was priceless too, Michael. But..." he turned... "Don't be scared to buy again."

I swallowed hard. "It's not that simple," I stated.

"I know... I know" he gestured. "I'm not saying that... I'm just saying, don't be scared to live. I think, your wife, she would want that for you. You're a great guy. That's why Rella loved you. I just," he hesitated. "You walking out here on this beach alone... I've watched you a few times, and you look as if you're waiting for someone. Part of me wonders if it's... Rella. However, another part of me hopes that you'll meet someone else. Sometimes it helps to know that you are lovable still."

"I don't think that could happen. Rella's love was a particular brand of wine, so to speak. With a drink like that, it's not like you can go back and settle for something else." I reasoned.

"I know but with wine, age is all about the timing. You never know when that bottle that has been stored for years, is ready to be opened." He looked out at the horizon. "Maybe what would have been weak yesterday emerges strongly today."

I waited as I let his words sink in. They were powerful. "I guess, only time will tell," I reasoned. Man did I ever want to get off of this subject.

"I don't know." He looked down at my left hand. "Just remember, you're the one with the watch." He patted me on the back. "Take care, Michael. Look me up if you're ever in Port Austin again." He smiled as he parted away...

I looked down at my watch... still frozen at the time before Rella's death. It hadn't ticked since then.

"Should I let time start again?" My heart asked.

I couldn't help but tear up. Maybe it was time... to finally move forward? I reached and turned the little dial on my Rolex. I couldn't help but be soothed by the small, subtle tics, starting again. The sound of its ticking was like a pumping of a heart. A heartbeat that had just begun to beat again... And a new breath of life was breathed into me...

* * *

Again, the evening drifted into night… I was in a daze, in a way. My life had been so dull and dark over the past few months. Now that hope was beaming through; it was as if my eyes had to readjust to the contrast between the two extremes. Pickles laid beside me. I was so comforted by his presence. Over the past few weeks, he truly had become my companion… I gazed at the stars knowing that my time was coming to an end here. I would have to go back soon… The thought filled me with worry… "Go back to what?" I asked myself..

I looked up to the sky as if asking God for an answer… What now? What do I have to look forward to?

Just then, I spotted the satellite moving slowly and steadily. My eyes filled with tears as I thought of my mom and Rella… Now, they were together… I tried to gather myself… Maybe this trip wasn't about finding what to look forward to; rather it was finding what to look for…

* * *

1 Week Later

Today was my last day on the beach and tomorrow; I was heading back home to buy a new home. I trusted Dad with a lot, but not so much for him to pick out a new house. It was time. I felt like everything here was coming to a close. I couldn't say that I knew if everything were better now, but I knew that there was enough that happened that I could call it worthwhile. I wasn't crying myself to sleep. I wasn't mad at God. I had a dog, and that was the best friend that I needed. Everything was coming to a close, in the way that I needed it to.

Pickles and I had spent the day, cruising in and around town. I bought a few things for my Dad and Mr. Salvador as a thank you. I wanted them both to know how much I appreciated them for all that they had done for me. If there was one thing I learned on this trip, it was how much I needed them. None of this would have been possible without them, and even though it was a nice getaway, I missed them both more than I could have ever anticipated. Plus, I was excited to see my Dad meet Pickles. He loved dogs, and I was sure he was going to be a great addition to the family.

"Come here boy," I motioned Pickles. "Time for our last evening walk. We're leaving out early tomorrow."

He followed obediently, as always. We went back to our old spot, right below the dead tree. As I stood there watching the glow of the sunset, Pickles sat next to me in silence, the kind of silence that brings so much comfort. It was a great place to watch the sunset since it was slightly elevated. The sun colored everything with a warm golden hue. Pickles and I just took it all in as we overlooked the water. There's something about a beach that can very quickly put you in the deepest of thoughts. I was content with the warmth of the sun that gracefully touched my skin, fighting the cold away. There was something soothing about the sound of the waves as they slid across the sand. If this wasn't heaven, I am sure that it was the beginning of it. I can say that this place helped me as it once did for my sweet Rella.

I remembered the first night I had arrived searching for this old dead tree and stumbling across Pickles. Not knowing that he was the little puppy who had once brought my Rella so much joy in her deepest despair. There was a poetry to it all, as I looked at him, I realized he had done the same for me. I was looking for hope... a sign... And he was just that. In such a short time, I had grown such an attachment for him. I couldn't help but be so thankful.

"What are the odds? Huh, boy?" I reached over to pet him, but before I could, he took off running.

"Pickles?" I questioned. He kept running faster. "Pickles!" I yelled as I chased after him.

"Pickles!" The dog was running so fast, I couldn't keep up. I realized then, just how out of shape I had become. Before I could help it, I slowed to a fast walk.

"Pickles!!" I could see him in the distance. It looked like someone had caught ahold of him. I picked up the pace, nervous for him. "Pickles!" I ran, as I approached the woman bent down petting him.

"Pickles!" I scolded. "What are you thinking?" I asked him. "Ma'am, I am so sorry." I quickly apologized.

"You should be, I'm highly allergic to dogs!" she replied

"Oh, my gosh, do I need to call an ambulance?" I said with great concern in my voice.

She laughed and said "I was joking. It was a joke; I love dogs. No harm was done."

I couldn't even push a chuckle because she scared me so much. "That's funny. You got me. Wow, good one." Even though by no means was I humored.

"I'm sorry, I shouldn't joke like that. You should know I was nominated for the worst joke telling in America," she replied

"Oh..... err..... I'm confused. I do not know if I should feel happy for you or sorry for you?" I responded.

"That was supposed to be a joke too, but at the moment I guess you can feel sorry for me," she said as she looked down playfully.

I let out and uncomfortable chuckle, "I am so sorry that my dog intruded."

"No, it's all right. He sure is sweet." She smiled as she continued to rub his head.

"He has a habit of this, I think." I realized it was the same thing he did to Rella as a puppy.

She laughed as she stood. "It's okay." She smiled. "I'm Scarlett Harrington."

"Michael Harvey," I introduced myself.

"It's nice to meet you and you too, Pickles." She turned to him.

He wagged his tail and barked. He seemed so excited and started licking her ankles.

"Pickles!" I scolded softly. "Stop that!"

She laughed. "No, don't worry. It's fine." She brushed her long dark hair back as she petted him again. She was dressed in dark blue jeans and a mustard-colored sweater. She had some indie song playing on her phone that was about being colorblind. A large Sony camera hung around her neck that seemed to weigh her small frame down.

I realized then that she was probably taking photos... working. "I'm sorry, we don't mean to interrupt you." I motioned to her camera.

"Oh, it's not an interruption." She smiled. "You were helping me."

I looked confused. "How so?" I asked.

"By staying still. I have been stocking you for some time now and have been wanting a great picture of you two to hang in my room. The only thing is; you keep moving." She said in a serious tone.

"Ugh... excuse me?" I replied. I never felt so nervous at the word stalking? Was she one of those... weird girls? This couldn't be good...

She blurted out in laughter as she use one hand to cover her mouth and the other to hold her camera close to her. Her nose wrinkled with every laugh. "I was joking again, but obviously it wasn't funny judging by the look on your face. Your face had fear written all over it." She said with laughter still lingering in her voice.

I started laughing. "You are out of control. You got me good. I was so scared and had no idea how to run from you."

"I'm sorry," she said with more laughter spilling out from her now.

"Again ma'am I am so sorry for interrupting you and your work," I replied with some laughter in my voice too.

She shook her head no and said, "You are not interrupting. I hope you don't mind, but I was taking pictures of you and your dog. The scenery and the color of the sunset made a nice shot but don't worry, you can't see your face or anything." She corrected quickly.

I was a bit embarrassed. How strange. "Oh, well, it's okay." I didn't know what else to say.

"You and Pickles standing, with that big dead tree towering in the background made it impossible for me to pass up that shot. That's what I love about coming out here. You never know what you're going to capture." She smiled as she turned to the water.

"It's beautiful isn't it?" I asked instinctively.

"It is... That's what I love about living here. The water... The sunsets... and the sunrises. I've been blessed enough to capture some incredible paintings by God." She took in a deep breath. "Some of Gods' most beautiful paintings only last for a short while. I believe it is because His beauty is so great that we wouldn't be able to handle it for too long. I think it is up to us to sit and wait for that right moment when... God shows His face and the glory that comes with it. In those moments, you have to ready to capture them."

I was stunned by her response. It was something Rella would say. "Yes... This beach is gorgeous." I responded.

"It is but the water is beautiful too. I like to sail when the water is right." She admitted.

"Wow, that seems intense." I thought of Rella and I and how we sailed.

She laughed. "It is... But, there is nothing like being with the infinite."

"What?" I couldn't help the chills form on my body from the very word.

"Infinite. That's the name of my sailboat." She explained.

"Oh... I see..." This conversation was getting to be too weird because she made me laugh and feel very similar to the way Rella made me feel. So I did what most men would do, I panicked and wanted to leave. "Well, ugh, we better let you get back to it." I motioned. "Come on Pickles," I called, but he didn't respond to my command. He just sat there and barked.

"Pickles...." I reasoned.

Scarlett giggled. "Sometimes they have a mind of their own."

"Yeah, they do." I agreed politely. "Pickles," I said in a firmer tone. By that, he got up.

"Well, it was nice to meet you Ms.." I couldn't remember her name.

"It's Scarlett." She corrected. "But.. umm..." she paused. "I don't want to be awkward, but I would like to give you some prints of you and your dog. I think you will like them, they turned out really good. I think you'd cherish them. Is there somewhere I could send them too, like maybe your address? I promise you I am not a stocker."

"Oh, it's okay, you don't have to do that," I said with laughter. It was time to go. She was weird. She was... familiar.

"I know but, I'd like to."

"Ugh, have you ever heard of Harvey Art Investments?"

She seemed shocked, "Yes I do. Do you work there?"

I smiled and said "Yes, I own it."

"Oh wow, you have an exquisite place. I have seen so many photos on your website, of the art that comes in and out of your place."

"Yes, well thank you we try to get the best. Here is my business card with my name and the address you can send the photos to." Why was I giving her my information? What? My mind held warning, but my heart didn't.

"Okay..." she waited, seemingly wanting to talk more, but I wasn't going there. Even though we were just talking, I felt like I was cheating on Rella because I liked how Scarlett made me feel. I like how without effort she pulled laughter out of me.

"Thanks, ma'am. It was a pleasure to meet you." I nodded. "Come on, Pickles." We walked back towards the hotel. Soon, it would be time to go, and after that little run in, I was more than happy too. It was strange. This girl was different... Like, I don't know... She reminded me so much of Rella, and that's whom I was trying to let go of from my life. For me, that was just another sign that it was time to head back home.

I needed to find a new balance again. A new way of life with the new perspective I had recently obtained. I couldn't afford anything that would interfere with the progress that I had made. I came here in search of something and found something, neither of which I could name. Rella was able to find her joy and laughter again on this beach. I smiled at Pickles and couldn't help but smile too at what had just happened.

"An old dog, with the same old tricks, huh buddy?" I smiled. Oh, the irony. Maybe that girl just needed a laugh too. I hated the phrase 'everything happens for a reason', but as much as I didn't want to admit it... it seemed that on this beach that was no less, than entirely accurate.

6 Months Later

CHAPTER 21

THE OLD HOUSE CREAKED LIKE never before, however, the sound had a presence to it. As much as there was to do in this old house, still, to me, it was worth it.

I'll never forget my Dad's reaction when I showed him this old thing, out in the middle of nowhere.

"I'm buying it, Dad," I remembered telling him.

"I think you lost your mind on that beach out there, son. This old thing is a hazard."

"No, Dad... It's a haven." I said as that's how I thought of it, as my haven.

I realized that some would have thought that I bought it for Rella, but I didn't. It seemed that well, she found God here. She met him here on a weekly basis but me I met Him here for the first time. I look back on that time, and I know I did. That was something entirely independent of Rella. This house, the office upstairs is where I can say that I was saved. It wasn't a church; there was no priest or pastor. It was a solemn old place, where I surrendered my heart. It was a moment, where I first truly, allowed God to come into my life. And that, for me, that was the memory of this place, and that's why I wasn't willing to let it go.

I remembered when I came back from Port Austin. I was so anxious to get a grip on life. I wanted to get my routine back. A little bit of order, and that I did. Work was as great as ever. We had more bookings than we'd ever had this year. Financially, Dad and I were completely blessed. I'll never forget the gift he gave me last month on my birthday when he surprised me with the title of the building.

"You're the official owner now." He told me with the happiest smile on his face. "You will take it from here."

I never expected him to give me the business, but the truth was, Dad needed to start taking some more time off. He had started seeing the portrait artist in her mid-fifties. May Anne was her name. There was a new light in him that I hadn't seen before, and I couldn't have been happier. He came to the gallery from noon till close but had Friday's off. Most of the time, I knew he spent with her. That was okay by me. I was happy for him to be happy again.

Oddly enough, Old Man Salvador and I became closer than ever. Before I bought the house, I showed it to him and asked if he thought I'd be able to fix it up.

"Yes," he said, "With a lot of cash and hard work."

I hired him to help me. There was a lot to do, and I still had a lot to learn. Dr. Walters was great, but Salvador knew how to navigate this loss thing better than any other. He helped me understand more about God. I was intrigued with the things he would say. The wisdom he had was beyond what any schooling or education could offer. We enjoyed our time together fixing this old house for the last few months.

The first thing we had to do was seal all the doors and windows. That was quite the task. I loved the old antiqued windows, so I tried to keep the ones I could.

"Once we seal it off, then we'll be able to work on the inside. It should be ready in about a year," he told me. I'll never forget his shock when I told him that I was going to live in it during the reservations. He would have never said it, but we both knew he thought I was crazy.

With the water and electricity lines in, I opted for the move. I cleared out one room well enough to put my bedroom furniture in. By no means was my house pretty yet, but it was beginning to take shape. When the renovation is complete, the house would be worth a least a two million. The land added extra value, and I knew myself, it was a sound investment. Not just financially, but personally too.

The projects gave me a new sense of purpose. They gave me a reason to get up in the morning. It was something for myself, and that was the most medicinal gift I needed.

Pickles seemed to like it too. He'd sunbath on the porch all during the day, as if he too, had moved onto retirement with Dad. He was truly the best dog anyone could have. The rooms were coming together slowly. Salvador suggested we work from the bottom, up, but I insisted that we started with the office upstairs. There wasn't necessarily a lot of work to do, more so, just small repairs. The mahogany was as strong as ever.

"This here will last another hundred years," Salvador said.

I never forget polishing it for the first time. Beautiful. I had started to meet God there every morning since. I'd pull out that old Bible, and read a few passages. Nothing fancy, nothing formal, just simple. That was my new way of life. Simple.

There wasn't a need for a lot of décor in there. I suppose that's why it proved to be the easiest room to fix up as well. I put all my books in there, and I hung Rella's painting on a mantle behind the office chair. It had been almost two years since we first met… and nearly a year since her death. I hung it, not to remember her, but to remind me of the joy we once had together. The memories were no longer filled with pain, but of joy. Regardless of how long she was in my life, she brought happiness while she was here. In all of this. Finally, I was able to see that.

I heard the old truck pulling up now. Salvador and I were going to be working on the bathrooms today. I went downstairs to greet him.

"Hey, Salvador! How are you?"

"I'm good Michael. I'm ready to get those bathrooms cleaned up, how about you?"

"Yes, sir. As ready as I'll ever be." I agreed. The bathrooms were always the worst and the messiest. But, I knew we'd get it done.

In a way, Old Man Salvador became like a father figure to me. Not to replace my Dad or anything, but he just had that spirit about him. I think too though he'd never say it, I reminded him of his son. We were both a help to the other, and it was nice. Fulfilling.

"So, we've already got all of the water lines and plumbing done, but we need to make it look great now. I don't know how you've gone so long with that dingy sink, son."

"Hey, it's nicer than what I had in college," I admitted.

Mr. Salvador shook his head. "I had better than that when I fought in foreign jungles, son."

I laughed. It was pretty bad. I was excited to get it done. We had all of the fixtures and furnishings picked out. They were ordered a few weeks back and had been sitting in the hall for some time. The whole project was just one step at a time. Again, that too was cathartic. One step at a time. Just like one day at a time.

We were knee deep in work when I heard another car pulling up the road. One thing about living out so far was that I could easily see and hear what was going on outside.

"Who could that be?" I asked. I heard Pickles starting to go crazy.

I went downstairs and found him barking and howling. "Pickles," I called. "Calm down. Who is it?" I asked as I opened the door.

I saw the little red slug bug driving down the road. Pickles continued to bark loudly. I had no idea who it could be.

The car came closer, but I couldn't make it out. As it shifted into park, I was shocked by who I saw.

"Scarlett?" I asked... I remembered the young brunettes name as if it were yesterday. Not that I wanted to admit it, I had been thinking about her ever since our first meeting on the beach.

"Hello, Michael." She waved. "I'm so sorry to drop by like this, but I went to the gallery and your Dad just gave me your address."

"Oh, okay." I wondered why she was here?

"I have the photos from the beach that I took a few months back. I'm sorry it took me so long; I just now got the time to make this trip. I wanted to bring them by personally." She smiled from ear to ear.

"Wow," I didn't know what to say, and I couldn't help but be a little flustered. "Thanks so much."

I took them, as we stood on the porch.

"You didn't have to do that." I gestured.

"No, I know, but I wanted to. They turned out great like I said. I even won an award for one of them."

"Wow," I was slightly embarrassed. I looked a mess. This girl was here, and it seemed a little awkward and a bit forward.

She seemed to grow uneasy too. "Well, I just wanted to drop them off to you. My card is in there too, if you ever need anything."

"Oh, okay." I lifted the envelope up. "Yes, will do. Thank you so much."

"Yes," She smiled politely.

Pickles then started barking like crazy as she walked down the steps.

"Pickles, stop!" I commanded as he ignored just as quickly. "Pickles!"

"What's the matter fella?" Scarlett asked as she reached down to pet him.

He wagged his tail.

"I'm sorry. He just wants attention from you, I guess." I shrugged my shoulders.

"It's alright. I don't mind." She petted him a bit more. "Well, I'd better go."

"Yeah, thank you." I came and grabbed pickles by his new collar, to hold him back. She got in her car. "Bye, thanks again!" I waved.

Pickles continued to go nuts. "Come on boy. Let's go inside." I all but pushed him through the front door. Salvador came down the stairs.

"Everything alright?" he asked.

"Yeah." I pointed to the front door. "A girl came by to drop off some photos." I tried to explain.

"Some photos?" he asked.

"Yes, ugh, when I was on vacation. From a distance, she got some pictures of Pickles and me. She went by the gallery to drop them off, and Dad sent her this way.

"Sure is a long way to drive, just to drop off a picture." He hinted.

"Yeah..." By that point, I couldn't help but to be a little curious as to what the envelope held.

"Well, let's see." I agreed as I opened the envelope. There were about ten photos inside. I looked through them, and even I couldn't dispute the beauty. They were gorgeous. I fanned through, admiring the images... Until I got to the last one... I stopped.

"It couldn't be..." I said aloud. "No, way," I said as my heart started to pound harder than I have ever felt it.

I was shocked at the image I saw. A picture of me, at the beach... the dead tree, stood tall in the foreground as if it had something to prove. The ratted dog, Pickles... standing right beside me in the distance. The sunset illuminated our silhouettes, surrounded by the warm golden tones of the lights hitting the water. The clouds... The sun.

I all but fainted. "It just couldn't be." I ran upstairs and down the hall to the office. I held up the photograph to Rella's framed painting. The images were identical. Completely identical. The painting that Rella loved so dearly that reminded her of the beach she had visited to... It was me and Pickles. The picture was the paintings' direct reflection. I couldn't help but fall to my knees as my tears fell. I was shocked and shaken by the moment.

"God, what are you telling me?" There was no way. This was impossible.

I waited for an answer. No verbal one came, but it all started to hit me. Rella's hope... The beach... Pickles. This house... God... The little black Bible. The story of the red chord in the window to spare the lives of.... Scarlett... Scarlett.

"Scarlett?" I asked... As soon as I uttered the words, the light seemed to peer through the window the same way I had seen it before with Rella.

I heard Old Man Salvador come in. "Michael, are you okay?" He sounded concerned.

"Yes..." I paused. "I just." I didn't know where to begin. I held up the picture in my hand and pointed towards the painting.

I could hear him take a deep breath. "I'll be," He said.

"Salvador, what does this mean?" I looked to him for answers. "Everything... Pickles... The painting... I held the Bible in my hand... The story of the thread with Rehab. It was Scarlett in color, right?"

He nodded yes slowly but still in shock looking at the two pictures. He looked back at me, somewhat stunned.

"The woman who took the photo." I swallowed. "Her name is Scarlett." Even saying it, gave me chills.

Old Man Salvador walked over to me. "Son...you've asked me before, how I hear God. How he talks, yes?" He asked.

I shook my head yes. "He talks, just like this." He held the picture out to me. "The feeling in your heart. That's God."

"But... I mean... Rella... I just... I don't..."

"Michael." Salvador grew serious. "How much do you have to lose before you decide to live again?"

The words echoed in my brain. I'd heard them before... Jack... The house! How much is the house worth? I looked around... It all fit in this perfect puzzle.

"Oh, Salvador." I looked at him in shock. "Nothing more! I'll lose nothing more! I'll be back!"

I ran downstairs and grabbed my keys to my car! The sports BMW... was this why I had a need for speed? I couldn't get out the door fast enough. I put them in the ignition as quickly as I could, turned and hit the gas. I was going so fast down the open road, but I had to catch her.

I was speeding until I spotted the old red beetle. I started to honk my horn!

"Beep, beep, beep, beep, bbbbeeep!" I laid on it, to get her attention. I saw her pull over.

I hurried to catch up. She was on the road right before the highway. I pulled over behind her and got out of my car.

It was no coincidence where we were... Rella Lane... I teared up. I knew without a shadow of a doubt that there were no such thing as coincidences... everything was on purpose. This was it... The new beginning.

"Scarlett!" I said winded, as she got out of her car. I ran to her. I didn't know what I was going to say. What I was going to do... I could only focus on closing the gap between us.

"Scarlett..." I breathed as I met her face to face.

She looked at me in a way that held expectance. With a smile, she said... "What took you forever?"

THE END